IF YOU AIN'T READ GOD'S REJECT (BOOK 1), YOU'LL BE LOST LIKE A MF!

GOD'S REJECT BY KING PEN GEMINI
(Formerly Known As AHMAD GEMINI RAY)

WELCOME TO 10-5

WELCOME TO 10-5

The Devil's Advocate

KING PEN GEMINI

Billy Ray, Bridget Ray

Iconic Creations Entertainment

CONTENTS

GOD'S REJECT i
Dedication x

Prelude 1

Lucifer's Journal PT.1: So Far Away From Home 4

1 Visions of Destruction 5

Lucifer's Journal PT.2: I Am.... 11

2 The Father, The Reject, & The Reject's Son 12

Lucifer's Journal Pt. 3: LETTER TO THE PATHETIC HUMANS PT. 1 (FIRST DAY IN GOD'S PRISON) 19

3 What's a God To a Prince? 21

4 The End Is Only Beginning 27

5 Bloodline Deception 35

6 Made In My Image 43

7 Family Secrets Revealed 47

8 I Have Dreams of HELL 54

9 WELCOME TO 10-5! 59

10 Let's Get Down To Business 64

11 Deadly Alliance = Ultimate Defiance 69

Lucifer's Journal PT.4: LETTER TO PATHETIC HUMANS PT.2 (DAY 10 IN GOD'S PRISON) 74

12 Am I My Brother's Keepa?! 76

13 Am I My Brother's Keepa?! PT. 2 84

14 When Darkness Meets The Light 92

LUCIFER'S JOURNAL PT.5: WHAT IS LIFE? (DAY 365 IN GOD'S PRISON) 97

15 GOD'S PLANT (PLAN) 99

16 Bloodline Rebellion/Special Guests 107

17 Heavy Is The Head That Wears The Crown & Mighty Is The Hand That Holds The Cane! 112

18 Holy Matrimony & Unholy Murder 117

19 Ten Years Later And Armageddon Is NEAR! 123

20 Final Chapter of The End of The Beginning! 129

FUN FACT ABOUT GOD'S REJECT 135

CONTINUATION OF GOD'S REJECT PT.1 137

CONTINUATION OF GOD'S REJECT PT. 2 141

CONTINUATION OF GOD'S REJECT PT. 3 143

CONTINUATION OF GOD'S REJECT PT. 4 145

CONTINUATION OF GOD'S REJECT PT. 5 151

CONTINUATION OF GOD'S REJECT PT. 6 157

WHAT'S NEXT? 159

MERRIAM WEBSTER'S DEFINITION OF LOVE, SEX, AND HEARTBREAK 161

CHAPTER 1: WRITER'S BLOCK & FAMILY BUSINESS 163

CHAPTER 2: AND THEN THERE WAS CUE? 173

CHAPTER 3: SIPPIN TEA WITH TEE INTERVIEW 181

CHAPTER 4: CUE IS HERE TO HELP YOU 189

CHAPTER 5: A WARM & WET WELCOME TO VEGAS 195

FIVE CHAPTERS OF A PREVIEW LATER 201

DRAFT & FIRST CHAPTER OF BLOODLINE DECEPTION 203

I LIED 225

DRAFT OF A KINGPIN'S MEMOIR FIRST CHAPTER 227

THE END 231

CURSE OF CAIN: EYE OF THE GEMINI PREVIEW (INTRO) 233

Dedication to My Dad

This book is dedicated to my dad, Mr. Billy J. Ray. Thank you so much for allowing me to take you and your life and turn it into the craziest, most gangsterest, supernatural shit ever. You are truly my muse for this entire Welcome to 10-5 book series! Love you forever.

-King Pen Gemini (FKA Ahmad Gemini Ray)-

First Printing, 2024

Prelude

Time. Where did it go? Did it disappear? No. It just passed by. But why? Is it because since the last time you heard from me, my brother was put on the cross to die? Is it because Moses parted the Red Sea? And during that time, the Pharaoh of Egypt rejected his God and embraced me? Is it because slavery of the black race took the world by storm? And the civil war left so many people to mourn? Is it because there have been so many evils in the world since God rejected me? That time has escaped all of our grasp, and the results of all of this evil is what you all have seen and still will see? Time, where did it all go? I don't know. And I don't give a shit. Because now the year is 1936, and peep this. Just like God has his chosen few, I do too.

One of my chosen few was a small child. A baby if we are to be a little more specific. A baby born into a family that God took a liking to. This child's name was Joseph James Williams. Born and raised in Leeds, Alabama, August of 1936. Parents, Willie Joseph Williams Sr and Esther May Williams. Oldest brother, Willie Joseph Williams Jr, (Aka Willie Jr). All three of these people were kind-hearted people. Didn't question a fucking thing that came out of the bible and was obedient to the scripture. These people were poor, didn't have much, but were always able to feed others in need, always helping someone out. And God always made a way for them to get whatever it was that their hearts desired. So I knew that these three could not be touched and that God had a great plan for this family. Their faith was too strong. Since I knew that, I had to corrupt Willie and Esther's second-born child. That's right, Joseph James Williams. Because I had to ruin something that God meant to be good, and any child born into a family like that was destined to come out good. But not Joseph, noooooooooo not him. Because he was my special little project.

When Joseph was a baby, I would wait until everyone in the house was asleep and go into his room and hold him, play with him, and tell him what his destiny truly was. I did this from the moment he was born. I had to get an early start on corrupting him. I would make him fall asleep by walking around the room with him and telling him stories of how hell was built from the moment God cast me from heaven and how it had evolved into a city called Cleveland, Ohio, and how the center of it was a street/neighborhood called East 105th Street. Before I would make this beautiful brown-skinned baby with a head full of hair fall asleep, he would grab my long jet black dreadlocks and beard and giggle and laugh. I enjoyed him so much as a baby. Some might even say that I fell in love with this child as if he was my own. I even made it so that he was the only human that could even see me. As time went by, I continued to do the same thing every night. And then the next thing I knew, Joseph was five years old, and Willie Jr. was fifteen years old.

Joseph and his brother had to go to church with the family every Sunday. Every time they walked into the church, Joseph always asked his parents and his brother the same questions. "Why is Jesus white? Why we don't know what God look like but we know what Jesus look like? How come I don't ever see God, but I see the Devil all the time?" They always ignored him because they were hoping he'd just shut the fuck up. So when he would come home and get ready for bed, I would be right there sitting in his rocking chair waiting for him.

He would climb into his bed and turn his lamp off and look at me and ask me a series of questions every night, especially when they left church. But one night, Joseph and I had a conversation that disturbed me to a certain degree. He had gotten into bed and looked over at me and began to ask questions.

> "Lucifer, why doesn't the bible acknowledge Cain as your son?"
>
> "What do you mean Joseph?"
>
> "Well, don't you think that it is unfair that the bible talks about how Adam and Eve had Cain and Abel, but the bible doesn't mention that you're Cain's father?"

I'd never told Joseph about Adam, Eve, Cain, or even Abel! But I refused to show this child how disturbed I was because I was grooming him since he was born to rule hell. It would make me look weak if I were to show him that anything rattled me because then he would not follow in my footsteps. So I responded calmly.

"Well, Joseph, it is a long story, but how do you know that Cain is my son? I never told you that."

"My brother Junior told me. God speaks to him just like you speak to me."

"Have you ever told your brother that you speak to me?"

"No."

"What about your parents?"

"No, I haven't told anyone about you. My parents wouldn't believe me, and my brother would try to turn me against you. But I like you. You're my best friend."

"You're my best friend too. Which is why you are going to be the true ruler of this universe. You just watch."

After that conversation, Joseph went to sleep, and I sat there in Joseph's rocking chair with a bit of fear inside me. At that moment I realized that God was waging a war against me just as I was waging a war against him. But the last time that we went head to head, he defeated me and that is what scared me. If he was speaking to this child, he was grooming him to be his prophet on earth. And a prophet of God's is a dangerous being. So I got out of the chair and walked through the Williams's house and when I got to Willie Jr's room, I had all intentions of killing him. But the second that I touched the doorknob, the door shocked me and shined a bright gold light. That is when I realized that God was protecting him. So there was only one thing that I could do. And that was to create the biggest fucking gangsta the world had ever seen to terrorize everyone. Someone who would not only rule hell, but raise hell, and kill anyone who got in his way. Including his own brother because I was not going to let my father get the upper hand on me! Not again! Not This Time.

Lucifer's Journal PT.1: So Far Away From Home

I'm so far away from home.
I'm no longer the heir to the throne.
Cast from my father's empire,
Because of my greedy desires.
I was born to be the king of heaven,
But I became the king of liars.
I am destructive,
Everything I touch turns to fire.
I'm unpredictably shocking,
I'm like a live wire.
My goal is to watch the universe burn,
And burn through heaven's gates.
I want the world to feel my pain,
I want my father to feel my hate.

CHAPTER 1

Visions of Destruction

I have groomed so many evildoers in this world. From motherfuckers like Haman, Jezebel, Pharoah of Egypt, fucking Herod, shit, even Judas, and so on. But in the end, they were not good enough to help me rule hell. They were not good enough to carry out my evil deeds. They just didn't have it in them to do so. I don't know. Maybe it was because I couldn't groom them from birth like I could Joseph. I didn't know how or why at the time, but I was connected to this kid from the moment of his conception. And when he was born, that connection got stronger. I had never felt a connection like that with anyone except for my son, Cain.

Joseph was very quiet around most people growing up. When he was five, he was always by himself, reading a book and writing poetry. Joseph had a lot of friends and family around him, but Joseph was always looking to learn and expand upon his knowledge. He was very observant of people, places, and things. When the other kids around him were playing, Joseph would find a nice shady spot under a tree and watch everyone while reading a book. Joseph's mother would always try to get him to play with the cousins he grew up around, but Joseph declined every time. One day, I sat beside Joseph under a shady tree disguised as a chubby black child with nappy hair. By doing this, I could make myself visible to everyone else instead of just Joseph. I asked Joseph why he didn't play with the other kids. Joseph's response was, "Because I like to be alone. I like my books. I like writing my poetry."

I was disappointed to hear Joseph say that. And right before I could give him a negative response, his brother Willie Jr. walked up to greet us. He leaned over, kissed his brother on the forehead, and said, "You staying outta trouble lil trouble maka?" with a huge smile on his face. Joseph responded with a laugh and a chuckle. Then Willie Jr. locked eyes with me and stared into my soul.

"Who is you," said Willie Jr.

"Names Chuck," I said in my child disguised body and voice."

"Who your kinfolk? Cause I ain't neva seen you round here."

" Oh, I's just visiting my aunt Charlotte James. I's from Mississippi."

" Well, it's a pleasure to meet you, Chuck," Willie Jr. said as he looked at me suspiciously.

Willie Jr. reached out to shake my hand, and when our hands locked with a firm grip, I felt like I couldn't breathe, and my body went numb. The next thing I knew, I had a vision. A vision of me standing in front of my father again. Both of us are standing in his holy throne room across from one another. His dreads and eyes turn to the color of pure gold. My eye pupils turn to the shade of red. We speak nothing to one another and then charge at one another. In the same vision, I see two men floating in the sky on Earth. Both of them look like Willie Jr. and Joseph, except older. The sky is dark, and lightning is striking the earth's atmosphere. The two brothers began to fight to the death. In an instant, my vision went away. It came and went like a flash. I instantly drew my hand back from Willie Jr, and he looked at me with a smirk. Then he leaned over and whispered, "The wicked will be no more; though you look for them, they will not be found." Junior then smiled at his brother Joseph and said, "I'll see you at home, lil trouble maka," and the tall, muscular, dark-skinned teenager walked away.

I switched to the original form God had given me, and I looked down at Joseph with tears in my eyes. Joseph looked at me and asked me, "What is wrong, Lucifer?" I just stood there in silence while fear filled my heart. After a long, awkward silence, I told Joseph, "Go home." As Joseph walked away, he turned around and said, "I guess I will see you later?" I nodded yes, and he continued to walk home.

After that day, everything became more and more challenging for me because Willie Jr. did everything in his power to stay close to his brother. He even had Joseph sleeping in his room with him. Every night, Joseph would be in Willie Jr's bed, and Junior would sleep on the floor. Junior would read the bible to Joseph until he fell asleep. During that time, Joseph would ask him questions about God. One night, right before Joseph's birthday, he wanted to ask his big brother some questions.

"Junior. Are you telling the truth about talking to God?"

"Yeah lil trouble maka."

"Why does God come to you and not the rest of us? Does that make the rest of us less special?"

"Noooo. Don't you ever think that. We are all special in God's eyes. He loves us all and uses some of us to do his good deeds."

"So are you like an angel?"

"No, I'm no angel lil trouble maka."

"Lucifer is an angel."

"Let's talk about Lucifer. Does he really talk to you?"

Joseph did not respond initially. He looked at his brother and said, "I speak to no one." Junior smiled, kissed his brother on the forehead, and said, "Let us pray before we go to bed." The two got down on the floor and said their nighttime prayer.

Once they were done with prayer, Junior put his brother to bed and walked outside in the backyard. Junior took a deep breath, looked to the sky, and said, "Lucifer, you can come out now. No need to hide in the shadows or in the disguise of children." I came from beyond the shadows of the night and walked toward Junior. I stared at the tall, strong, dark-skinned young man, and he stared back at me.

"Your eyes glow a bright red, Lucifer. There is no need to be on the defense. I called you for a peaceful conversation," Junior said in a deep Southern accent.

"What the fuck do you want from me?"

"God told me about you, your capabilities. But to prey on a child? Since the day of his conception? That came as a surprise to him. You didn't even do that to Jesus when he was born."

"Your brother is special."

"That I know, which is why I will save him from you and your chaos and destruction," Junior said as he walked toward me.

"You cannot save your brother, not from me."

"Lucifer, Lucifer, Lucifer, I have seen the future. It is dark. It is cold. It is painful. It is scary. It can all be avoided. So, I come to you, a prophet to an angel of chaos and destruction, asking you. No, I am *begging you* to let my brother go. It will not end how you think," Junior said with tears in his eyes.

"I'm supposed to let him go just because you asked me t...."

Before I could finish my sentence, Junior grabbed me by my arm, causing my eyes to roll to the top of my head. Just like the last time Junior touched me, I had visions that came in flashes. I could see God defeating me in yet another battle and locking me away in a prison made of fire and brimstone filled with lost souls. Then I saw a young man with a bald head and a beard standing before me surrounded by fire, with his wings extended, an evil grin, and one red eye. With a deep, raspy voice, this individual said, "The world is mine!" Junior finally let me go, and the visions had disappeared.

"How did you...."

"God gave me vision," Junior said.

"Who... What... How... Why?"

"This is what can happen if you do not repent and stop your chaos and destruction. I cannot say who that was or what he will become. The only thing that I know is that whoever that is. Whatever that is, it is something that can destroy all of mankind. It can destroy God. It is strong enough to kill you. That thing is an offspring of my brother. We cannot stop him from being born, but without chaos and destruction, we can prevent him from causing armageddon. Because that is what he will bring," Junior said.

"HM. I don't believe it. There is no way that my father would create something that would become more powerful than me. Not even my brother Jesus is stronger than me. Anything stronger than me can indeed destroy this entire universe. I am the only thing that comes close to defeating God and comes close to bringing the entire universe to armageddon. You show me false visions to make me fear a future that I will own."

"No, I show you the visions that God has given me. And God is the truth," said Junior.

"God is a deceiver. God is a murderer."

"God is your father, and I think that it is time that you go home and speak to him about what can happen if you do not stop what you are doing," Junior said.

I looked at Junior but did not respond. I turned my back to him and looked at the sky lit up by the stars God had created just for me to marvel over.

"I will speak to my father, but under one condition."

"Tell me, and I will deliver the message," Junior said.

"I want to sit with him and only him. I have not spoken to my father since our battle before Christ. When he cast me from my home and my throne. No angels, no demons, just us. In the Garden of Eden."

"I will deliver the message."

I left Joseph and Junior's home and went to Hell, which was East 105th Street in Cleveland, Ohio. There, I had a house built by my very own worshippers. A throne was created for me to sit on in that house. In deep thought or reflection, I would sit on this throne and try to figure out my next move. But this time, nothing came to mind except all I had done since I could walk the Earth and dwell with the humans. I had done a lot of good in the beginning. Yet there was a lot of evil I had done. A lot of tragedies I had caused. I began to wonder if it was all for nothing. If there was a possibility that the entire universe could be wiped out by one individual. My goal was not to destroy but to rule.

With everything destroyed, there would be nothing to rule. Therefore, I had to sit down with my father and come to a compromise.

Lucifer's Journal PT.2: I am....

I am the son.
I am the son of the one who created the sun.
I am the son behind the reason that the one who created the sun, created it.
I am the son who went through pain just so the sun could exist.
I am the son who's dna lights the sun in order for it to share the sunlight kiss.
Everyone marvels over the morning star when it rises,
But I am the morning star that everyone despises.
People look at God's sun as one of his many gifts and prizes
But I am the son that everyone criticizes.
I am the son that God rejected,
While the sun is what all has accepted.
How could I be bested,
By someone or something that I vested.
Completely replaced,
By a half-human race.
I am
God's Reject.

CHAPTER 2

The Father, The Reject, & The Reject's Son

When God created me, there was no light. There was only darkness. And in this darkness, some way, somehow, he created me. It is a mystery of how we both came into existence. I never knew the details of how either of us became. But I remember being very small and looking up to my father amid the darkness and asking him, "Father, what is the opposite of darkness." He responded, "You, my child. You are the opposite of darkness." After he said that, he ripped one of my dreadlocks out of my head and squeezed it tight until it turned into a hot, beaming ray of light. He tossed it into the atmosphere, and it lit up heaven. Then God said, "Let there be light!" He picked me up into his arms, and he said to me, "You are my light, my star, my muse to create, my son. Therefore, this beautiful creation will be considered the morning star, the *sun*, if you will." I remember thinking, "Wow, my father named the most beautiful creation after me," feeling happiness and joy. I still feel happiness and joy when I look at the sun. It reminds me of when there was no one else except for us. I miss those times. I miss him occasionally, but there is no going back to how things were, not after all that has happened between us over the centuries.

After a long time of reflecting in Cleveland, I decided to return to Alabama to the Williams's place of residence. Before stepping on the property, I was approached by a tall, brown-skinned angel with black wings and long hair. It was my brother, Michael.

"Not much has changed about you, brother," said Michael,

"What the fuck do you want, Michael."

"I have come to take you to the Garden of Eden. As you may know, your access to come as you please was revoked after that battle you had with Father. Due to your havoc over the years, it was time for a new watcher of the Garden. And that watcher is me."

"You know, if I remember correctly, you enjoyed many of the gifts that the earth had to offer as well. Your lust for the mortals was ridiculous. You were addicted to them. Yet you still remain an archangel."

"Unlike you, I repented and asked our father for forgiveness."

"Well, let me ask you this? How does it feel to come second to me?"

"I don't know, Lucifer, how does it feel to come second to Jesus?"

Michael's question made me very angry, and I responded, "Take me to the garden, you bitch." Michael smirked and teleported me to the garden. It was still beautiful. It was amazing how a place such as this existed on earth, yet I could not even walk through it without the permission of the watcher of the garden or God himself. Anyway, I followed Michael through the garden as he led me to our father. Once we reached our destination, my father, God, was sitting underneath the replenished Tree of Life. The apples hanging from it were gold, like an Egyptian Pharaoh's palace.

God, as always, was dressed like royalty, gold from his head to his feet. He looked as strong as ever. Still tall, black as night, long dreadlocks, long beard, and gold eyes.

"Welcome back to Alkebulan, my son," God said as he extended his arms to hug me.

"You shall receive no hugs from me. Let us talk about your *prophet*."

"What about him?"

"He showed me a vision of what could be the future. I didn't like what I saw."

"Ah, yes. The future, that is why you are here. I almost forgot. Well, here is the thing, Lucifer. The moment that you slept with Eve, you created an imbalance in all universes. Things began to spiral. Chaos, destruction, sin, it took over in more ways than you could imagine. And a lot of those things I could not stop, but this is something that I could possibly avoid if you work with me. If you don't work with me, then universe can possibly be wiped away," God said.

"That thing that Junior showed me..."

"He is an offspring of the one you call your successor. And he is someone that you should fear."

"Why? No other creation is more powerful than you and I. Not even Jesus."

"That is something that I thought too. But things changed because I made a mistake."

"What do you mean, *YOU* made a mistake? You are *PERFECTION*," I said sarcastically.

"Well, son, I loved you so much that I couldn't kill you. And even though you betrayed me, disobeyed me, I couldn't let you walk the earth powerless. I also could not let something that you created just die."

I stood up, and I walked closer to my father as he paced the garden's ground. I looked deep into his gold pupils and asked him, "Could not let something that I created die? What are you trying to tell me?" He began to shed tears, put his hand on my shoulder, and said, "Cain." I backed away from him in disbelief. I had just known that I saw my son's skeleton in West Eden, his mother's. God had left my son and my love to die. But I realized that I was wrong as God further explained things.

"Cain was sent to West Eden, which is now known as East 105th Street in Cleveland, Ohio, thanks to you, to die. But I thought I saw some good in him when I saw that he was trying to create life and start another garden without any sunlight or water. I heard his cries at night. Seen his nightmares. Nightmares of him killing Abel. He begged me for forgiveness in his prayers. I appeared before your son one night and asked him if he would repent. Unlike you, he said yes. Therefore, I thought he was redeemable," God said.

"You *thought*?"

"Yes. *Thought*. So I took Cain to heaven with me and taught him everything I taught you. Cain sucked it all in like an empty vessel. I sent him back to Earth with my words and scriptures, and the next thing I knew, it was chaos. Better yet, I will show you my son."

God put his hand on my face and showed me a vision of the past. I saw my son in the spitting image of God and myself. He was walking through heaven with my father, thanking him for giving him a second chance in life. He swore that he would not be like his father (me) and continue to spread God's law. God let him back into the world, and he spread the word of God and worked as his prophet for years. Until one day, he'd come across a beautiful woman, a necromancer and medium that I had blessed with wicked powers and abilities—the Witch of Endor. The Witch was a very beautiful woman with dark skin, a slim body shape, green eyes, long kinky hair, and a scar above her eye from being beaten by her father as a teenager for trying to wake the dead.

Cain was supposed to go to Endor to speak with King Saul. Before Cain reached King Saul, he was distracted by the beautiful witch. She knew what she was doing by distracting him. How could she not when I had taught her everything that she needed to know about seduction, magic, etc. She stepped from behind a wall leading to King Saul's palace, and she stared at my son's beauty as he stared at hers. She smiled, walked toward my son, and said, "Mighty, mighty Prince of Darkness, you are more beautiful than what the women across the lands say you are." Cain backs away from the witch and says, "I am here to see the king. Please step aside, beautiful lady." But the witch is very persistent. She walked closer to Cain and put her hands through his head, which was full of light brown dreadlocks. Her eyes glowed the color red as she leaned over and whispered in his ear.

"Prince, please do not reject me, for you are the son of the King who blessed me. Let me serve you."

"I am sorry. Although you are very beautiful, I am here to see your king."

"Why come to see my king when I can make you feel like one," The Witch said right before she kissed Cain's lips.

The moment she kissed my son, it was over. He said to the Witch of Endor, "Take me to your home." She led him inside the palace where she resided because she worked as King Saul's medium. Once they arrived at her room, she pushed Cain onto her large-sized bed with silk sheets. She looked down at him, smiling and chuckling as she slowly removed her clothing.

Cain became fully aroused and sat up on the edge of the bed and grabbed the beautiful witch by her waist. Filling his mouth with her left breast while playing with her clitoris. They both moaned in pleasure until Cain stood tall over the beautiful, naked witch and lifted her by her beautiful derriere. She wrapped her legs around him, and they shared a passionate kiss. He then laid her on the bed and climbed on top of her. He inserted his penis inside of her tight and wet pussy and began to stroke her with his long and girthy manhood slowly. As Cain moaned softly, the beautiful witch gripped his muscular arms and screamed in pleasure while biting down on his shoulder. After a while, they shared another kiss as he continued to stroke her slim and tight body.

Later, Cain turned over the woman's body and began to penetrate her from behind while grabbing her long and kinky hair. Both of their moans grew louder and louder until they both were relieved sexually. After Cain and the beautiful witch were finished having an incredible sexual encounter, Cain laid down beside her, staring at the ceiling and breathing heavily.

"Beautiful woman, I do not even know your name."

"My name is Aclima. And I am here to serve you, dark prince."

"How do you know who my true father is? Why do you refer to me as the *dark prince*? I have been brought back to the light by my father's father."

"I can feel your father's power, his darkness, coursing through you. I have encountered your father, for he is the one who gave me my gifts. He spoke of you but is not aware of your false death."

"Gifts? Dead?"

"This is why you must join me, prince. Let me serve as your princess and your father's servant. The three of us together can be so powerful."

Cain stood up, walked to the balcony unclothed, and stared at the sky. With a look of confusion and disbelief, he said, "God told me that my father wanted nothing to do with me. He never mentioned that he was under the impression that I was dead. Why would he do that?" Aclima walked over to my son and wrapped her arms around him while kissing his back.

"God does not love you, prince. He only uses you as his servant as he did your father."

"No! He saved me when he could have let me die after what I did to my brother. And what are these gifts that you speak of? My father was cast from heaven. He should not have any abilities to bless anyone else with abilities."

"God did not strip your father of his power. In hopes that he would find peace in loneliness in the world and return to heaven, but it never happened. Lucifer is very much alive and powerful, and he blessed me with the power of foresight and necromancy. I can speak to the dead, raise the dead, and see upcoming events. Your father is the true God, not the God that you serve."

Cain returned to the room from the balcony and put his clothes on. You could see the rage in his face. Aclima walked over to Cain and said, "My prince, where shall you go?" Cain looked at Aclima and responded, "Take me to your king." Aclima got dressed and led Cain into King Saul's dining area. King Saul sat before his royal army at the dining table, stuffing his face. The fat, brown-skinned, bearded king looked at Aclima and Cain while chewing before speaking.

"Beautiful witch woman. Who stands before me while I eat and drink."

"I am Cain, son of Lucifer, who is the son of God. God sent me here to speak to you about raising the dead to aid you in killing the Philistines in war," Cain said before Aclima could respond.

"Cain? Son of Lucifer? Impossible. You do not look like the direct descendant of an angel. And everyone knows that Adam is your father. Legends tell it!"

"Legends lie false king," said Cain as his eyes began to glow red.

"You do not sca...."

Before King Saul could finish his sentence, Cain teleported from in front of the king to being behind him and slit his throat with his cutting knife. He then looked at the king's general and Aclima and said, "Raise the dead, kill the Philistines." then he took the form of King Saul and sat at the head of his dining table.

Lucifer's Journal Pt. 3: LETTER TO THE PATHETIC HUMANS PT. 1 (FIRST DAY IN GOD'S PRISON)

YOU ALL READ YOUR SCRIPTURES AND REBUKE ME! YOU ALL GO TO YOUR CHURCH, AND PRAISE.... YOUR.... GOD! AND THEN WHAT? YOU JUDGE ONE ANOTHER! YOU DECIEVE ONE ANOTHER! YOU BETRAY ONE ANOTHER! AND WHEN YOU SONS OF BITCHES FUCK UP, WHAT DO YOU SAY?! WHAT....DO.... YOU.... SAAAAAAAY! YOU ALL SAY, "THE DEVIL MADE ME DO IT!" "MAAAAAAAAAADE ME DOOOOOO IT!" WHERE IS YOUR ACCOUNTABILITY!? WHEN WILL YOU FUCKING SKIN SACKS REALIZE THAT I AM TEMPTATION?! NOT FORCE! I GIVE FREE WILL! AND YOU ALL DO WHAT YOUR HEARTS TRULY DESIRE! AND THEN YOU BLAME ME! FOR ALL OF THE FUCKED UP THINGS IN THE WORLD! WANNA BLAME SOMEONE FOR ALL THAT YOU SEE!? LOOK IN THE FUCKING MIRROR! OR MAYBE YOU'RE ALL JUST AFRAID TO LOOK! BECAUSE IF YOU SEE WHAT IS STARING BACK AT YOU, YOU WILL HAVE NO CHOICE BUT TO OWN IT! YOU HAVE TO OWN A PART OF YOU THAT YOU WANT TO RUN AWAY FROM! BECAUSE YOU ALL CAN'T FACE THE FACT THAT YOU ALL ARE A BUNCH OF INSECURE, PATHETIC, UNINTEL-

LEGENT, JUDGEMENTAL, UNHAPPY, UNHEALED, INCONSIDERATE, SELFISH, DEPRESSED, UNFULFILLED, WEAK, AND FLAWED PIECES OF SHIT! I HAVE NO CHOICE BUT TO FACE MY UGLY SIDE! BUT GOD SHEILDS YOU PATHETIC HUMAAAANS!!!! JUST SO YOU CAN DISAPPOINT HIM ALL OVER AGAIN! BUT WHAT ABOUT ME?! I HAD TO PAY THE PRICE FOR EVERY MISTAKE I MADE! AND FOR WHAT?! MY BROTHER DIED FOR YOU ALL'S SINS! AND FOR WHAT?! SO YOU ALL COULD CONTINUE TO BE A BUNCH OF FUCKING WORMS?! FUCK THAT AND FUCK YOU ALL! YOU STUPID HUMANS!!!

CHAPTER 3

What's a God To a Prince?

God removed his hand from my face and ended the vision. He looked at me with a blank stare.

"This is not possible. I saw Cain, his skeleton. Eve, her skeleton," I said with hurt in my voice.

"All a part of my plan," God said.

"And what you just showed me?"

"Not a part of my plan. After Cain killed King Saul and took his form, he stayed in his form for at least a few years during the day. On top of that, he had plenty of children with that wicked witch. He became a danger to society, and he became a danger to me."

"He fought you, didn't he?"

"Let me show you," God said as he put his hand across my face to show me another vision."

God showed me another vision. This time, it was Cain standing in heaven shirtless with his right eye glowing red. Five angels were lying on the floor dead. Twenty-six angels were waiting to attack him, and one thousand one hundred and ninety-four angels were guarding God on his throne. Cain's hands were dripping blood from ripping the throats and hearts of the first five angel's out. He stared at the twenty-six angels before him and ran towards them to attack. The moment that

Cain attacked, God's angels attacked with their weapons. Cain's hands turned into claws, and his teeth grew sharper and sharper as he fought.

Cain dodged every blade that the angels swung at him. He used his sharp nails to cut each angel open from head to toe. When Cain got to the last angel out of the twenty-six, Cain grabbed him by his hair, bit into the angel's neck, and drained him of his blood. Then he ripped his throat out and spit it out. Then he reached God's heavenly throne, stood before the one thousand nine hundred and ninety-four angels, and said, "Come, fight me! You pathetic, worthless COWARDS!" His voice echoed throughout the throne room. Michael was standing behind God's throne, and he ordered the angels to attack my son. While they ran towards my son, he gave them all an evil grin, and he screamed to the top of his lungs and put both arms in the air with his hands wide open. Then he quickly waved his hands down, and the one thousand nine hundred and ninety-four angels turned into ashes. God was about to step up and fight Cain, but Michael blocked his path. Michael looked at Cain with anger.

"You wanted to prove a point, Cain? You did it," Michael said.

"You all lied to me! And FOR WHAT! TO PUNISH ME! PUNISH ME FOR EXISTING?! I DIDN'T ASK TO BE BORN! I DID NOT ASK FOR YOUR SON TO DECEIVE YOU! LIE TO YOU! I LOVED YOU! SERVED YOU! AND YOU LIED TO ME, GRANDFATHER," Cain screamed with tears in his eyes.

"You're just like him, Cain. Lucifer was filled with anger, hate, envy, and pain. And it was all because life was not what he wanted it to be then. But I had something great in store for him, like I did for you. And in the beginning, I wanted to kill you, but I couldn't do it because I couldn't kill your father. I love your father, and I love you," God said.

"Then why did you treat me like you did in the garden? Why did you praise Abel when he did not work as hard as I did? You treated me like I was nothing. Then you sent me away after his death where I was supposed to die. Then you told me my father wanted nothing to do with me, which was a lie. You let my mother die. Was that a lie, too," Cain asked softly.

"Everything I've ever done was for a reason. A reason that I cannot explain. I am sorry, Cain. I am sorry that your life has been hard. But your actions cannot continue. Now I will give you the same chance I gave your father," God said.

"And what is that?"

"Repent, son. Repent, and I will forgive it all. I will give you everything your heart desires."

"Then give me my mother, my father, and take away my pain. I am alone."

"You have me. And as long as you have me, you will never be alone."

"In that case. I...WILL... NEVER... REPENT!"

God shook his head and said, "It begins again," as he shed tears. Michael attacked Cain, and Cain dodged Michael's attack, grabbed Michael by the neck, and lifted him off of the ground. Cain looked at God with an evil grin, and God looked at Cain with a look of surprise on his face. Cain dropped Michael on the ground, spread his dark wings, and charged towards God. As he charged, Jesus appeared out of nowhere and blocked Cain's attack, knocking him to the ground. Cain shook his head from being dazed and looked up at Jesus. Jesus stood over my son and said, "I may look like your father, but I am not your father. I love my father, God, and will do anything to protect him." Cain smiled and said to Jesus, "You are nothing more than a defective copy of an elite prototype." Cain was about to attack Jesus. When he did, God came off his throne, and Michael stood in a fighting stance.

They all stood around Cain, ready to attack. Cain laughed and posted up in a fighting stance.

"You mean to tell me it will take all three of you to take on little ole me? I'm only half angel," Cain said sarcastically.

"You must be stopped, you're worse than Lucifer," said Micahel.

"I am not worse. I am better than my father."

"Either way, Cain, you will be stopped," Jesus said.

Cain threw the first punch at Michael, and Michael dodged the punch. God, Jesus, and Michael fought my son in hand-to-hand combat together, but they struggled. God finally was able to land a punch, but it did not affect Cain. Instead, it made Cain angrier, and his right eye, which had turned completely red, shot a beam out and burned a mark in God's chest. Jesus came from behind Cain and wrapped his arms around him. Michael ran up and punched Cain in his upper body multiple times at hyper speed. Cain's body was changing at a very fast pace while in combat. He looked as if he was transforming into a beast. It was inhumane. Cain ended up breaking out of Jesus's arms, and he screamed uncontrollably. He looked down at his hands, arms, feet, and legs. He was turning into some type of beast. Then Cain held his head while screaming in pain. God, Michael, and Jesus backed away from him and watched his transformation.

The final stage of his transformation was his horns. Horns grew from Cain's head and a tail from a backside. After completing his transformation, Cain said, "Now, who is your God?!" God, Michael, and Jesus looked at my son with shock and fear. They pulled their power together and attacked him all at once. Jesus charged at Cain and held down his legs. Michael jumped on Cain's back and held on by his throat, and God stood there saying a spell in Enochian to kill Cain. Before the spell was finished, Cain let out an enormous scream and teleported out of heaven's throne room. The three of them looked at each other with an expression of confusion.

God lifted his hand off my face, taking the vision away from me as he had done the last time.

"I made a mistake by letting your son live," God said.

"You made a mistake by lying to my son. You made a mistake by deceiving him and using him."

"I did not deceive him or lie to him. I saved him."

"I have no time to sit here and argue with you over my son. I want to know where he is now and what this has to do with my successor?"

"He is out there somewhere. But your so-called successor, your advocate. His father shares our blood. And he and his children are the last of our bloodline in the human race."

"WHAT?!"

"They are the descendants of Cain, and that vision that Junior showed you, that man is an offspring of Joseph. If you continue to speak evil into Joseph, it will be passed down to future generations in the bloodline. And then armageddon will begin. This is why I told you, son, to stay away from the humans. I knew it would cause destruction, but I didn't think it would birth beings more powerful than us."

I thought about what God was saying to me and showing me, and for a moment, I was going to go along with him and do the right thing. But then I said to myself fuck that shit. If I was going to do this, I needed something in return. I wanted access to The Garden of Eden again. Especially now that it was an extension of heaven and wholly removed from Earth. I wanted access to all of the universes that God created. I wanted to control the timelines of every universe. I wanted to be the balance of life and death. I wanted it all. I wanted to coexist with God. So, I made it clear to him what I wanted. God *rejected* me yet again.

When he *rejected* me again, I punched the Tree of Life as hard as I could, and I walked away from God toward Michael so he could take me back to the earth/universe he put me in.

"If you walk away, son. This means a war unwinnable for all of us," God said.

"The moment you made the Garden of Eden an extension of heaven and removed it from the rest of the universe, deceived me, my son, and took away the love of my life, this became an unwinnable war. At least for you."

"When you walk out, my son, there is no coming back to negotiate an alliance."

"Good. Because the last person I would ever wage an alliance with is your ass. Michael, let me the fuck out!"

Michael opened the portal for me to exit the Garden of Eden, and as soon as I walked out of it, I was back at the Williams's home. Night had fallen, and I was ready to see my successor before he slept. So I teleported into his room and sat in the rocking chair beside his bed. Joseph was excited to see me, and I was excited to see him. He got out of bed, hugged me, and said, "Lucifer, I thought you had left." I responded, "I will never leave you. I will always be here." He got back in bed and demanded that I tell him a story before he went to bed. And so I did. He went to sleep, and I walked out of his room and into his parent's room. I watched them sleep for a long time until I grew bored and walked to Junior's bedroom door. This time, I was not there to kill him. I was there to speak with him. I gently knocked on the door. When he answered, I walked in and told him, "There will be war, and in this war, your God will die." Junior responded, "He who has evil in his heart will never succeed. For his mind is clouded by the unnecessary evils he creates." I chuckled and walked out of his room. From that moment forward, I knew that I had to hurry up and get Joseph to live up to his full potential to become my weapon and provide me his offsprings so I could use them to my advantage.

Junior was too good to turn, like I said before. A prophet for the lord at such a young age and was without sin. And I couldn't even kill him if I wanted to because of two reasons. God protected him, and who knew what type of beast was within him when provoked? From what I saw in the visions God showed me, he could've been like Cain, if not worse. I had to move with caution.

CHAPTER 4

The End Is Only Beginning

As it got closer to Joseph's eleventh birthday, Junior, at twenty-one, decided to leave Leeds, Alabama, and do what all prophets do. Spread God's word to help make the world a better place. What a waste of fucking time, right? Anyway, when Junior announced that he was leaving, it took a toll on the entire family. But no one took it as hard as Joseph. Joseph grabbed his brother and begged him to stay while crying and screaming. Junior squatted down and said,

"Lil trouble maka, no need to cry. I will be back. But God needs me more than you, mama, and pop right now. You have to understand that when God calls on, you come lil trouble maka."

"I don't know what to do without you, Junior. I have no friends, I don't fit in with anyone else in our family, and kids pick with me in school. You're the only one that understands me. You're my best friend," Joseph said with his eyes filled with tears.

Junior hugged his brother tight, kissed him on the forehead, and said, "No matter where I go, what I do, I will always be with you. All you have to do is close your eyes, open your mind up, and think of me. When you think of me, call for me. So I want you to close your eyes and think of me now." Joseph closed his eyes.

"Good job, Joseph. Now, what do you see," Junior asked as he watched Joseph close his eyes.

"I see you. I see your face, Junior."

"Good Joseph, now I want you to think in your mind without saying out loud what you want to tell me that you don't want Mama and Pop to know."

"I broke the vase in the living room and blamed it on the dog," Joseph said in his mind.

"I knew it was you. I just never said anything about it," Junior responded by speaking to Joseph telepathically.

"How'd you hear me," Joseph asked as he opened his eyes with an expression of shock.

"I can speak to you in your mind. It was a trick God taught me," Junior said as he winked at Joseph.

"So we can do that all the time?"

"All the time. I will always answer," Junior said as he and his little brother embraced one another one last time before Junior's departure. "I love you, man," Junior said.

"I love you too, Junior," Joseph said with tears rolling down his face while hugging his brother.

Junior finally lets go of his little brother after holding him as if it would be the last time they see one another. Junior then hugged and kissed his mother and father goodbye. Afterward, he hopped in a car with a neighborhood friend and drove off into the sunset. Joseph stood in the front yard of his home and waved at the vehicle as it drove off while crying until he couldn't see it was out of sight. Joseph finally walked away from the house and wandered the streets of Leeds as if he was lost and didn't know his way.

While wandering the streets of Leed's, Joseph stumbled across his uncle's barn, where he and his gang loaded hooch. Joseph had a sad look on his face as he slowly approached the barn door. When he knocked, you could hear a big, heavy voice yell, "WHO IS IT!?" Joseph announced himself, and a big, burly man dressed in a tailored suit and a bowler hat with a shotgun on his shoulder opened the door. He looked down at ten-year-old Joseph and said, "GONE ROUND BACK," and pointed toward the back of the barn.

Joseph walked to the back of the barn, where his uncle Timothy Knight and henchmen were loading the hooch. His uncle was smoking a cigar and drinking a gallon of hooch straight out of the bottle in his three-piece brown suit and pink shirt. Timothy was a very light-skinned gentleman with a bald head and a scar across his right eye from being cut with a blade. He stood at five foot four, had hazel eyes, and was very muscular. Timothy saw his nephew and had a look of shock on his face. He put his bottle of hooch down, ran over to his nephew, picked him up, and hugged him excitedly. After putting Joseph down, Timothy looked at his nephew and saw the tears rolling down his face.

"What's wrong with you, boy," Timothy exclaimed in his strong southern accent.

"Junior left Leeds," Joseph said sadly.

"Well, I'm sorry to hear that. I know y'all are close. So what you come here for? Ain't got no business here in my place of business."

"I don't know where to go or who to go to. Junior always spent time with me and took me fishing. I don't have many friends. So I'm lost without my brother."

"Well, that's a shame, boy. You may have to find another hobby and more friends."

"Hobbies like what?"

"Well, you're round ten. You're old enough to work. Want a job?"

"What kind of job, Uncle Tim?"

"Well, I could use someone to load these gallons of hooch. You think you could do that after school every day and on the weekends?"

"Yes, sir."

"Perfect, but you know you cannot tell your mama or daddy. That would make them very angry. I need you to tell them you're going to play some baseball with your friends. Got it?"

"Got it."

Joseph hugged his uncle and left to go home. Timothy walked from the loading dock to his office, where I stood waiting for him in an all-red suit, wearing black Edwin Clapps and a black button-up with a red tie. He looked at me and said, "I did it, Lucifer. I held up my end of the bargain." I grinned at Timothy and gave him a briefcase filled with one hundred dollar bills. "You did, and you have been rewarded. Now, what will you do with all of that money?" Timothy opened up the briefcase and stared at the money with an evil grin on his face, and said, "I am going to run this fucking town, Lucifer. I am going to run this fucking town."

Now before I finish, I know what y'all are probably saying right now. "Lucifer ain't worth shit." Or, "He's a sleazy motherfucker." The truth is, I don't give a fuck what you worthless humans think of me while reading this shit. Cause this is what I do, I'm a fucked up mothafucka that does a lot of fucked up shit. I knew that getting Joseph to come to the dark side would be complicated, like a bitch that is not in the mood to fuck when you are. So I had to wait for the right moment and use the right person. And nobody can bring your ass down or fuck you up more than your own family. So with Timothy, also known around Leeds as "Night Time," being thirty years old, in a life of crime, well dressed, well-liked, and charming?! He was the cool uncle who could influence Joseph without Junior standing in the way! So, I took advantage of that and made a deal with Timothy.

Timothy was so greedy for street power that he was more than willing to make a deal with me to sacrifice his nephew for money. Money that he would use to put hits out on all of his enemies' families just to weaken them and take over their territory. Timothy was a ruthless son of a bitch, and was successful in all of the evil he had done in Leeds. He was so successful once he expanded on his opposition's old territory he was able to move more hooch and open up after-hour gambling joints, nightclubs, and whore houses throughout the whole city. The mothafucka even had white cops on the payroll. In the South in 1946. Crazy right? And while expanding his empire, his nephew, Joseph, was right there at age ten, loading up hooch, making deliveries to all of Timothy's places of business, watching his uncle's every move.

Joseph started falling in love with the lifestyle that his uncle lived. It is evident from how he always bragged about his uncle to his classmates at school. Joseph always talked about how Timothy had a nice house and nice cars, how everyone feared and respected him, and how Timothy had a lot of money. On top of that, he had a lot of ladies. Joseph was impressionable at seeing these things, so he said to his classmates, "I want to be like my Uncle Tim when I grow up."

After five months of lying to his parents and brother, whom he spoke with daily telepathically about what he was doing after school and on weekends, Joseph's father became suspicious of what he was up to. He began to notice things people just "happened" to give Joseph, like a new pair of shoes, comic books, or candy from the candy store. All because Joseph would do "odd jobs" for the people in the community. Now, Joseph's father, Senior, was not an educated man. But he definitely had a PhD in "I Know That's Some Bullshit University." So one day, after working his side job on the railroad, Senior went to Junior's school and stood outside the building from a distance. He watched his son be dismissed and decided to follow him after school.

Joseph led Senior straight to Timothy's barn off the swamp. Senior ran up as Joseph approached the barn doors, collared his son tightly, and lifted him off the ground.

> "Odd jobs, huh? Odd JOBS," Senior screamed while collaring Joseph.
>
> "Pop, please put me down," Joseph pleaded while crying."
>
> "How could you, son? After all the good we tried to teach you? You come from a God-fearing house. Not the streets, yet you up here with your uncle while telling us you're playing baseball and working odd damn JOB," Senior exclaimed as his deep voice broke.
>
> "I'm sorry, Dad. Please put me down."

Senior dropped Joseph on the ground, looking down at him with sadness and disgust. Senior snatched the barn door so hard that it broke off the hinges. The six-foot-seven black man with a pot belly and muscular arms, shoulders, and chest rushed into the barn and said in his heavy voice, "KNIGHT! GET YOUR ASS DOWN HERE NOW!" Timothy came from his office upstairs dressed to kill as always, with a big cigar in his mouth, a grin on his face, and two of his henchmen.

"My broke ass brother in laaaaaaaw. I didn't know they let niggers off the railroad so early in the day," Timothy said while laughing with his henchmen.

"You and I had a deal. Or did you forget," Senior growled.

"Of course, I remember. I get your business as long as I leave my sister and Junior out of all my dealings. Because yo ass wanted to be a better man for your family."

"Yet you broke your word."

"Big Man, I didn't break my word. You said that when my sister was pregnant with Junior. You didn't say shit about Joseph. Besides, he's about the same age I was when you and Big Joe Joseph had me doing your dirty deeds. What's the big deal?"

"I don't want my sons in this mess! I raised them better!"

"AAAAHHH. I understand, so this life was good enough for me, but not the boys, right? See, that's where you have life messed up, Big Man. See, before you were their father, you were my father. Or did you forget that after me and my sister's parents were killed by the coward ass Klan, you moved my sister and me into that house on your farm? You and your brother taught me everything about y'all business. Shit, you even put a gun in my hand to kill them damn Klansmen. All five of em. ALL FIVE OF EM! And all I have your boy doing is loading some hooch and paying him decent so he can have some money in his pocket. And you gone come in here and look your big ass nigger nostrils down at ME?! I don't think so," Timothy said sarcastically.

"You little high yellow bitch I will kill you if you ever come near my son again."

"But Jesus wouldn't do that, now would he? Mr. God-fearing man," Timothy said sarcastically.

Senior took off the straps of his overalls and his shirt. Then, he began to rush at his brother-in-law at full speed. Timothy's two henchmen attempted to stop him, but he clotheslined the both of them. He proceeded to pick both men up by in each hand by their throats and threw them through the ceiling of the barn. While standing in the center of the barn with the sun beaming on his dark skin through the holes in the ceiling, Senior gave Timothy an evil stare. In a demonic voice, Senior said, "You should know better than to fuck with my kids!" The next thing I knew, I saw black wings extend from his back, his muscles grew bigger, and his eyes glowed a bright red as if they were fire-filled.

Timothy stood and stared back at Senior without showing an ounce of fear. Then he decided to walk up to the large, angry man who was beginning to take the form of a beast. Timothy stared into Senior's fire-filled eyes and grinned an evil grin.

> "Thou shalt not kill. And you just broke that commandment twice in one day. Shame on you, Big Man," Timothy said sarcastically.
>
> "I will break it three times today," Senior screamed in his demonic voice as he lifted Timothy off of the ground by the collar of his shirt.
>
> "You won't. Because your son is standing right outside that barn, watching you, listening to you, afraid because he didn't know that his father had the blood of the devil in him. But I've seen you. The real you. Not that churchy churchy church church hard-working negro you pretend to be. This form of the beast you show me is nothing. I saw it that night you.... You know what, never mind. Just put me the fuck down."

Senior grinned and tossed Timothy across the barn. Causing him to land in a bale of hay. Then he turned around and looked at Joseph. Joseph looked back at his father with fear in his eyes and a face full of tears. "Go home, now, and never return here again," Senior said. Joseph stood there frozen in a state of shock. "NOW," Senior exclaimed. Joseph jumped from being frightened by his father's voice and appearance and ran as fast as he could towards the house on the farm. Senior proceeded to punch Timothy repeatedly in his face and body for a while.

After giving his brother-in-law a royal ass whipping, Senior stood over to his brother-in-law, looked down at him, and said, “Next time, I will forget about how much you once meant to me,” and then returned to his regular form before walking out of the barn. Timothy lifted his head hay, breathing heavily, and said, “He who is without sin among you, let him be the first to throw a stone. You bitch,” and then laid his head back in the hay while laying flat on his back.

CHAPTER 5

Bloodline Deception

By the time Joseph arrived home, he was entirely out of breath. I don't think I'd ever seen that boy run so fast. He charged through the house's front door, dashed right past his mother, went straight to his bedroom, and slammed the door. His mother, Esther, looked surprised because Joseph had never run into the house and went straight to his room, especially without speaking to his parents. Esther began to walk towards Joseph's bedroom until Senior teleported and appeared in front of his son's bedroom door, blocking his wife. Esther looked at her husband's face and could see sadness. She said, "Let's go outside and talk." They walked around their farmland, and Esther got straight to the point.

"The last time you had that sad look on your face was when Tim saw you in that raging form after our parent's death."

"Unfortunately, it wasn't the last, as you know. But since Joseph was born, I have been able to hold that demon inside of me. But today, I couldn't, and our son saw it.

"Senior, what triggered it."

"Knight," Senior said as he broke down and cried. "Our son is working for him, loading hooch in the old barn, and I believe he is helping deliver it too. Joseph has been lying to us for months. He wasn't getting his money from doing odd jobs for townspeople. He wasn't playing baseball after school and on weekends. The boy was working for your damn brother."

"Timothy would not do that. Senior, my brother would never involve our children in his business. He knows better," Esther said as she covered her mouth while crying.

"Knight has changed sweetie. He's different. He has only two things on his mind, money and power. I didn't teach him to be greedy in that business. I wish I never brought him into it. Then, just leaving him to run it all. I am so sorry."

"We were kids ourselves. We didn't know any better. All of us were orphans and didn't have anyone to fall back on. Besides, whether you taught him the business, he still would've found his way into this mess. You only taught him what you and your brother Big Joe knew. May God rest his soul. I hate that we never found the white men who killed him."

"Yeah, me too, but it still don't make it right, Essie. And now it is all coming back on me. I am going to pay for all of my sins through our son. Our baby boy," Senior said as his voice cracked like a bitch.

"You cannot help the fact that you were born with these abilities. But God saved you. He saved you the day that Junior was born. God showed you that you could turn your life around for your family, and you did that. He knew that you were destined for something greater as he does Junior, as he will Joseph. This is why he showed you the light to escape that life of crime. Even if it meant we'd struggle and be poor in the process. But when has God ever let us go without food, a home, or some type of income, and we can still help people?"

"I believe you're right on a lot of things you just said, sweetie. But I don't know if God can save Joseph. I think that only Junior can. I feel Joseph's energy shifting. He's different. His energy feels similar to Knight's now. He may grow up to be worse than your brother and myself. I am afraid for that boy."

"God has him, Senior, you have to have faith. And you have to talk to your son about what happened today."

Senior looked down at his five-foot-two, full-figured wife, with long hair, big pretty eyes, and freckles, and picked her up, held her tight in his arms, and kissed her. Afterward, Senior walked back into the house and knocked on his son's door three times. After knocking, he entered the room only to see an empty bedroom and an open window. He stood in the empty bedroom, let out a deep sigh, and said, "That boy is going to be trouble. God, please save him," as he looked out the window.

Joseph ran to the pond where he and his brother used to fish. He stood there staring at the pond, and I appeared in a red suit before him. I put my hand on his shoulder. He looked up at me and said, "I'm scared." I looked down at him and said, "You have nothing to fear because you are the one who will be feared in due time." He hugged me and cried, and I consoled him.

"My dad, he was a monster. I have never seen him like that," Joseph said.

"That is because you, your father, and your brother share the same blood as God, Jesus, my son Cain, and myself. Your father doesn't know, but your brother does."

"Why you never told me," Joseph asked me as he cried.

"I didn't know until recently myself, Joseph. But you will be okay. I will guide you through life and teach you how to control your power, but first, I want you to close your eyes and think of me. Once you think of me, let me take control of your body and mind."

Joseph followed my instructions, and I entered his body and possessed him. I needed to expedite the process of Joseph being my protege. So, after I got inside of his body, I took over his mind as well. Then, in Joseph's body, I headed back to the house. While approaching the house from the backyard, I saw a car arrive. Once it stopped, Junior got out and yelled, "MAMA, POP, I'M HOME!" Senior and Esther ran out of the house, greeted their oldest son, and walked into the house with him. At that moment, I knew I had to put on my best damn Joseph act.

So I ran into the house and ran straight into Junior's arms and cried tears of joy as he would. Junior picked me up and said, "Lil TROUBLE MAKA! I HAVE MISSED YOU SO MUCH." After holding me for a moment, he threw me from the dining room to the living room. Everyone stood up with a look of surprise on their faces.

> "Boy, you mean to tell me you go away for a few months, and you done already lost your damn MIND," Esther exclaimed.
>
> "That ain't my brother," Junior growled while getting in his fighting stance.
>
> "What," Esther asked.
>
> "It's Lucifer. He has control over Joseph's mind and body, mama. That ain't Joseph."

I finally got up and stood before the family. I spoke in Joseph's body and began to levitate off the ground.

> "So you figured it out, Junior. You're smarter than I thought you were," I said with an evil grin.
>
> "There is no way the devil is in our home, son," Senior exclaimed.
>
> "Dear God, please take this demon out of our ho...."

Before Esther could finish her prayer, sentence, whatever the fuck, I had snapped my finger and broke her neck. The bitch was really starting to work a nerve. Senior and Junior both stood there and looked down at Esther's lifeless body lying on the floor. Junior then screamed and charged at me. While charging at me, Senior got down on his knees, holding his wife in his arms. Screaming in agony because the pain of losing his wife must've been pretty fucking immense. But anyway, I charged back at Junior. While we both charged at one another, we drew our fists back to hit one another, but lightning struck the living room floor before we could land our punches. Propelling Junior and I backwards.

I was stunned at first, but once I snapped out of it, I couldn't fucking believe it. It was that punk-ass brother of mine, Jesus, and the angel of death, Grimm. Standing in the middle of the floor with two other angels.

"Grimm, collect the Queen of this household and take her to my father," Jesus said.

"Yes, holy prince," Grimm responded as he signaled for his angels to take away Esther.

"This bitch. Go back to your fucking cross already and die again. I am about sick of your shit. You're nothing more than a lesser version of me. And you're no prince, bitch I am," I exclaimed.

"This ends now. Let go of the boy. Joseph, young man! I know you're in there. And I know you're not the one doing this. But I need you to fight Lucifer. You cannot let him control your mind like this," Jesus said.

"Mothafucka, he can't hear you. He's sleeping in there. By the time he wakes up from this, he ain't gone remember shit," I said while laughing.

Senior got up from the floor after Grimm and those punk ass angels took Esther away, and he charged at me in his beast form while screaming, "GIVE ME BACK MY SOOOOOOOOOOOON!" While throwing a punch, I caught his fist, swung him around the room, and released him. Causing him to fly out of the living room window. After that, Jesus and Junior came after me throwing every punch they could, but I ducked and dodged all of them bitches. Then I let out a loud screech, causing Junior and Jesus to grab their ears. While they were in pain, I teleported outside where Senior was. I looked down at Senior and said, "You were right. God can't save Joseph," and I reached down and snatched his heart out of his chest, bit into it, and threw it to the ground.

"Noooooooooooo," Junior screamed. He ran out of the house as blood from his ears rolled down the side of his face, and tears flowed down the front. I let out another screeching sound and weakened Junior and the great-value version of myself (Jesus), and then I disappeared before their eyes. They looked so stupid and confused. It was shameful. Jesus looked at Junior and said, "He didn't go far at all. He is near. We will save your brother. Follow me." While they were trying to find me, I had teleported to Timothy's house. I then separated myself from Joseph's body and let him fall to the ground. While unconscious, I picked him up and made all of his father's blood disappear from his body. I shook him to make it seem like I had just found him lying there in the middle of the road. He finally woke up and had a look of confusion on his face.

"Lucifer, what happened," Joseph asked.

"A lot, my child. I need to tell you something."

"What is it?"

"Remember when you were standing at the pond crying?"

"Yeah, so what?"

"Well, from my understanding, your uncle knocked you out because he was angry about the situation that happened with your father. He blamed you. Then he went to the house, and he... he... he killed your parents."

Joseph broke down and cried in the middle of the road in a fetal position. He then looked up at me, exposing his face, and his eyes had turned a bright red as if they were filled with lasers. "How did I end up here," Joseph asked me. I had to think of something, and something really quick, because even though the kid was eleven years old. He was no stupid mothafucka.

"I found you unconscious. Lying on the ground. I didn't want any more harm to come to you. And once I found out what your Uncle Tim did, I brought you here. To seek your revenge."

"I cannot believe he would do such a thing. I have to call on Junior. He's all I have now," Joseph said while crying.

"Noooooo, noooooooo! There is no need to call on him. You have me. I will help you, guide you. And right now, you need to take this and knock on that door and avenge your parents. What does the bible say? An *eye for an eye*," I said while handing the eleven-year-old Joseph a handgun.

Joseph took the handgun and knocked on his uncle's door. When Timothy answered the door, he looked down at Joseph and said, "I ain't got time to be fighting with your daddy no more. You see what the fuck he did to me. So take your ass home, and don't come back here." As Timothy was about to close the door on his nephew, he noticed that he was crying and he had a gun in his hand.

"Now, wait a minute, boy, what the hell happened? And why do you have a gun," Timothy said while holding his ribcage.

"You killed my parents."

"You little mothafucka, have you lost your damn mind? What are you talking about? I killed your gotdamn parents? Hurting your mother or that nigger giant Willie would never come to mind. Even if he did beat my ass earlier," Timothy said while grunting from the pain he was in.

"My parents are dead, Uncle Tim, and I know you did it!"

Timothy dropped to his knees and began to cry. He then whispered to himself, "My sister. Oh my God, not her. How?!" Joseph lifted the gun and put it to his uncle's head. He cocked back the hammer slowly. I came up from behind Joseph and placed my hands on his shoulder. Timothy looked up at me with a face full of tears and an expression of anger.

"You son of a bitch. You did this. You have fooled my nephew into believing that I would do harm to my family," Timothy said.

"Well, did you not have your nephew around all of your ill elements and was getting ready to teach him more about your business? Shame on you for not being responsible for your actions."

"You set this up. You set all of this up. You had all of this planned from the jump."

Timothy looked beyond Joseph and me, seeing Junior and Jesus from afar. He yelled, "Nephew, help me!" Before Junior and Jesus could make a move, Joseph pulled the trigger and shot his uncle in the head. I looked back at Junior and Jesus, gave an evil grin, and looked down at Joseph and said, "It is time for us to go." Joseph looked at his brother and waved at him, and before their eyes, we disappeared. Junior ran over to his uncle's lifeless body and begged Jesus to bring his family back. Jesus could only stand there and cry while looking down at Junior with a sympathetic expression. At this point, I knew I owned Joseph and had him brainwashed enough to be able to persuade him into doing all that I needed him to do for me to rule this entire universe. At least, that's what I thought at the time.

CHAPTER 6

Made In My Image

When Joseph and I disappeared the night of his parents' and uncle's death, I teleported us to the roof of my home, located on Hathaway Avenue off of East 105th Street, the hell I created on earth. Night had fallen, and the weather was warm. Joseph looked at me and asked, "Where are we?" I looked at him and responded, "This is your empire." Joseph walked to the edge of the roof and looked at the view.

"This is the place that you spoke of for all of these years," Joseph asked me with tears in his eyes.

"It is."

"Lucifer, this is beautiful. It doesn't look like hell. I never expected Cleveland to be so big and busy. It looks like paradise."

"One day, you will inherit it. All of it."

Joseph broke down and cried, then ran up to me and hugged me. He looked up at me and said, "What about God? Won't he be mad?" I looked back at Joseph, and with a grin on my face, I kneeled and wiped his tears.

"Why worry about God? If God really loved you, would he have let your parents die that way at the hands of your uncle? What did they ever do to anyone? They were good people. They followed his laws. They went to church faithfully and look at how he abandoned his children? But I will never abandon you. So don't worry about God. Fuck him! And fuck Junior too. Look at how he abandoned you to follow *GOD*! Now, would someone who loves you leave you like that?"

"No, I guess not," Joseph said as he continued to cry.

"Exactly. Boy, all you have is me. Your family in Leeds don't give a shit about you. Your brother doesn't give a shit about you. God, don't give a shit about you. It's just you and me," I said as I pulled Joseph in and hugged him. "So now that it is just us, I need you to tap into your full potential and become the king you were born to be."

"Yes, Lucifer. Anything for you."

After that quick visit to hell, I took Joseph back to Leeds. He expressed his concerns about not having a place to stay now that his parents were dead.

"Lucifer, where will I go? I have no place to lay my head."

"You will live in the house that your parents were killed in."

"I can't do it!"

"You can! And YOU WILL! YOU WILL DWELL IN YOUR PAIN FOR YOU TO *BECOME THE KING YOU WERE BORN TO BE*!"

I teleported him to his home, and when we walked in the door, he stared at his mother's blood on the dining room floor. He looked around the house with an expression of sadness and said, "Where is Junior Lucifer?" I looked at Joseph and said, "I don't know. But, like I said, fuck him. I am all that you need. Now, let's clean this place up." I snapped my fingers and put everything back in place as it was before I killed Joseph's parents.

Joseph went to his bedroom and cried himself to sleep. While he grieved his family, I walked around the house, and then I looked down at Essie's blood. I squatted down and touched it, and another vision came to me in a flash. Except this one felt different. I was physically there in the vision. I saw the same bald-headed man I'd seen in a previous vision standing in an office on the top floor of a skyscraper. The color of the office was black and red. The bald man had the same beard as in the last vision, except his wings were not expanded. Now that I think of it, he favored Timothy a lot.

Anyway, this man was wearing a black turtle neck, black dress slacks and shoes, an Allah medallion around his neck made of gold, a gold watch, black and gold sunglasses, and a gold pinky ring. He had a touch of gray in his beard, and he was drinking a glass of scotch. The man spoke to me while he stared out the office window as it stormed outside, holding a cane with the head of a snake with ruby eyes.

"I always liked storms. Do you like storms, Lucifer," the man said in a deep raspy voice.

"I do," I said while looking at this strange man suspiciously and cautiously.

"I know you do Luci. I know you do."

When he turned around, he took his glasses off, displaying the scar across his right eye and his red pupil. Then, behind him appeared Cain with his hand on the man's shoulder.

"Fear not, father, it is only a dream until it is not," Cain said to me with an evil grin.

"Yeah, what he said," said the man.

"What the fuck is thi....."

Before I could finish my sentence, I was suddenly standing in a park on a fall day. I saw the same bald man, except he was younger. He was walking hand in hand with this absolutely gorgeous young lady. She was short, kind of slim, light-skinned, and had long natural black curls. She was wearing a cream-colored pantsuit, sunglasses, and a fur jacket. The bald man wore brown slacks, brown dress boots, a brown turtleneck, and an overcoat.

The bald man looked at her with so much love and smiled. She smiled back at him and said, "We have been together for years, have children together, and you still look at me and smile like you did when we first started dating. Why?" The man looked back at her, and with an expression of sincerity, he responded.

"Because I never thought that I could have someone like you. Someone so sweet, so pure with intentions, so good. Someone that just made me want to leave this life behind. You have no idea how much you mean to me. If you did, you would never ask me a question like that. I love you so much," said the man, pulling the gorgeous woman closer to him by her hips.

"I love you more, my short, bald king. I just hope our kids don't start to lose their hair and look like a cue ball like you," the gorgeous woman said in a jokingly manner while laughing.

"You know what? I take everything back that I said," the bald man said as he laughed.

"Just shut up and kiss me, Gemini."

The two kissed, and afterward, I was back in my reality. Standing in the very spot where Joseph's mother was murdered. It was weird because out of all the other times I had visions, I had never felt like I was actually there. It was as if I had physically traveled in time. I didn't know what to make of it at the time, but shit was starting to get weird. But don't get it twisted because shit only got weirder. After my experience with that vision, I realized I had one goal. Finding out *Who.... The.... Fuck..... Was.... "Gemini?" And why was he with Cain?*

CHAPTER 7

Family Secrets Revealed

Joseph laid in bed for at least five days straight after we returned to his family home. He didn't speak a word to me or even to himself. He didn't get out of bed to eat, drink, wash his funky ass. Nothing. After the fifth day, a knock was on the front door. Joseph ignored the knock. Another knock was at the door, and Joseph refused to budge. There was silence for a moment, and then all you could hear was a loud "BOOM" echo through the house. Joseph hopped out of bed and stood in the middle of his bedroom with fear in his eyes.

There was another moment of silence. Joseph crept to the door of his bedroom and slowly cracked it. He saw nothing and no one. Joseph opened the door entirely and slowly walked out of his room. He entered the living room cautiously and saw the front door lying on the floor but saw no one in the house. He called for me out loud, but I did not respond. Instead, a soft, smooth, and raspy voice with a strong Southern accent said, "*I wouldn't call myself Lucifer, but I can bring hell depending on the day.*" Then, a tall, dark-skinned man with a long braided ponytail stepped inside the home wearing a white suit and a cane with the head of a snake with ruby eyes. He looked down at the eleven-year-old boy and smiled, displaying a mouth full of gold teeth.

The man resembled Joseph's father. Five more men walked inside the house behind him, and Joseph recognized them. They were

Timothy's henchmen. Joseph began to walk backward away from the men until he backed into a wall. The men walked toward him, but the man who resembled his father got close to Joseph, kneeled, touched Joseph's face gently, and said, "Yup, you my brother's boy, alright." The man instructed his henchmen to take Joseph to his car. Joseph put up a fight, but they finally got a hold of him, tied him up, blindfolded him, and put him inside an all-white Rolls Royce. They pulled off, and moments later, the car stopped. Joseph began to breathe heavily, and the dark-skinned man said, "Ain't no need of being scared, boy, you with family now. Now stop all that damn heavy breathing. I've got something I want to show you." Joseph was untied, and the blindfold was removed. Joseph looked out the car window and saw that they were at the barn his uncle Timothy used to do business out of. "Get out, boy, let's go in. And don't try to run," the man said. Joseph followed instructions, exited the vehicle, and entered the barn with the strange man. They both stood in the center of the barn and stared at one another for a moment.

"I know a million things are going through your mind right now. Like, who is this nigga? Where did he come from? And why is he a better-looking version of my pappy? Well, nephew, I be your uncle," said the man who resembled his father.

"That is impossible. White men killed my father's brother."

"HA! That's what he told you? Naaaaah, see that ain't true. Not true at all. See, your father was an awful individual before he turned his life over to *God*. He was a murderer, a hooch runner, a pimp, and had his hands in policies and shit. He was a deceitful liar and betrayed me, his brother. Then, he handed off our business to that little high yella bitch Timothy fucking Knight."

"My father was not that kind of man. I know he has a past, but...."

"But you didn't know your father, and neither does Junior. You're only eleven years old, boy. You don't know nothing about nothing yet. But you will soon," The man said after cutting Joseph off mid-sentence.

"I am so confused. If you have been alive all this time, why not take vengeance? Why are my uncle's men standing beside you? Where did you even come from? All these years, and you're back in Leeds?"

"You ask a lot of questions. I like that. Well, let me tell you. Your father, Knight, and myself went to New Orleans to make a deal with Italian mob boss, Don Johnny Santino from Cleveland, Ohio. He was traveling through the South because he was looking to expand his business from the North to the South. He was willing to sell us the purest heroin and coke he had for a decent price. I wanted that deal. But Willie wanted to think on it for a day or two. Johnny granted us twenty-four hours. I argued that we could make so much more money if we ran drugs through our clubs and whore houses. Your father disagreed. He felt that drugs would be a liability rather than an asset. We got into a heated argument, which turned into a fist fight. A fist fight that caused us both to turn into something we weren't."

"Turn into something you weren't? Like what? Beasts?"

"Exactly that. Something that I had no idea we had the ability to do. Wings expanded from our backs, our hands turned to claws, our teeth grew sharp, and horns grew from our heads. Knight was really young, and unfortunately, he got hit in the eye during our fight."

"I thought that scar came from a blade."

"No. It came from these hands of mine. But it was an accident," The man said as he looked at his hands.

"So tell me the rest of the story."

"Well, Senior sliced my throat with his claws. And it caused me to bleed out. The thing is, my brother left me for dead and dumped me by an alligator swamp in New Orleans. I guess he was expecting me to be eaten. I don't remember seeing anything but darkness after he sliced my throat. But later, I saw a light. And in that light, I saw a tall, skinny, bald-headed man with a dark hooded robe and wings. He looked down at me and ran his hands across my face, removing any dirt and mud off me. Afterward, he ran his fingers across my throat and closed the open cut. He then said to me, "Distant son of Cain. You are not ready to see the other side yet!" And then he disappeared."

"Who was it that brought you back to life?"

"Grimm, *The Angel of Death.* Once I woke up, I walked back in the city and entered a bar. I was filthy. Everyone looked at me like I was a crazy man. I ordered myself a drink, and Johnny Santino was there. I wasn't expecting that. He approached me and asked me what happened. When I explained that my brother left me for dead, he advised me not to return to Leeds. Instead, he gave me a job running drugs in New Orleans and changed my name to Silky Whispers."

"Why Silky Whispers?"

"Because of how my voice sounded after my throat was cut and how smooth I am. Because this uncle got some style to him! But anyway, I built a multi-million dollar criminal empire in New Orleans and kept a very low profile. And since I couldn't return to Leeds, I had no choice but to have some of my men from New Orleans travel to Leeds and go undercover. I wanted them to prove themselves to your father and be recruited. They were successful, and they worked for your father. Then, after your father, they worked for Tim. And now that you have done me the honors of killing that uncle of yours, you left room for me to return. And with all of my money, power, influence, and brute force, I have successfully retaken over Leeds. And everyone in Tim's organization is on my payroll now."

Joseph put his head down, stared at the ground, and began to cry. He tried to speak words for a moment but could not get them out. Silky kneeled, put his hand on Joseph's shoulder, and said, "Calm down. Just breathe." Joseph finally calmed himself down and responded to this newfound uncle he had.

"My mother and father are dead."

"I know. And despite all we went through, I hated to hear that Willie died. I still loved him, which is the reason why no harm came to any of you. Shit, I was even proud to hear he'd become a God-fearing man. It made me proud to see that he had become more than I'd taught him to be. Where is your brother?"

"I don't know. I haven't seen him since the night of our parent's death." Joseph said as he began to cry.

"HM. Got it. Well, I want you to know that you are not alone. You've got me, and you have a lot of cousins. I will send one of them here to live with you until it is time for you to branch off on your own. I will make sure you are taken care of. I will also make sure that you continue to work as you did with your Uncle Tim, and I'll teach you everything you need to know and more."

Joseph nodded in agreement and hugged his uncle. Silky called for one of his henchmen to take Joseph home, and when Joseph exited the barn, Silky said, "Luci, baby, reveal yourself. We need to talk." I was shocked when he said that, but I revealed myself to Silky.

"Here I am. Now, how the hell did you know I was here?"

"*I am blood of your blood and flesh of your flesh.* I can feel your presence. You may be able to cloak in the shadows, but your sinister energy is always present."

"Well, what the fuck do you want, *Silkster*."

"Call me that one more time, and I will unleash the wrath of Cain! And to answer your question. I want the same thing as you. I want to see Joseph grow into the king he was born to be. I want his offsprings to carry on my legacy. Your legacy. I have seen what the future can hold. I may not be alive to see it all come to fruition, but I can help you start the process. My greatest revenge is to corrupt my brother's children after what he did to me."

"Okay, and what do you want from me? Money, power, women?"

"I am not *Knight*, as they called him. I am feared. I am a God in my own right. There is nothing you can provide me that I don't already have. I know that my brother and his wife are with God. I know they are watching over their children. And I know that Junior is with them in heaven. Strategizing with your father and brothers to take you out. OH, and by the way, that shit you pulled with possessing my nephew's body and mind? Hell of a way to use his body to kill Willie and Essie," Silky said with a smirk.

"How do you know all of this, you slick-haired son of a bitch."

"When I was brought back to life, I was aware of the supernatural powers I possess. One of them happens to be vision of the past and the future. And the future? It is really fucking dark. Joseph's grandson, *Gemini*, will be too much for any of our bloodline to handle. Which is why it would be best for you to control him. It'll be the greatest fuck you to my brother, your brother, and your father."

"You know of *Gemini*? You have *seen* him?"

"I have, and if we play this right, the future will be just how we want it to be. Just trust me," Silky said while winking.

"If this is what you really want, I am all for it."

"Good. Now, my plan is long-term. And I know what your hell looks like in West Eden. I mean, Cleveland. It is amazing how you guided some of the most corrupt people to that place. East 105th Street is terrible, yet beautiful. I've been there. My Italian bosses run a couple of neighborhoods in Cleveland. But not East 105th Street. I will see to it that he learns everything he needs to know, corrupts as many people as he needs to, and blesses them with evil deeds and thoughts to serve your army in Cleveland by the time he reaches the age of sixteen."

"Damn. *Blood of my blood. Flesh of my flesh.* I think I am going to like you," I said as we both laughed sinisterly.

"In that case, let's give 'em all *hell* then, Luci baby."

The two of us shook hands and shared a smile and a laugh. And for the first time in years, I felt like a proud father. The first I felt this was when Cain killed that punk ass Abel. Couldn't stand that little bitch.

But at this time, I knew that I would unleash hell in the heavens and on earth.

CHAPTER 8

I Have Dreams of HELL

Five years had passed since Silky approached Joseph and took him under his wing. Within those five years, Joseph continued to live in his family home on the farm, but he was not alone. Silky's oldest son, Julian, stayed in Leeds to ensure Joseph was safe and cared for. Julian ensured Joseph stayed in school and tended to his responsibilities in their criminal organization. Now, don't get me wrong, Julian was no Junior. Joseph still missed his brother, but the two cousins had a close relationship, and Joseph looked up to Julian like a big brother.

Julian was not only in Leeds to take care of Joseph, though. He was also there to run the city's crime organization under Silky's control. By the time Joseph was sixteen years old, Joseph had become Julian's right-hand man. Before you could get to Julian, you had to go through Joseph. And at that age, no one wanted to go through Joseph. Because he'd grown to be one ruthless son of a bitch, but a charming son of a bitch, and handsome too. He stood at five foot eight and a half. One hundred and forty-five pounds of ripped muscles, beautiful dark brown skin, freckles, and jet black slicked back wavy hair. The ladies loved him, and the fellas wanted to be him. He was desired, he was feared, he was revered.

He was so revered that he impressed many mafia bosses throughout the South and the North. Joseph was brilliant, cold, and calculated, and he had the tongue of a serpent. Slicker than a mothafucka. Joseph was becoming who I wanted him to be. And it was all thanks to Silky. But by sixteen, it was time for Silky to cut him loose and let him leave Leeds, Alabama, and go to Cleveland. Exactly where he belonged. The perfect opportunity came when Joseph and Julian made their monthly trip to New Orleans French Quarters to deliver Silky's cash in the summer of 1952.

During this trip, the two cousins ran into their father's employer in the French Quarters, Don Johnny Santino. Johnny was a short Italian man with an even shorter fuse. In his day, he was the most feared man in Cleveland, Ohio. But that is another story for another day (or book.....hint, hint). Any fucking way, the two cousins walked into Silky's juke joint, where there were entertainers and prostitutes. As soon as the two walked in, Silky greeted them with a big hug. Joseph was holding bags of cash and said to his uncle, "It's great to see you, old man." Silky grabbed his nephew, kissed him on the forehead, and said to the two young men, "Follow me. We have a guest that wants to see you two."

Silky walked his son and nephew to the V.I.P. room in the back of the juke joint, and when he opened the door, Johnny was sitting in a chair while a beautiful, full-figured black woman in lingerie sucked his Italian sausage. Johnny yelled, "You don't stop until you've got all of the cream out of my cannoli, ya hear!" The prostitute continued to suck him off, and finally, Johhny grabbed the back of her head and held it in place while he came in her mouth. Once he had ejaculated in her mouth completely, he paid her and sent her out of the room.

"I swear, out of everyone who works for me that has whore houses, you've got the finest whores Silk. In every city and state you run," Johnny said as he zipped his pants up.

"Tell me something I don't know, and I will be surprised, Johnny. I know you remember my son Julian and my nephew Joseph."

"How could I forget the brain of the organization and the brute muscle? These two are running Leeds like kings! And it looks like these kings bring gifts."

"Don Santino, it is always a pleasure. I wasn't expecting to see you here tonight. And I definitely come bearing gifts," Julian said, shaking Johnny's hand.

"Is that my money," Silky asked.

"It is. There's about two million in these bags," Joseph said.

Silky and Johnny looked at one another with an expression of surprise. Joseph put the bags on a table and opened them to show his uncle and Johnny the cash.

"Well, well, well. If a money pit is the devil's pit, I'm always riding with the devil," Johnny said as he pulled a wad of cash out and stared at it excitedly. "How the hell are you two making so much money in a small place like Leeds? Every month, you earn more and more."

"As much as I would love to take the credit for it all, I have to give credit to this little cousin of mine," Julian said as he put his arm around Joseph's neck. "This man right here has not only helped me run Leeds. He has helped me expand into other territories and cities in Alabama. We running shit from Birmingham to Montgomery. He figured out how to make peace and not war among other gangs. They buy our drugs, we supply them with weapons and women, and they answer to us. Which means they answer to you, Don Santino."

Johnny laughed and clapped his hands while pacing the floor. He looked at Joseph and then at Silky with a sinister look.

"I like that. I like that a lot. But I have to ask you something, Julian. Do you think you can continue to run Alabama without Joseph," Johnny asked.

"Why would you ask my son something like that, Johnny? He learned from the *best*!"

"He definitely did Silk. He definitely did. But I am asking because I have heard a lot about Joseph here. I hear that Joseph is smart. I hear that Joseph knows the streets. I hear Joseph is charming. And on top of that, he is ruthless. I like ruthless. I like ruthless a lot. And I need someone like Joseph in Cleveland with me."

"*Me*? Cleveland? Why me," Joseph asked Johnny.

"Because I already have your family running shit in the South. Louisiana, Alabama, Mississippi, and Florida. But I can't expand outside of Little Italy and the Collinwood area. I need Woodland, I need Superior, I need Saint Clair. I need Cedar. I *NEED East 105th Street.* And I need someone with brains and muscle. And that is you, Joseph."

Joseph looked at his uncle and cousin in confusion as if he wanted them to confirm whether he should take the offer to work with Johnny Santino and move to Cleveland. Julian had an expression of happiness and sadness at the same time. I don't know. The shit was weird. But Silky, on the other hand, was smiling harder than a mothafucka. Because this is the moment he and I had been waiting for.

"Don't look at us for permission, Joe. Where does your heart want to go with this? You wanna go to Cleveland, or do you want to go back to Leeds," Silky said.

"I'm not sure, Uncle Silky. Leeds is home. But I saw Cleveland the night my parents were killed. And I must admit what I saw was beautiful."

"How did you see Cleveland the night your parents died," Johnny asked.

"I saw it in my dreams. But it felt real. I was on a street called "*Hathaway*," standing on top of a brick building. It was amazing."

"Well, that must be some of that voodoo shit y'all practice down here because there is a building with four houses connected on that street," Johnny said.

"I guess. I don't know. All I know is that the night my parents died and I killed Tim, everything else was sort of a blur afterward. I just remember laying in my bed, crying myself to sleep. Then, a few days later, Silky kicked in my door. I don't even remember seeing my parents when they died. It is almost like certain things were erased from my mind."

"Maybe that is a good thing, Joseph. No need to carry that burden of those memories for the rest of your life," Julian said.

"He's right, boy. Now let's get out of our feelings and talk about what you're going to do. This is a major city we're talking. Shit like this don't come too often," Silky said.

Joseph looked at his uncle and back at Johnny and said, "If I come to Cleveland, I want that building I saw in my dreams. I don't know what it is about that street and that building, but I want it." Johnny smiled at Joseph and said, "You know what? You've got it." The two shook hands, and my prophecy had been fulfilled. Joseph was going to my hell on earth. So now shit was really about to get dark!

CHAPTER 9

WELCOME TO 10-5!

A few weeks after Joseph and Johnny's last encounter, Johnny had everything set up on Hathaway for Joseph to move to Cleveland. Johnny bought the building Joseph wanted, a beautiful car, and a legitimate business bank account. Johnny transferred ownership of everything to Joseph even though he was only sixteen. Silky got the call that everything was ready for Joseph, and Silky traveled to Leeds to tell his nephew personally at the house on the farm. He informed his nephew that everything was all set in Cleveland and that he could leave whenever he wanted to. Joseph decided that it would be best for him to leave by the end of the week, which was within three days of him receiving the news.

Silky agreed with his decision and brought Joseph's plane ticket that day. Later that night, Julian took Joseph out to celebrate his promotion. While the two boys were out having fun, Silky stayed behind at his brother and sister-in-law's home, drinking whiskey and smoking cigars. While he smoked and drank, I decided to join him while he still had some privacy.

"You did it," I said to Silky as I just appeared out of nowhere.

"You took Joseph to Cleveland the night his parents died, didn't you? And then you made it out to be a dream in his head."

"I did, why do you ask?"

"Joseph has known who you are and what you are since he was a baby. Don't you think it is only a matter of time before he realizes that things that may seem to be dreams are actually reality? Or that maybe, just maybe, he will remember what happened the night his parents were killed? How they were killed?" Silky asked as he took a sip of whiskey.

"Silky, don't bitch up on me now."

"I'm just saying. I've seen what can happen in the future. You've seen what can happen in the future. We're literally one mistake from our plans all turning to shit. Lucifer, if he ever finds out the truth about a lot of things, he will turn against both of us, and it will be deadly. We won't win."

"We will, Silky. We will."

Silky took another sip of his whiskey and went to sleep that night. After that night, Silky spent as much time with Joseph as he could, advising him on how to conduct himself in Cleveland and what to look out for. Then, the day finally came for Joseph to leave for Cleveland. Joseph said his goodbyes to his crew and his favorite cousin. And finally, he was on that mothafuckin plane to Cleveland. While Joseph was on the plane, I disguised as a regular passenger and sat next to him while he read a book.

"Long time no see, young man," I said to Joseph.

"If it ain't the devil himself. Haven't seen you in a while."

"But I've definitely seen you. And I am proud to see you are finally leaving Leeds to start a new life. You are becoming the king you were born to be."

"Becoming? I've been the king. I just don't have a throne yet."

"You will once you touch down on East 105th Street."

"But why should I settle for one street or neighborhood? When I can take over the entire city? The entire state?"

"What are you saying, Joseph?"

"I am saying that if I am going to run something, I don't just want a portion of it. I want it all. This white man ain't doing me no favors by buying me a house car and giving me bank accounts.

Shit, after all of the work I have put in? The people I've killed? This is retribution. Fuck Johnny Santino. My uncle may shuck and jive to his bullshit. But me? I am just playing along to get along. So that I can get what's mine in the end. And Cleveland, that shit is mine."

"Don't you worry about the enemies you will make? Your enemies up north will be far more relentless than your enemies down south."

"I don't worry about enemies, Lucifer."

Joseph fell asleep on the flight after that. And the entire time he slept, I thought about who the hell I was talking to at that moment. I wasn't talking to some naive child anymore. I was speaking to a man, and a dangerous one who didn't even know what the fuck he truly was yet because he had yet to unleash his powers. After a few hours, Joseph's flight touched down in Cleveland, Ohio. Johnny Santino was the first person Joseph saw when he walked outside of the airport.

Johnny stood in front of his limo with a cigarette in his mouth and said, "I've never been more happy to see you, kid. Let's get those bags in the trunk." Johnny took Joseph's luggage, threw it in the trunk, and entered the limo. Johnny instructed the driver to pull off and take them to the nearest whore house to celebrate. Joseph declined the invitation to go.

"You've got to celebrate, Joseph. You're in Cleveland now!"

"We can celebrate another time. Right now, I want to see my new home my new car, and I want to get some rest and get down to business tomorrow," Joseph said dryly.

"Goddamn. In that case, Butch! Take this young man to his new home," Johnny said to his driver. "You really are about your business. I respect that. But if you are going to work for me and with me in Cleveland, I will need you to loosen up a little bit."

"I understand, Don Santino. I just cannot celebrate until I have learned how this city operates and who is running everything."

"Damn, no wonder Alabama is making all that damn money. You and your cousin keep y'all heads on tight. Okay. I want you to get some rest today and tonight. Tomorrow, we will get straight to business, and I will teach you everything you need to know about the city."

After a while, Joseph and Johnny pulled up on Superior Avenue and East 105th Street. Joseph's face lit up like a fucking Christmas Tree. "It is literally everything I dreamed up," Joseph said while looking out the limo window. The streets were filled with people. The roads were beautifully paved. There were businesses everywhere, beautiful homes everywhere. And it was busy as hell. Ha, get it? Busy as *HELL*? Well, if you don't, then fuck you. Anyway, the limo driver turned onto Hathaway Avenue, and they finally arrived at Joseph's new four-unit brownstone home. When Johnny and Joseph got out of the car, Johnny handed Joseph his new driver's license that said he was twenty years of age, the deed to his home, all of his banking information, the title and keys to his car, and the keys to his new home.

Joseph stood in front of his new building with the biggest smile. Johnny patted Joseph on his shoulder and said, "Let's go see your new home." The two walked into one of the fully furnished units of the brick building. Joseph thanked Johnny for everything, and Johnny nodded his head. While Joseph walked around the three-bedroom unit, he asked Johnny, "This entire building is really mine?" Johnny responded, "The entire building. You earned Joe." Joseph shook Johnny's and Johnny left the house. I appeared before Joseph as soon as Johnny pulled off in his limo.

"*Welcome to East 105th!* Look at how far you've come, Joseph. How does it feel to own everything and live by yourself?"

"It feels like I belong here. I just wish I had my parents and my brother to share my fortune with. I've tried calling Junior telepathically for years, and he won't answer me. But I know he's alive. I can still feel him."

"What did I tell you when you were younger?"

"You told me fuck my brother and God too. But I won't give up on Junior. I love my brother, and I still miss him."

When Joseph said that, it pissed me the fuck off. But I kept it cool and responded calmly.

"You are entitled to feel how you feel, Joseph. Now that you're settled in, what are you going to do?"

"I am going to bed. I have a lot of work to do in the morning. I want to walk in this neighborhood and meet the people, and then I have to meet up with Johnny. Goodnight, Lucifer."

Then the son of a bitch went upstairs and went to sleep. Although I was happy to see Joseph in Cleveland and reside in the hell I made on Earth, I felt something was off. Joseph's energy was different. He was becoming more and more ruthless. Now, I have dealt with a lot of evildoers, but never ones that were in my bloodline. And now I was starting to wonder, would Joseph do to me what I did to God in the future if he continues to change. Would I pay for all of my sins through the child that I started slowly corrupting from birth? Who knows. Well, I know, but you all who are reading this don't. So just keep fucking reading because the story ain't over, you bastards.

CHAPTER 10

Let's Get Down To Business

Joseph was an early bird. He started every day around four in the morning. He would have his coffee, toast, and cigarette and then do what he had to do. But since he was in Cleveland now, he skipped breakfast and walked around the neighborhood. He walked and observed everything and everyone. He walked into different businesses and met the owners. He met his neighbors who were up and walking around getting ready for work. He studied the city's infrastructure. While he took his walk around, I appeared before him in disguise as an older black man in his seventies on a cane.

"How do you like your new home so far?"

"I've been walking around and meeting new people for the past four hours, and I must say, this place has potential. But this place doesn't seem like hell."

"Why would it? See, when I first came to West Eden, this was nothing but dry land. There was no life. And the people that came here were lost souls with no place else to go. Some people came here to die. So as time passed and evolution happened, it was time to blend in. But remember, what you see is sometimes fiction, and what is beneath the surface is always fact. You'll learn soon enough that you are residing in hell soon."

As soon as I said that, Joseph walked by an alley where there was a beautiful woman and two men standing over a bloody man. The woman stood at five foot seven and had a body out of this fucking world. She wore a beautiful dress down the knees and high heels. The two men were dressed in suits and big as hell. They were beating the shit out of this guy on the ground, and the woman said, "I want my goddamn money by the end of the week. And if I don't get it, my partner Scat will visit you. And I don't think you want to see Scat!" Joseph stopped and stared at the woman and her henchmen as they beat this man to a bloody pulp. The woman finally looked up and saw Joseph. She smiled and waved at him, and afterward, she and her henchmen got into their vehicle and pulled off.

I looked at Joseph and smiled as he stood in the middle of the sidewalk, processing what he had just witnessed. I said to him, "Still think this isn't hell?" Joseph looked back at me and then looked at his watch and said, "This is going to be interesting. Let me get back to the house. Johnny is picking me up." Joseph walked to his new home, and as soon as he arrived, Johnny was waiting for him in the limo. Johnny rolled his window down, releasing all the cigarette smoke, and said, "What are you waiting on? Get in." Johnny's driver, Butch, opened the door for Joseph, and he proceeded to get in the vehicle. When Butch drove off, Johnny offered Joseph a cigarette. Joseph declined.

"How are you enjoying your new home," Johnny asked.

"It's different than the South, that's for sure."

"Yeah, that southern hospitality doesn't exist here. And everything is in the open. At least in this neighborhood."

"So, what can you tell me about East 105th and all of it's surrounding areas?"

"You've got some Jewish businesses, some black businesses as you've already seen, I'm sure....."

"I'm talking about the people who actually run it," Joseph said as he cut Johnny off while he was talking.

"Straight to the point. I like it. But that's the thing. Right now, no one runs this area. There is no structure there. No politics.

Just criminals trying to take whatever they can. A lot of underground gambling, no sign of drugs, really. Illegal sales of alcohol. Policies. Extortion, racketeering. Same thing as down south, but not as sophisticated. Which is why I need you here."

"You want me to take it for you."

"Yes, but this area is the start of it all. I want all of Saint Clair, and I want all of Superior. I want Chester, Carnegie, Cedar, I want Hough and more. I feel that you can make that happen by any means."

"I can, but it won't be diplomatic from what I have seen so far. As I said, it's different than the South."

"It might not, but I trust that you know how to handle things without drawing too much attention to yourself."

Johnny and Joseph talked for a bit longer in the limo, and after a ten-minute drive, they arrived at a restaurant called Gaurino's. The restaurant appeared closed, but the owner let the two men in. They walked to the back of the restaurant, where twelve men sat at a table, eating, drinking, and smoking. All Italian men, of course. Johnny greeted all twelve men with a hug and a kiss on the cheek, then introduced Joseph.

"Alright, everyone! I'd like to introduce a friend of mine. This here is Joseph Williams. He has been my muscle of the South for some years. Now, he has moved to Cleveland to help us get things in order. Get some of our territory back. Over the years, this thing of ours has been slowly weakening for several reasons. It's time we get our shit back. So we will treat my friend Joseph with the utmost respect and follow his lead to regain our strength."

The other men looked at one another with an expression of disdain. One don at the table stood up and said, "Permission to speak?" Johnny responded, "By all means, Don Bernardi."

"The fuck do we need with a moolinyan? We've been able to handle our business for a long time. We don't need a fucking darkie coming into this thing of ours. For what? Only for it to make us look weaker. We can't handle our own affairs, so we call a nigger to do it," Don Billy Bernardi said.

"Didn't I say you would show my friend some fucking respect, or did you not hear me," Johnny said angrily.

Joseph calmly raised his hand and smiled. He looked at the men in the room and said in Italian, "May the *moolinyan* speak?" Everyone was shocked to hear a black man speak Italian. Johnny responded to Joseph in Italian, saying, "Proceed, my friend."

"Don Barnardi, your name rings out in the South. You are known to be a *nigger* lover. And to have many *nigger* children. Because you love to sleep with *nigger* whores. You spend so much money on pussy that you need to take loans from us *niggers* when you run out of money down South. So, if you want to know why you need this *MOOLINYAN*? It's because your commission has you as an unfortunate liability. Your only strength lies within the union of your commission, but you contribute nothing So, so, so sad," Joseph sarcastically said.

"You son of a bitch," Don Barnardi exclaimed as he pulled out his revolver pistol on Joseph. "I will blow your nigger head off!"

Joseph walked towards Don Barnarti, took the barrel of the gun with his hand and put it to his own head, and said, "Now blow my *nigger* head off!" Everyone in the room looked surprised, and Don Barnardi's hand trembled as he held the gun to Joseph's head. Joseph looked at the frightened don, laughed, and said, "That's what I thought." Joseph took the gun out of Don Barnarti's hand and placed it in his waistband.

"Think I'll keep this pearl handle you have here. Let's consider it an apology and a welcome to Cleveland gift huh," Joseph said while laughing.

"I have never been a fan of the blacks, but I think I am now," Don Marlon De Nado said as he smiled. "He's got balls."

"I saw something before we got here. I also heard a name," Joseph said as he walked around the table.

"Well, don't just beat around the bush, spit it out," Johnny said.

"I saw a woman in an alley, beating a white man for some money. She said a name. Scat. Who is she, and who is Scat?"

"Scat some half and half. Half black, half Italian. He's fucking insane. And he has killed about ten of my men in the past year. He moves a lot of heroin and guns. That woman? Had to be his partner, Mary Ann Mabel. She's from the South. Shit, she used to work for us," Johnny said.

"*Used to*?"

"We killed her husband right here in this restaurant, in front of her. He was about to do something that would've been a problem for us. It would've ended everything we had," Johnny said.

"Well, why kill him and not her?"

"We didn't see her as a threat at first. Because let's be honest. Who is going to take orders from a woman? She's rare, though. We thought she'd be weak without her husband. But she's stronger than he was. And now, just like many crews throughout the city, we have no control over hers. She is just one of many problems that we have to solve. But we can't get close to any of these people for obvious reasons. But you? You're the right color. Nor a bad-looking man. You've got style. You've got the devil's tongue. You're slick. And you're dangerous. That's why we need you here, Joseph."

Joseph picked up a pack of cigarettes lying on the table, took one out and lit it, and said, "Fuck it, I'll do your dirty work. But once this is over, I think I'll go back down South. And visit Cleveland periodically. You fucking wops are making me homesick." Then he left the restaurant and asked Johnny's driver to take him home.

CHAPTER 11

Deadly Alliance = Ultimate Defiance

Joseph wasn't trying to stir up any trouble in Cleveland. He wanted to make peace, not war. So, instead of stirring up a pot of bullshit, he observed the city for about two or three months. Once he gained an idea of who was who and what was what, he began to make his move to approach specific individuals. The first three people he approached were Mary Ann, Scat, and Abdul. Now Mary Ann was a beautiful, light-skinned woman with long curly hair and a had a body like a muthafucka. She was bad enough for me to fuck. And God knows I love a fine-ass human woman to stick my dick in. I mean, I was the first one to fuck Eve..... Anyway, the bitch was bad. Scat was light-skinned, tall, hazel-eyed, and always smoked weed. Then, there was Abdul, a Muslim brother who had just moved back to Cleveland from New York. He moved back to Cleveland a month after Joseph arrived. He was light-skinned, had dark brown eyes, and was a pretty slim guy.

The three of them owned a candy store on East 105th Street, and they sold more "*candy*" than you could think of. One day, Joseph walked into the candy store, and the first person he saw was Mary Ann. She smiled and spoke to Joseph. Joseph nodded and looked around the store.

"How are you enjoying Cleveland, Bama? I know this is a long ways from Leeds," Mary Ann said.

"I see you've done your research, Mary," Joseph said as he chuckled.

"There's no need to research someone I already know."

Joseph turned around and looked at Mary Ann with an expression of surprise.

"How the hell would you know me, beautiful woman."

"Meet me at Dearings at six o'clock, and we will talk about everything. Also, I have someone for you to meet."

Joseph agreed to meet Mary Ann and walked out of the store. Four hours later, Joseph drove to 1035 East 105th Street. When he exited the car, an older black gentleman greeted him at the door and said, "Welcome to Dearings, young man! Come on in and get some of this good ole food! You in V.I.P!" Joseph had an expression of confusion, and the man guided Joseph to a private dining room. When Joseph entered the dining room, Mary Ann was smoking a cigarette, Scat was standing on the wall playing with a switchblade, and Abdul sat at the table playing solitaire.

"Thank you, Mr. Dearing! You can go now," Mary Ann said as the establishment's owner walked out.

"Okay, let's get straight to the point here, Joseph. There is no need to introduce ourselves. You've been observing everyone for months now. You know who all of us are, and we know who you are," Abdul said as he continued to play solitaire.

"Yes, indeed. And if you know who I am, then you know who I work for," Joseph said as he sat beside Abdul to play solitaire.

"We definitely know who you work for. And we know your uncle is as well. We used to work for Silk and Johnny Santino." Mary Ann said.

"Ooooookay? And?"

"And Silky and Johnny turned their backs on us. Johnny killed my husband because he wanted to make peace with the Irish. The bloodshed was becoming too much. When my husband was killed, there was no more order or structure. Things got bad. And when things got bad, Silky didn't support us like we supported him when your father walked away from him."

"You knew my father?"

"Everyone knew Willie Joseph, boy. He was a legend in the streets back in the day. The only black man to kill a Klan Man and lived to tell the story. On top of that, Leeds was the place to be. We were part of your uncle's crew before the split between the two brothers. And when the split happened, we were the only original crew members that stuck beside your uncle. We were the only ones who knew he was still alive from Leeds. But if we are going to be honest, I see why your father cut Big Joseph's, I mean Silky's throat and left him for dead," Abdul said.

"Because of the drugs, right? That's the reason why my father did it."

"Hahaha! Is that what your uncle told you? No. Your father didn't like them Italians. He'd turned down their offers on drugs and all kinds of stuff many times. He didn't want anything to do with them after what happened to your mother," Abdul said.

"What happened to my mother?"

"Our mother," Scat said as he stood on the wall, flipping his switchblade.

Joseph stopped playing solitaire, stood up, looked at all three of the individuals in the room, and said, "*My mother,*" in a stern tone. Abdul gently grabbed Joseph by the wrist and said, "Sit down. You have no enemies here. No need to get aggressive. Just listen." Joseph sat down and looked at Scat very closely. He began to see the similarities between Scat and his uncle Tim.

"How," Joseph asked

"That fat, greasy son of a bitch Barnarti raped her back in the day when she, your father, Silky, and Tim visited Cleveland once. I don't know the full details, but I do know that she couldn't raise me knowing that I was conceived out of pain by a white man. So, she gave me to Momma Mary and her husband."

"I couldn't have children, and I loved your mother and father. Despite their life of crime, they always cared for people and looked out for their own. Your father was such a good man, willing to raise Scat as his own, but your mother just couldn't do it. And my baby here was born in 1923 and I took him off their hands."

"Three years before Junior was born," Joseph said while sitting in a daze.

"I know this all may come as a shock to you. You come to Cleveland with a goal and are hit with all this. But understand this, Joseph. We are not here to do any harm to you. I genuinely mean that. That's why I wanted you to come here today. Because I wanted you to meet your brother, and I wanted you to know where we stand," Mary said.

Joseph stood up and walked over to the bar in the private room. He poured himself a stiff drink. His eyes filled with tears, but would not let them drop. Then he looked at Scat and walked over to him.

"I'm sorry that I never knew you. Sincerely. And I am sorry you have to share the same blood as that fat greasy bitch," Joseph said as he stared his brother in the eyes and patted him on his shoulder. "I always knew there were holes in Silky's stories. And as far as Johnny is concerned, I never liked him. I can't stand that fucking wop. And Barnarti? Barnarti is another one in the commission that I would love to get rid of."

"Well, it sounds like you have the plan to commit sins on some biblical shit," Scat said.

"I do. But before I do, I need to get every black gang leader and gangster on board with us. We need to come together and play our cards right. Get more organized, come together as a unit, serve the Italian's purpose for a while, and then when it is time to strike, we strike. But we cannot let them know what our plans are. We cannot show emotion. And we must always stick together," Joseph said.

"You're basically talking about starting our own mafia," Scat said.

"Why not? We have the capabilities and the resources. We're just divided."

"But when we start a war with the Italians, Silky will come out of the woodwork to take us all out. He has a lot of muscle, power, and influence everywhere," Abdul said.

"I don't give a shit what he has. I will take care of my uncle. So, are you three with me?"

Scat, Abdul, and Mary Ann looked at one another, nodded, and all three said in unison, "Yes!" Joseph grinned and said, "Good, now let's take this shit over!"

Lucifer's Journal PT.4: LETTER TO PATHETIC HUMANS PT.2 (DAY 10 IN GOD'S PRISON)

For the first time, I sat down and read the bible. This shit is some good shit. Very fucking entertaining. In *2 Corinthians 11:3* it says, "But I am afraid that just as Eve was deceived by the serpent's cunning, your minds may somehow be led astray from your sincere and pure devotion to Christ." DAMN! I like that shit. That's some deep shit right there. Now, it is said that the bible is made up of God and man's words combined. I don't know. I just know whoever wrote this shit was spitting some real facts on that part. Because it is basically saying you bitch ass humans are weak-minded as fuck! I have witnessed so many people move further away from God, Christ, and themselves for superficial pleasures. People wanted money, they wanted cars, they wanted status, dick, pussy, power. And they would sell their souls to me just to have it all. Shit that you can't take with you when you die. But I *ALWAYS* got a kick out of how you humans have so much *vanity*. Which is my personal favorite sin. Because, like I said before, you fuck turds have free will. But you all become so self-absorbed that *vanity* becomes your weakness. And you all let it destroy you from the inside out. It is almost hilarious. Because you all make my job so much easier. I guess you humans have no clue that pride and ego will kill you all before the serial killer next door will. But still, you all are God's favorite? Ants are more intelligent than you all. A fucking monkey is more intelligent than you all. But I am locked away in a prison for my sins! I regret ever telling God to create you bitches sometimes. If it had not been for me, you all wouldn't exist. You all thank God for your existence when you should all be thanking me! AND YOU KNOW WHAT?! YOU KNOW WHAT YOU FUCKING WHORES?! WHEN GOD CREATED YOU ALL, HE MADE YOU ALL BORING, WORSHIPING PIECES OF SHIT WITH ONLY THE PURPOSE TO SERVE HIM! WHILE I WAS DOWN HERE WITH YOU ALL SHOWING YOU ALL A GOOD FUCKING TIME! BRINGING JOY INTO YOUR LIVES! I WAS RIGHT HERE! I WAS RIGHT HERE! I WAS RIGHT HERE! WHERE WAS HE?! WATCHING! WATCHING AND JUDGING YOU ALL! BUT HE LOVES EVERY SINGLE ONE OF YOU! YET I SIT INSIDE OF A PRISON CELL! IN MY OWN VERSION OF HELL, PAYING FOR THE SINS THAT YOU ALL HAVE COMMITTED DUE TO THE TEMPTATION YOU ALL FOLDED UNDER! DUE... TO.... VANITY! FUCKING VANITY! BUT THE TRUTH OF THE MATTER IS, IF YOUR RELATIONSHIP WITH GOD WAS TIGHT, HOW CAN ANYTHING OR ANYONE ELSE INTERFERE?! NEWS FLASH YOU FUCKING CUNTS! IT CAN'T, AND IT WON'T! SO DEAR PATHETIC HUMANS I PRAY THAT MY BLOODLINE WILL BRING ARMAGEDDON AND END YOU ALL! FUCK YOU ALL! SINCERELY, THE DEVIL HIM FUCKING SELF!

CHAPTER 12

Am I My Brother's Keepa?!

A few nights after Joseph met with Abdul, Mary Ann, and Scat, Johnny called Joseph in the middle of the night and woke him out of his sleep. Joseph hated being disturbed during his slumber, but he answered the phone.

"I need your ass to get to my house now," Johnny said as soon as Joseph picked up the phone.

"Sounds serious, Don Santino."

"There's a car waiting for you outside now. No need to get dressed. Just get in the car. Butch is outside now."

"Say no more. I will be there."

Joseph walked outside in his red silk pajamas and silk robe, greeted Butch, and Butch opened the door for Joseph to enter the vehicle. On his way to Johnny's house, Joseph asked butch a few questions.

"Butch, how long have you been working for Johnny?"

"Since I was twelve years old."

"You like it?"

"I'd die for Johnny and his family."

"*Got it.* Do you know why the Don calls me to his home this late?"

"You'll see."

Butch and Joseph pulled up to Johnny's home on Murray Hill in Little Italy. Joseph entered the house and walked to the dining room where Johnny Santino, Johnny's thirteen-year-old son, Johnny Junior, Julian, and Silky were drinking coffee. Silky sat with his legs crossed, wearing an all-black suit, with his snake-head sword cane in his hand. "Have a seat, boy," Silky said as he pulled out a chair for Joseph to sit in.

"Why the fuck am I here at 2 am? I was asleep dreaming about a beautiful woman with full breasts dancing in front of me," Joseph said sarcastically.

"Good to see you too, nephew. We've got an important job for you to do tonight."

"Well, it better be worth my time."

"You need to burn down a building. It's an Islamic temple that Abdul attends, and I want him dead," Silky said smoothly.

"Okay, and it took you and Julian to come up north for this shit," Joseph asked sarcastically.

"Who the hell do you think you're talking to, boy? You watch your damn tone with me. Now, Butch is going to drive you there. He knows what building we're talking about. But before you burn it down, make sure everyone in that bitch is dead. And don't worry about why we're here. Just do as you're told" Silky said.

"Okay."

"You don't have any questions? You don't want to know why we have you doing this," Don Santino asked.

"I could ask, but it wouldn't guarantee you'd tell me the truth," Joseph said as he shrugged his shoulders.

Don Johnny Santino instructed his son, Johnny Junior, to give Joseph a gun with duct tape on the handle and trigger. Johnny took the gun and sarcastically said, "I need to change clothes. All red silk pajamas ain't gone work." Julian had an all-black outfit ready for Joseph to wear and said, "You don't have to do this." Joseph smirked and responded, "I do this shit for fun. It's nothing," as he changed clothes in the dining room. Joseph and Butch left the house and drove to the building Joseph was instructed to burn down. The ride to the location was silent for a while. And out of nowhere, Butch spoke.

"I've been instructed that if you don't burn this place down to kill you."

"That so?"

"Yeah, but I don't want to do it."

"Wanting to do something and doing it are two different things, Butch."

"Just burn the fucking building down, so I won't have to kill you."

The two pulled up in front of a building that had Arabic writing on it. A sign on the front said, "Temple 79" on 79th and Euclid Avenue. Joseph looked at the building and said, "I hear people inside. What are they doing? What are they saying" Butch began to laugh and responded, "Probably chanting some monkey babble." Joseph gave Butch a cold stare and got out of the car, and said, "This shouldn't take long, you fucking deigo." Joseph walked into the building and realized that it was an Islamic temple. There were women, children, and elders inside praying.

He stood there and watched them as they prayed. Once they were finished with prayer, Joseph noticed that Abdul was one of the people inside the temple.

"My brotha, Joseph! Assalamu alaikum," Abdul said as he hugged Joseph.

"I don't know what to say. How to respond."

"You say wa alaikum salaam. *It means unto you peace.* What are you doing here?"

"Abdul, Butch is waiting outside for me. Silky and Johnny sent me here to kill everyone in the building and burn it down. But I am not going to do that. Number one, this is a holy temple. Number two, I don't kill innocent bystanders and civilians," Joseph whispered.

"They didn't tell you why?"

"No, they didn't."

"Is Silky here? In Cleveland?"

"Julian, too."

Abdul rubbed his chin and looked at the ceiling while in deep thought. He then placed his hand on Joseph's shoulder and said, "You must go to the Imam. Warn him first. He will have a plan. He's upstairs. Joseph began to walk upstairs. The closer he got to the top, the darker it got. Once he reached the top, there were candles lit, and there was a man on the rug on his hands and knees. He was praying in Arabic with his back to Joseph. Joseph did not want to disturb the Imam during prayer, so he waited for him to finish. Once the Imam finished, he sat down on the rug Indian style. The Imam still sat with his back facing Joseph.

"You've come with a warning," said the Imam.

"How do you know," Joseph asked.

"I know many things."

"Well, I don't want to hurt anyone in here, so I am asking you to get your people out of here," Joseph said as he pulled his gun out of his waistband. "I don't want to hurt you, but I will. So just do as I ask."

"No need to pull out guns, *trouble maka*! You are in God's house."

Joseph dropped his gun and walked slowly up to the man from behind. He looked down at his hand, and he noticed that the man was wearing his father's ring on his pinky finger. Joseph walked around to the front of the man, and when he saw his face, he had the surprise of his life. Joseph dropped to his knees, and tears began to roll down his face. He crawled towards the man on his knees and wrapped his arms around the Imam's neck.

"This isn't real. You're not really here. It has to be a dream," Joseph said as he cried.

"Nah, lil trouble maka, this is real, and I have missed you so much," The Imam said as he hugged Joseph and cried tears of joy.

"I missed you too, Junior! I missed you so much!"

Joseph looked at his brother again and touched his face to confirm that he was really reunited with him. He smiled and said, "Junior, I have so much to tell you, but I will need you to follow my lead and get your people out of here." Junior responded, "I already know. I will get them out of here as soon as possible. You do what you have to do." Junior went downstairs and instructed everyone to scream while Joseph shot his gun. They all did so and then snuck out of the back door.

After everyone ran out of the temple, Joseph rigged up the oven in the kitchen to explode. He ran out of the temple and ran straight to Butch's car. When he hopped in the car, he screamed, "DRIVE YOU FUCKING DEIGO! DRIVE!" Butch took off like a bat out of fucking hell, and within a matter of seconds of Butch pulling off, the building exploded. Shortly after the explosion, the police, fire department, and ambulance sped right by them. After a while of Butch driving, Joseph realized that they weren't going in the direction of Little Italy.

"Where the fuck are we going, Butch?"

"Outwaite Homes. A lady is waiting there for you. Pretty black woman. Prostitute. You're going to fuck her tonight. And she is going to tell the cops that you were there fucking her fucking brains out all night. Understood?"

"Understood. After all of this shit tonight, she better be the best in bed."

"She's new. Your uncle recruited her. Picked her personally for you. She's a virgin, I believe."

"Damn, I've never had a virgin before."

"They're very tight, Joseph."

Joseph and Butch finally arrived at the apartment building, and Butch gave Joseph the apartment number. When Joseph arrived at the unit, a beautiful dark-skinned woman with big and lovely breasts, green eyes, full lips, short black hair, and a backside that was out of this fucking world. I mean… I was kind of jealous of Joseph because he was going to fuck her and not me. Anyway, she greeted him in a sheer white nightgown and invited Joseph into her apartment. Joseph was so mesmerized by her beauty that he couldn't take her eyes off her.

"Wow, you look beautiful," Joseph exclaimed.

"You're not bad yourself, Joseph. My name is Julie, and your uncle hired me to show you a good time tonight. Now let me get you out of these gassy-smelling clothes," Julie said as she assisted Joseph in removing his clothes. "You have really nice muscles, Joseph."

"Thank you. Can I be honest with you, Julie?"

"By all means."

"I want to have sex with you. But I don't want to have sex with you. I just want to sleep here tonight and go home in the morning. I am so tired. I went through a lot tonight."

"I understand. You're more than welcome to sleep in the room with me."

"I think I am okay with sleeping on the couch, Julie, thanks."

Joseph laid on the couch, and Julie went to her bedroom. After lying down for an hour or so, Joseph became restless. So he turned on the television in the living room and watched "The Stu Erwin Show." Julie came out to the living room and sat next to Joseph on the couch.

"I'm sorry if I woke you," Joseph said.

"You're fine. I have a hard time sleeping at night anyway, honestly. Besides, I love this show."

"Stop it. Are you serious?"

"Um, yeah! This and "*I Love Lucy*!" Ricky Ricardo is so handsome. But not as handsome as you."

Joseph looked over at Julie, smiled, and kissed her gently. He laid her on the couch and removed his underwear, exposing his fully erect penis to her. Julie looked down at Joseph's penis and said, "This will be my first time ever doing this." Joseph responded, "I will be gentle. I promise." The two shared another kiss, and Joseph inserted his fully erect penis inside that fine-ass woman's vagina slowly. He pumped her slowly, in and out, in and out, in and out. The two moaned with pleasure while in the missionary position. After a few minutes, Joseph ejaculated inside Julie.

Julie looked satisfied with the sex, but she said to Joseph, "I want more. That was nice." Joseph responded, "I am not a machine lady."

Julie got up from the couch, grabbed Joseph by the wrist, and guided him to her bedroom. Then she pushed him onto the bed, played with his penis for a while, and put it inside her mouth. She sucked him off until he was fully erect again, got on top of him, and slid down on his penis up and down repeatedly until they both climaxed.

After their fantastic sex sessions, Joseph and Julie talked about how she ended up working for his uncle. It appeared that Johnny Junior recruited her for his father. She had just lost her parents and needed money to survive at the tender age of seventeen. She was initially meant to have sex with Don Santino, but because of Joseph being ordered to burn down the mosque, her virgin pussy would be his reward. The two of them talked until sunrise. It wasn't long after Joseph had fallen asleep, Silky was standing over Joseph, shaking him awake. Joseph looked up at his uncle, disoriented.

"You did good last night, nephew. You made it look like an accident. Time to get you home."

"I just fell asleep not too long ago, so leave me."

"Get your ass up, Joseph."

"Get your ass out of my face Joseph Williams, and let me get some sleep," Joseph said to his Silky.

"You little nigga I will kill you if you ever call me by my birthname, you understand me? KILL YOU," Silky exclaimed as he snatched Joseph out of the bed by his throat.

"I cannot believe my father actually named me after a man who would burn down a holy temple."

Silky held Joseph by his throat and stared him deep into his eyes. Silky had fear in his heart. I could sense it. Honestly, so did I because Joseph was beginning to rebel—something he never did.

"Get dressed and get your ass in the car," Silky said as he released Joseph's throat.

"You owe me an explanation behind this one. I hope you know that, Silky."

"You'll get that. I owe you that much," Silky said as he walked out of the apartment.

Joseph got dressed, kissed Julie on the cheek while she slept, left two thousand dollars on her nightstand, and left the apartment.

CHAPTER 13

Am I My Brother's Keepa?! PT. 2

Joseph entered Silky's all-white Cadillac limousine and deeply stared Silky in the eyes. He showed so much anger in his facial expression.

"Now, I have been a loyal soldier to you. Done everything in my power to make sure that your criminal organization was secured. Make sure that all of your enemies that were a threat were dead. But I have never burned down any place of worship IN MY LIFE! AND TO KILL INNOCENT PEOPLE! THAT'S NOT MY CODE OF CONDUCT, AND YOU KNOW THAT!"

"I don't know where all this heart you got is coming from. But I am getting quite sick of it. Now, this is the third time you got smart with me, boy. And you can best believe that you being my brother's child is not what is saving you. You're only here because you're needed at the moment. Now, you want to talk about a threat. That place was a threat. The man who ran that place was a threat. A threat to Johnny's business. Our business. That man called himself saving souls and shit. And his bullshit religion brainwashed the majority of those people. People that used to work for us. Not only had he opened temples here in the north. But down south, too. He was destroying everything we built. Everything you built! Just like your father would have done!"

Joseph looked at Silky with so much anger. I could see the fire in his eyes and tell he wanted to kill his uncle.

"You knew. That is why you came to Cleveland. Because you knew."

"Yeah. I knew. I knew he was still alive. I found out after about a month of you moving to Cleveland. Out of nowhere, all of these damn temples kept popping up. EVERYWHERE! And then, one day, I saw a temple being built right across the street from my business in New Orleans. And a young man dressed up in a nice suit and bowtie walked over to me as I watched the workers work on the building. I saw him, and I could not deny my brother's blood. He looks just like Willie. He walks like him and talks like him. He greeted me and handed me a flyer to invite me to one of his temples. We conversed for a little while, and he told me about Islam and all that shit. About a month after my first interaction with him, the temple across the street from me was finished. I decided to attend one of the services. During his service, he spoke about how "*God*," or "*Allah,*" had protected him for many years and how you must pray for your loved ones. Then he brought up his mother, his father, and his brother. And when he mentioned that. It was all the confirmation I needed."

"Wow, great fucking story, Silky. But why didn't you tell me he was still alive?! Before me killing him?"

"Why would I tell you? I wanted it to be a surprise. The boy was beginning to take all of my dealers, my whores, and change their lives. I was losing money. So, I made it my business to see that you would take him out. And you're the only one that would've been able to get close to him. He probably didn't recognize you."

"He didn't recognize me at all, Silky. Not at all," Joseph said sadly while lying through his damn teeth.

"Exactly, so save your tears for someone else. Because let's be real. He left your ass, for all those years. I found you and provided for you. So don't give me that, *I'm my brother's keeper bullshit.*"

Once the driver arrived on the corner of East 105th and Hathaway Avenue, Joseph ordered the driver to stop and let him out. Before Joseph exited the car, Silky grabbed him by his wrist.

"I know it wasn't easy what you did. But trust me when I say you did the right thing. You did, nephew. Junior was only going to cause more of a financial crisis for us. And in order for us to afford the lifestyle we live, we must always always protect our business first. It comes before everything. Money will always come first. You understand?"

"Of course I do, Silky. I just need to overcome the fact that I blew my brother up. But I'll be fine," Joseph said sarcastically. Still lying through his damn teeth.

"Of course. I understand, smart ass. But listen, I have killed, raped, beaten, and robbed a lot of people for many years. Innocent and guilty. And here I am, forty-something years old now, and I am used to it. Doesn't bother me at all. You will get there in due time."

"Right," Joseph said as he stepped out of the car and closed the door.

"Oh, one more question, nephew. How was that sweet virgin pussy? Good, wasn't it?"

"Stupendous," Joseph said dryly.

"Plenty more where that came from," Silky said as he laughed.

Joseph forced a laugh, and Silky pulled off in his vehicle. Joseph walked back to his house from the corner of his street and passed out on his way there. Moments later, he woke up in his home on the couch. While trying to figure out how he got home, he looked around the living room and saw no one. But he could hear someone in his kitchen. When he walked into the kitchen, he saw his brother preparing breakfast.

"Lil trouble maka, you sure do have a lot of swine in here. You're going to have to change that. It's not good for your health," Junior said as he continued to cook breakfast.

"Junior, what happened? I felt all of this... this power coursing through me. This ridiculous amount of strength and I just....

And how did you find me and.... What's going on," Joseph said while looking confused.

"You passed out on the sidewalk. And I just happened to be in the neighborhood. And that feeling you have is the blood of Lucifer boiling in your veins. Only a matter of time before I have to teach you how to control that angel demon blood. Now eat. You've had a long night," Junior said as he fixed Joseph a plate at the kitchen table.

"You're just going to fix me breakfast with a smile on your face and act like I haven't seen you in six years. And the last time I did see you, our parents were killed, I killed our uncle, and you just abandoned me."

"There is a lot you don't understand, Joseph. I had to do a lot of things to be able to see you. God needed me."

"God needed you," Joseph said as he stood up from his seat at the kitchen table.

"Yes, Joseph. God needed me."

"Fuck God! I NEEDED YOU! I NEEDED YOU, AND YOU ABANDONED ME," Joseph exclaimed as he began to cry. "You said even when we were apart, I would always be able to reach you in my mind! And I called for you, and called for you, AND CALLED FOR YOU! And I never got an answer."

Junior stood up from his seat, hugged his brother, and said, "Get it all out." His brother fell into his arms and screamed at the top of his lungs.

"Joseph, we are not average at all. We are the direct bloodline of God and Lucifer themselves. And sometimes, with our blood and destiny, we will lose more than we win. But when we win, we win. And God..."

"Fuck your God! God took our parents," Joseph exclaimed as he pushed his brother away.

"Joseph, I have seen what the future can look like if you continue on this path of crime. You will lose everything, and your offsprings will wreak havoc! Our uncle Silky is doing the devil's work, and so are you!"

"You know about Silky, huh? What else you know?"

"I know about our brother Scat. I know about your plan to go to war with the Italians and our uncle. I know about you being Lucifer's puppet. I know it all. Which is why I am trying to save you. Because God has shown me so much. Let me help you. Let me help what will be our family. Let me save your soul before it is too late."

"Go to hell, Junior."

"We're standing in a house off of East 105th Street. I am already in hell. Let me show you a few things," Junior said as he touched Joseph's forehead.

Joseph's eyes rolled to the back of his head, and he saw Gemini standing on Tecumseh Court at night in the rain, surrounded by three men dressed in all-black street attire. Gemini stood there with black dress slacks on, a red turtleneck, and an overcoat, and had what appeared to be Silky's snakehead sword cane in his hand. He was in a rage and was pacing the ground looking down at a man on his knees with his hands tied behind his back.

"YOU KNOOOOW..... I HAAAAAAATE! AND I MEAN ABSOULTLY HATE TO BE DISTURBED WHEN I AM READING BEDTIME STORIES TO MY TWIN BABIES! BECAUSE WHEN I PUT MY BABIES TO BED, I GET TO SPEND QUALITY TIME WITH THE MOST BEAUTIFUL WOMAN IN THE WORLD! A WOMAN THAT MAKES ME SMILE EAR TO EAR! BUT HERE I AM! STANDING IN THIS PISSY-SMELLING ALLEY, GETTING READY TO KILL WHO I THOUGHT WAS LIKE A BROTHER TO ME! AND I CAN'T UNDERSTAND WHY! OF ALL PEOPLE WHY WOULD YOU DO THIS TO ME MAN?! TO ME! I TOOK CARE OF YOU! YOUR FAMILY! MADE SURE YOU DIDN'T HAVE TO DO A DAY IN JAIL! MADE SURE YOU DIDN'T LOSE YOUR LAW LICENSE! MADE SURE YOU

BECAME MAYOR! AND YOU'RE TRYING TO PUT ME AND MY FAMILY BEHIND BARS?! AND FOR WHAT?! A SECOND TERM! WELL NOW YOU DIE!"

Gemini pulled his sword out and stabbed the man on his knees repeatedly in the chest! Gemini told the henchmen, "Make sure my mother knows the deed is finished." After that vision, Junior showed Joseph another vision where Gemini was sitting in Joseph's office in a mansion. He sat in a chair as an older Joseph sat on his desk in satin pajamas and a robe.

"What happened? Because last time I checked, you were supposed to get out of this business. Raise your children. Tend to your wife. We agreed upon this," Joseph said to Gemini.

"I had to protect the family, Dad," Gemini said.

"By brutally murdering the mayor of our city? That's the DUMBEST THING I EVER HEARD!"

"HE HAD EVIDENCE ON YOU, ON MA (Grandmother), ON UNCLE DRE, MY MOTHER (Actual mother), AND ME! WHAT WAS I SUPPOSED TO DO!"

Joseph paced the floor. Then he looked up at a tall, burly, bald man and shook his head in disappointment.

"Andre, I hate to do it, but he cannot stay in this state," Joseph said to the tall, burly, bald man, Andre.

"I know, Pop, I know," Andre said tearfully.

"You must leave our world, son. It pains me, but you must go away for a while," Joseph said to Gemini.

"What's a while?"

"I don't know yet. But as far as your crews, your territories, all of your businesses and rackets, they belong to the family as of right now. Andre and I will see that your family is taken care of. You know that."

"I can't take my children with me?! My wife?!"

"Sorry, nephew. It would be in their best interest to stay, and you know that," Andre said to Gemini.

Gemini sat in the chair at the edge of his seat and buried his face into his hands. Joseph placed his hand on Gemini's shoulder and consoled him.

"I love you dearly, son. And even though you are my grandson, I have always considered you my son. I have had you since you were born. You've done a lot to protect this family, including killing Shawn Love, and going to war with your other side of the family. I will always appreciate everything you have done for us, but Gemini, this was too much. You kidnapped and killed the mayor of our city on our territory. That's not a good look. It isn't like you to be this reckless. Because the Gemini, *I know*, would've watched the mayor's routine every day for a week or so. See where he got his coffee. Set it up for one of our people to go undercover as a barista and poison the mayor's coffee one morning, and that's it. This was a rushed job and a sloppy job. And this is the worst body we could have on us. So tell me, son, who put you up to it? Was it my daughter?"

Then, the visions ended. Junior removed his hand from Joseph's face, and Joseph was back in their reality.

"What the fuck was that you just showed me," Joseph asked.

"It was only a partial of what the future could look like. And that man, *Gemini*, is the key to armageddon. He will be one of the most powerful of all of your offsprings. And he will rebel against God, Lucifer, everyone."

"God has given you a false vision. I don't believe that, not for a minute."

"Joseph, I need you to listen to me. Lucifer is going to use you and your children as weapons to overpower God and heaven. We cannot afford for that to happen. He will use you and all of your children to corrupt the world and recruit followers. Why do you think you are here? Him and Silky are working to make you the greatest weapon for their benefit! If you continue to let this happen, you will lose your soul. Your children will lose their souls. The sake of the world is in your hands. Understand that you are like Adam in the garden. You're amongst temptations that will corrupt you. ONLY IF YOU LET IT! But brother, I will save you if you let me!"

"It ain't up to you. And you've got some nerve walking up in here talking about Lucifer! He was the only one there for me when we lost our par..."

"I AM SICK OF THIS!!!! LUCIFER IS THE REASON WE LOST OUR....."

Before that bitch could finish, I made myself visible. I refused to let Junior tell Joseph what really happened to their parents. I put my hand on Junior's shoulder and teleported instantly to open land in the center of the earth that no one else could access. The sky was dark, and we were surrounded by dead trees. We stood across from one another, and Junior gave me a frightening stare. I knew what he really wanted. And I was definitely going to give it to him. So I watched him take off his shirt and all of his Islamic jewelry as he slowly turned into a beast. Once he was finished transforming, I grinned and said, "Now that's what I'm talking about!" Junior growled, spread his wings, and charged at me.

CHAPTER 14

When Darkness Meets The Light

Junior charged at me and threw a punch towards my face. I was able to block it, but I would be lying to you all if I were to say the shit didn't hurt because that shit hurt like a mothafucka. He even pushed me back a little with that punch. He threw another punch, and I blocked it. Then he just started throwing them so fast I couldn't keep up. He finally landed a blow to my stomach and knocked me into a tree. I held my stomach while in pain because believe it or not. This bitch hit harder than God. I'd never fought one of my offspring like this before this moment. But I could see how Cain gave my father, Michael, and Jesus a run for their money!

Anyway, this son of a bitch stood there before me with his horns exposed, his wings spread, his claws out, and his teeth were sharper than a fucking razor! But I'm Lucifer. I ain't no bitch. I stood on my ten toes and channeled all the power I had. I spread my wings, and I said, "Bring it on bitch!" Junior chuckled and said in a demonic voice, "I've been waiting a long time to show you this form, Lucifer. For all the pain you've caused, for all the havoc you're responsible for, it is time for you to be locked away." Then he charged again. This time, I dodged his attack, and I watched him fly into the sky. When he reached a certain height, he came directly at me like a meteor, feet first. I grabbed Junior by his ankles and slammed him into the ground as hard as I could! But that stopped nothing. He was so filled with rage and power it was almost as if he could not feel anything. He jumped up and repeatedly punched me in every part of my body in hyperspeed.

After he beat the shit out of me, he took his finger and opened up a portal filled with fiery flames and souls falling from the sky. He grabbed me by my throat and was about to throw me inside of it. But before he could, Joseph appeared out of nowhere, snatched Junior by his wings, and threw him across the open land! Junior landed on the ground harder than a ton of bricks dropped from a skyscraper building. I looked at Joseph with an expression of surprise and fear. The next thing I knew, I heard Joseph speaking in Enochian.

> "You and your God will bow before me," Joseph exclaimed in Enochian.
>
> "To be in the presence of God is to be in the presence of love. To be in the presence of Lucifer is to be in the presence of lies," Junior said in Enochian as he stood up on both feet. "I don't want to fight you, Joseph, so step out of the way," Junior said in English.
>
> "I won't let you hurt him!"
>
> "Then you leave me no choice, brother. If I have to lock you away with him, I will. Just to save the universes from being destroyed."

Joseph slowly turned into a beast and said, "I want to see you try!" Joseph and Junior charged at one another with all of their might. Both of them threw punches and kicks at one another and were blocking, ducking, and dodging one another's blows. Joseph made some distance between the two of them and shot red beams out of his eyes! Junior flew between the beams while flying towards Joseph and got close enough to punch him in the stomach. Sending him flying across the open field. Joseph became angrier and he began to grow larger in size. His horns began to grow longer and his wings grew wider and darker. His wings and horns caught fire, but his body went through another transformation.

Every other part of his body was turning back to human, except his wings, horns, claws, and teeth.

Joseph stood in the middle of the open field and said, "You think your precious *God* can beat me?!" Junior and I looked at Joseph because I didn't think either of us could believe what we were looking at. I was scared shitless. At the same time, I was glad he was on my side. But, Joseph began to levitate off of the ground, and he shot another beam out of his eyes. This time, he was successful in hitting his brother/target. His beam burned Junior severely, knocking him to the ground. Joseph stood over him while speaking in Enochian. He said, "Your God cannot save you now. Can he, brother?" A ball of hot energy began to form in the palm of Joseph's hand, and he was getting ready to throw it at Junior to end his life. He stopped and began to scream saying "NOOOOOOOOOOO!" He grabbed his head, flapped his wings as hard as possible, and disappeared. Leaving me and Junior in the center of the earth alone. I was bent on one knee holding my abdomen while Junior laid on the ground. Both of us were too weak to fight.

"How! How did he become that powerful?! How did he even find us?!"

"He found us because he can feel our energy. Yours more than anyone else's because he is connected to you the more than anyone in our bloodline. He is starting to change. Which is why he passed out earlier today. He is overwhelmed by his powers. They are so overwhelming that it compromises his mind until he knows how to control it. Which is why he couldn't decide if he wanted to kill me moments ago. Because he fought his true nature."

"He fought his true nature? The fuck is that supposed to mean," I asked as I groaned in pain from Junior hitting me and grabbing me by the neck.

"Our true nature is to choose the same path as you. A path of darkness. But the light in us sometimes fights it. Joseph is in a battle between darkness and light within himself. He will either choose God's light or your darkness," Junior said as he also groaned in pain from being knocked around. "Lucifer, you..... You still have the same light in you. Therefore, you must repent."

I finally stood up, and I said, "I will never repent. My father tried to get me to repent, but it will never happen." After I said my piece, I teleported back to Joseph's house, leaving Junior at the deepest part of the center of the earth. When I got back to the house, Joseph was lying on the floor in his complete human form, vomiting. He looked up to me and said, "Lucifer, what is happening to me? I don't know how I ended up at that place. How I turned into that monster. I'm scared." I looked at Joseph and I smiled. Because at that moment I knew if I showed him how to control that monster inside of him, I would control him even more.

So, I pretended to be sympathetic and kneeled to help him clean himself up.

"Joseph, I will help you control these powers of yours, but before I do, you must know that your brother is the enemy. He is not trying to save you. He is trying to make sure you don't become stronger than him and my father. But I think you're already stronger than your brother. Let me help you. I will guide you in becoming a great force in this universe. And together, we will rule. Reign supreme," I said as I helped Joseph clean himself up.

"I will follow only your word, Lucifer."

"Good, my child. Now, remember, you have a mission to complete. Cleveland ain't gone rule itself, Joseph."

"You're definitely right about that," Joseph said as he grinned an evil grin and passed out again.

I didn't feel like getting him up off the ground. So I just let him lay there. I stepped outside on the back porch, and Silky was sitting in Joseph's backyard, smoking a cigar with his sword cane lying in his lap. Julian was sitting next to him.

"Luci baby! You've got the stench of the deepest part of the earth's center all over you," Silky said.

"I do, Silk. And you look like you're up to something for you to be here. And with Julian?"

"I felt Joseph's energy level through the roof. We both did. It seems his energy wasn't the only one we felt, though. So, I take it that he didn't kill his brother. Which I already knew. But I will let it go for now. Because this may actually work in our favor."

"How so, Silky."

"The more Junior tries to pull Joseph to God, the further Joseph may get away from God. It is that simple," Julian said.

"That's all fine and dandy, but I am more worried about Junior than Joseph," I said while holding my abdomen.

"We can see that. It looks like he gave you a run for your money. Let me worry about him. You continue to do what you're doing with Joseph and all should work out fine," Silky said.

"It fucking better, Silk. Because I've never seen anything like I saw a few moments ago. So our plan better work."

LUCIFER'S JOURNAL PT.5: WHAT IS LIFE? (DAY 365 IN GOD'S PRISON)

WHAT IS LIFE?
LIFE IS WHAT YOU MAKE IT.
WHAT DO YOU MAKE OF LIFE?
WHATEVER YOU WANT.
WHAT IS LIFE?
LIFE IS AS SHORT AS YOU WANT IT TO BE,
OR AS LONG AS YOU WANT IT TO BE.
WHAT IS LIFE?
LIFE IS EITHER AN OPEN FIELD THAT YOU CAN'T GET ENOUGH OF,
OR IT IS A PRISON YOU'RE STUCK IN.
WHAT IS MY LIFE?
MISERY.
MY LIFE IS MISERY.
FOR MANY REASONS.
AND I WILL SUFFER IN THIS PRISON GOD HAS MADE FOR ME FOR MANY SEASONS.
ALL BECAUSE OF MY DECISIONS,

TO IGNORE GOD'S PROVIDED VISIONS OF AN INEVITABLE FUTURE.
ARMEGEDDON IS NEAR.
AND IT IS ONLY A MATTER OF TIME BEFORE I FACE MY GREATEST FEAR.
SINCERELY
THE ORIGINAL EVIL HIMSELF!

CHAPTER 15

GOD'S PLANT (PLAN)

When God made woman, he made man's weakness. Look at me. The first most powerful creature that God ever created. Yet I created chaos with the most beautiful woman to ever walk the earth till this day, Cain. And from Cain came an unfathomable bloodline that we all learned about more and more each day. Which poses a threat to everything and everyone. Including God and myself. And if I, a supernatural creature, have fallen weak for God's greatest, softest, sweetest creations. Just imagine how far a mortal man will go and has gone. ***Kings and empires have crumbled because of the woman. Lives have been taken over the woman.***

But now, at this moment, I was beginning to lose my advocate to a woman who was pure at heart and had a gentle soul. And she would eventually be his wife and the mother of his children. But I am getting beyond myself. Let me go back. It was a year after Joseph's battle with his brother. In that time, Joseph had accomplished so much. He gained the trust of the Italians one hundred percent. He brought all of the black gang leaders and gangsters together in the city of Cleveland. They all started a co-op behind closed doors to overpower the Italians and become independent. With Joseph's leadership, of course. But on the surface, they worked for the Italians and were loyal. Joseph was making millions and became the top earner for the Italians.

His right-hand man became his brother, Scat. Scat and Joseph grew very close and genuinely loved one another. Scat guided Joseph on many things in Cleveland and was a massive reason why Joseph had the success that he had. His core crew was Scat, Abdul, and Mary Ann. The four of them together were untouchable. And while they ran shit their way, there was no bloodshed in the city amongst the blacks. There was no black-on-black crime. Was there drug circulation, sure. But fiends weren't out on the block dirtying up the neighborhoods, and neither were the pushers. Everything was done underground—police proof.

Joseph was making more money in one city than Silky and Julian were making in multiple towns combined. One night, Joseph decided to celebrate all of the successes that had come to fruition within that past year. Plus, his seventeenth birthday was approaching. So he decided to book Cafe Tia Juana on East 105th and Massie for all of the black crews in Cleveland to party. They had live music, unlimited alcohol, joints were being passed around, and there were beautiful women every fucking where. But no one was as beautiful as the woman who walked in with one of Joseph's soldiers, Hosea Moses, aka Hosey Mo. Before Joseph knew the dynamic of his trusted soldiers' relationship with the beautiful woman, he did not approach her. Yet, he could not stop staring at her occasionally as she graced the room with her presence.

Hosey Mo, who was in his early twenties, slim, with a chocolate brown skin tone, wavy hair, and the craziest wheezy cough laugh you'd ever heard, walked up to Joseph and greeted him with an envelope while holding the beautiful lady by her hand. He guided her through the crowd of people in the club.

> "I've got a gift for yaaaaa! HAHAHAHAHAAAAA," Hosey said as he laughed. "It's like salad, but better! Probably healthier than salad. But cha can't eat it!"
>
> "Hosey, you sure do know how to put a smile on my face," Joseph said as he laughed. "I'm sure Johnny will be happy with this envelope."

“That ain’t for him. That envelope will be in Scat’s hands tomorrow. This is for your birthday. That’s a personal gift from me. For everything you’ve done.”

“I appreciate this, Hosey,” Joseph said as he hugged Hosey Mo.

“Listen, I want to introduce you to my best friend from childhood. Name’s Jean. She like a sister to me, cept she always ratting on me to my mama about the nasty women I sleep with! HAHAHAHAHAHAAAAAAAA!”

Joseph laughed so hard he almost spit his drink out. Hosey had a sense of humor that would keep you laughing all night. Joseph shook Jean’s hand and introduced himself while still being mesmerized by her beauty. Jean stood at five foot two, about a buck fifty in weight, curvy, light-skinned, with long, beautiful silky hair, high cheekbones, and a smile that would light up the room. She carried herself in a sophisticated manner but was very down to earth.

“It is a pleasure to meet you, Joseph,” Jean said while still holding Joseph’s hand.

“The pleasure is all mine, Jean,” Joseph said as he kissed the beautiful woman’s hand. “Tell me, how’d you become friends with this menace, Hosey?”

“Our mothers went to church together when we were children. Been stuck with him ever since. And he has been a menace his entire life!”

“And I ain’t gone stop being one till a honkey turn black,” Hosey Mo said as he laughed. “But my friend here needed to get out, have some fun. Her ole man just left her, so she all sad and lonely. Laying up in the house crying. Just sad man, just sad.”

“Well, you’re going have plenty of fun here, Jean. Especially if you save a dance for me.”

Jean shyfully smiled and chuckled and said, “You’ve got it, handsome.” Joseph walked over to the stage and stopped the live band from playing. He grabbed the microphone and gave a speech to all of those who were in the room.

> "Ladies and gents. I'd like to thank you all for coming to this party. Tonight is not about celebrating just me. But it is to celebrate all of us. We have stopped the bloodshed amongst our people and have made so much money together. We have shown that the black man and the black woman can stand hand in hand, shoulder to shoulder, and be peaceful and prosperous! We are truly the beginning of a new era that will determine the future of our children, and our children's children, and beyond. We must continue to stick together, always remember to love one another, and continue to make money together!"

Everyone in the club applauded and cheered Joseph on as he finished his speech. Afterward, the live music resumed, and Joseph ran over to Jean, grabbed her by the hand, and dragged her to the dance floor. They danced the night away and looked at one another with so much love in their eyes. I knew it was love because how they looked at one another is how Eve and I used to look at one another. The love was pure, energetic, electrifying, authentic.

But this woman, this woman, Jean. She had the light of an angel inside of her. A pure angel. A woman without sin. She could walk into a room and her light would just cast out every bit of darkness. I'd never seen any human woman like her with that kind of light and beauty. But I have seen a man like that. And that was Junior. I then realized that God had sent this woman to Joseph to save him from me. And when I realized that I kept myself invisible, I was going to sneak up on this woman and kill her. Cause her to have a heart attack or some shit. You know, make it look natural. But before I could get to her, God, who was also invisible in the room, stood in front of the two. He looked at me and said, "Your wickedness will not be tolerated this time. Walk away." I did just that because I didn't want to reveal myself in front of everyone. But I was mad as shit. This fucking father of mine was really playing chess. Ain't that a bitch. Mothafucka always got a strategy to overpower my evilness.

Any mothafucking way, after that night, a fucking crowbar couldn't separate Joseph and Jean. The two of them dated for months and got to know one another very well, mentally and emotionally, but not sexually yet. The reason was that she wanted to wait for marriage before sex. And even though Joseph had been sexually active for years, he never forced the idea of sex. He was patient with her. Despite his line of work at the beginning, she was patient with him.

They were also understanding of one another. They revealed many things to one another about themselves. Joseph even explained his bloodline and powers to her and showed Jean his beast side now that he knew how to control it. With her being a prophet and being able to see inside Joseph's past, she already knew who he was and what he was. And she still loved him.

One cold winter night in December of 1953, Jean and Joseph were laying on the floor, cuddling by the fireplace, watching the flames dance. Jean ran her fingers through Joseph's wavy hair and held him tight.

"I don't want to lose you, Joseph."

"You won't. I'm made of steel, baby. Ain't no taking me out," Joseph said as he laughed.

"I'm serious. We never discuss your work line and how it will affect our future. You basically run this city, Joseph. That makes you a target."

"Whatever I do in this life, it will never come back to our family. Baby, you have to trust me. I would never put you in any danger. Now look, you will be my wife, we will have ourselves some beautiful babies, and we will live a life of peace and happiness."

"There is no peace without God in our hearts, Joseph. And I know who has guided you all these years and how you feel about God. We've talked about this before. I've seen your other form, and I accept the fact that my children will share the same blood as the devil. But the blood that is inside the devil is the blood that God put there. You are God's creation. You just have to let your light shine through, honey."

"Everyone is not you, Jean. That light inside of me is very small. The last time I truly felt God's light inside of me was when my parents were still alive, and my brother was still with me. Now we both walk this city as if we're on two different sides. And I miss him like crazy. If God loved me, he'd mend my relationship with my brother. If God loved me, he would take my pain away."

"Joseph, God is what brought us together. Don't you see th...."

Joseph's phone rang and interrupted the conversation. Joseph answered the phone, and it was Silky. Silky wasted no time getting straight to the point.

"I know you didn't kill your brother, little nigga. And I was going to let it go since no one else even knew what he looked like but us in this thing of ours. But now you ain't got no choice. Because this motherfucker has built a humongous temple in the center of the territory, we were trying to take over on the west side of Cleveland. He is making national news. Preaching about the words of this *Elijah Muhammad*? Whatever the case may be, I need for your ass to get rid of him. NOW! AND I MEAN RIGHT NOW. BECAUSE IF YOU DON'T GET RID OF HIM? I WILL SEE TO IT THAT YOUR PRETTY LITTLE GIRLFRIEND THAT YOU LOVE SO MUCH IS DEAD!"

Silky said all he had to say and hung up the phone. Joseph put the phone down and said to Jean, "I have to go. Can we speak about this another time?" Jean nodded in agreement. Joseph ran upstairs, changed into an all-black outfit, and threw on an overcoat. Then he closed his eyes, channeled his brother's energy, and teleported to the new mosque temple that Junior just built. When Joseph arrived at the temple, Junior was sitting on the floor, praying and meditating.

"Which one of your masters sent you. Your uncle, or your so-called *God, Lucifer*?"

"Why are you making this hard for me? All you had to do was lay low and keep your fucking mouth shut! But here you are, building temples. *In GOD'S NAME! FOR WHAT*?!"

"Every lost soul needs a home, Joseph."

"They have a home. Or did you forget what *HELL* stands for?"

"Here Eternally Lives the Lost. I haven't forgotten."

"You really pissed off Silky. He wants your head."

"And if you don't give it to him?"

"Then he will kill the love of my life. The best thing that has happened to me since we lost our parents, Junior. I really love her. And this isn't just some kind of puppy love. I love her. And I want to marry her. I want children with her."

Junior stood up and faced his brother with a smile on his face. Joseph took a fighting stance.

"You're in love. You *ACTUALLY* fell in love. God said this would happen. God said he would bless you with a light. A woman that will accept you for all that you are. You've found that woman. Now, you'll do anything to protect her. But killing me won't do that. I said it once. I will say it again. You must get away from all of this. Forget Silky, forget Julian, forget Lucifer. Forget all of them. You, me, Scat. We can all be a family for once. I will look after you both. And your families. I promise I will."

Joseph looked at his brother as a tear fell down his cheek and said, "Not today, not any day." Joseph teleported instantly from his spot right in front of Junior and threw a punch. Junior was ready, so he threw one back. The two brother's fists met, causing a force to knock out all of the windows in the five-story white and gold temple. Yet again, the two were in combat, except this time, no powers were used, and no transformations took place.

Finally, Junior grabbed Joseph by the throat after throwing, ducking, dodging, and countering countless blows. He lifted Joseph off of the ground as they both cried.

"ALLAH! THE ALPHA, AND THE OMEGA! I PRAY THAT YOU SHOW MY BROTHER THE WAY AND PUT HIM ON A PATH OF RIGHTOUSNESS! GIVE HIM THE STRENGTH TO COUNTER ALL OF THE EVIL INFLUENCES IN HIS LIFE! SO THAT HE MAY BE ABLE TO LIVE THE LIFE THAT YOU ARE WILLING TO PROVIDE FOR HIM! PLEASE SAVE MY BROTHER!"

"NOOOOOOOOOOOOOOOOOOOOOOOOOOO OOOOOOOOOOOOOOOOOOOOOOOOOOOOOOO OOOOOOOOOOO!"

Joseph screamed so loud he caused Junior's ears to bleed. Junior grabbed his ears in agony and said, "Only death will stop me from saving you from yourself!" Joseph responded, "Well, the day of death has come!" Joseph charged at Junior, and something knocked the shit out of him. When Joseph regained consciousness, he saw an older, tall, brown-skinned man with a gray beard, wearing a black robe, with a syth in his hand. It was death. "It is not his time. Now tell Silky THAT," Grimm said as he looked down on Joseph. Joseph was too weak to attack death. So he laid on the ground and said, "This isn't over."

Joseph snapped his fingers and teleported to his house, where Jean had fallen asleep on the floor by the fireplace. Joseph kneeled on the floor and gently stroked Jean's face with his hand. "I won't lose you. I've lost everyone else. I cannot lose you, my sweet Jean."

CHAPTER 16

Bloodline Rebellion/ Special Guests

A few days after Joseph's encounter with Junior in the masjid, Joseph decided to visit his uncle in New Orleans. He met Silky at his restaurant in the French quarters.

"I've been waiting for you. What the fuck is going on with that brother of yours," Silky said.

"I have a message from Grimm."

"And?"

"He said it wasn't his time."

"Death only comes when he wants, but not when it is necessary. Well you and I need to come up with a plan, and fast. Do you see that across the street? That building? It is your brother's work."

"So, what you want me to do, blow it up? I wish you had this same attitude when it came to the Italians."

"The fuck you say to me, little nigga?"

"*Nothing*"

"That's what I thought. Now, like I said, you need to come up with a plan to take your brother. From my understanding, he is teaming up with the Jewish and Christian communities to bring all of *God's* children together. He is not only building mosques.

He is building synagogues and churches as well in honor of *Abraham*. We have to show them we mean business. They will not fuck up our business by spreading *God's word*. Not on my watch. So, I need you to figure out a way to kill your brother. Talk it over with Lucifer and see what he advises. That is, if you want to keep that pretty little thang you have prancing around you. Didn't I tell you not to let the world know your weakness, nephew? Now look at you?"

"Right, I will figure it out, unc."

"Besides that, I see you're earning well in Cleveland. Keep that shit up. And don't try no slick shit up there."

"Got it, unc."

"Now get the fuck out my face, Joseph!"

Joseph snapped his fingers and teleported to his childhood home in Alabama. It had been over a year since he'd been in Leeds. He walked through his home and looked at all the pictures of his parents and brother on the wall. "If God, really wanted better for us, why would he let my parents die," Joseph said out loud to himself. After he said that, he felt a breeze on his back. He turned around, and his parents stood there staring at him smiling.

"Mama? Daddy," Joseph said as he dropped to his knees.

"Son, please listen to us. You must get away from that brother of mine and Lucifer. They are leading you down a path that will not serve you or your children. PLEASE," his father's spirit pleaded.

"You have to remember the things that we taught you, Joseph. Think about all of the days and nights we sat up and discussed the scriptures. You were brought up in a *God-fearing home*. And now you've found yourself a *God-fearing* woman. If you don't change for anyone, change for her. And do it for your brother's. You all need one another," his mother's spirit said.

"I miss y'all so much. I will do anything, just come back to me. Please come back. I promise I will change. GOD PLEASE

BRING THEM BACK! MOM! DAD! COME BACK," Joseph pleaded as his parent's spirits began to disappear.

Joseph laid on the floor and cried his eyes out. "I HATE YOU GOD! I HATE YOU SO MUCH! SHOW YOURSELF YOU FUCKING COWARD," Joseph screamed. But God didn't show himself. But Junior did.

"Joseph? I didn't come here to fight," Junior said.

"Lucifer has always been there. You know," Joseph said tearfully.

"I know, Joseph," Junior said sympathetically.

"And I called for God many nights, despite what Lucifer said. But he didn't answer. You didn't answer. But Lucifer did, and Silky did, and I am so confused because I have everyone telling me what I should do and who is good for me. And I don't know what to do. I just know I want to live a happy life with the woman I love and I want to have my brothers in my life. But I can't have what I want. AND WHY CAN'T I HAVE IT ALL? I WANT IT ALL! I WANT IT ALL! I WANT IT ALL!"

"You can have it all. Just come with me. This is the last time I will ask you. Right here, in our home. Come with me, and all will be better."

Joseph nodded in agreeance and was about to walk to his brother and accept his invitation and brotherly embrace. Before he could, Silky appeared out of the blue behind Joseph, and Joseph froze.

"Don't you want to continue to be rich beyond your wildest dreams? Don't you want to be able to provide that beautiful woman in Cleveland with the life she deserves? The money, the cars? Put your kids in position to rule the world? I can provide that for you, nephew."

"Silky, as of today? You provide nothing for me. I provide it for myself," Joseph said.

Silky looked at Joseph suspiciously. Joseph grinned, and his eyes began to turn red. Junior said, "Joseph, please don't do it!" Joseph turned around and charged at Silky so fast that Silky had no time to defend himself. Joseph threw his hand into his uncle's chest and ripped his heart out. He proceeded to take Silky's cane sword and cut his head off. Afterward, he threw Silky's heart on the ground and stomped on it.

Silky was dead, and this time, Grimm did not appear to be coming to his rescue. Joseph looked at his brother and said, "I prefer to choose my own destiny, Junior," and disappeared before his eyes. Junior looked down at Silky's lifeless body, and I made myself visible to Junior.

"Damn, he really fucked Silky up, didn't he?"

"He is getting stronger by the day. And he's only seventeen. There is no way he's this much stronger than Silky at this age. Injure him, yes. But strong enough to kill him? No."

"So what? He got rid of an evil for you and your other religious groups," I said sarcastically while laughing.

"You know, I am only one decision from being Joseph and killing you for what you did to our parents, right? But God has tamed my monster. I have to save my brother from that monster inside him," Junior said as he gave me a cold stare.

"Good luck, little nigga," I said in Silky's voice while laughing, and I disappeared. Leaving Junior standing there looking like a dumbass.

I channeled Joseph's energy and teleported to his location, the French Quarters. He stood in Joseph's house and looked around it for a long time, holding his uncle's cane. "It's time to run things in the way that I want to," he said to himself.

"What about Julian? He is the heir to the throne," I said as I made myself visible to Joseph.

"I will deal with Julian."

"Well, I guess the time is now because he is walking in."

Julian walked into his father's house and noticed Joseph's hands were covered in blood, and he was holding his father's cane sword.

"You did it. You killed him."

"I did. I am sorry, Julian."

"Good. I am finally free. I no longer have to pretend to want this life. If you're wondering if I am going to fight you for the business. I'm not. I am leaving and going to Florida. And I am staying there. You and Lucifer can have.... *.this*," Julian said as he walked up to Joseph.

"So, this is it? You're out of the business? Just like that? You're turning your back on me, Lucifer, the family business," Joseph said.

"Joseph, I never wanted this. My mother was a whore that worked for my father. She just happened to get pregnant with me. When I was six years old, Silky killed her in front of me, right there in this courtyard. I wanted to kill him so bad. But I never experienced the amount of power that you and Junior did. So you have a great life, Joseph. And if you were smart, you'd choose God over this despicable reject that created us," Julian said as he looked at me. "I'm going to pack my things and get on a train to Florida. I will write and call you. I love you little cousin. It's been a ride," Julian said as he hugged Joseph.

"I love you too, man," Joseph said as he hugged his cousin. "If you ever need anything, I will take care of you. I don't need any of your father's secret stashes. Take it it all. And when you need more than that, there's more where that comes from," Joseph said.

The two cousins released one another, and Julian walked over to me, looked me in the eyes, and spit in my face. Then he walked away and proceeded to pack his things. After Julian took one last look at his father's home, he said to Joseph, "Burn it down. Please?" As Julian walked out of the house, Joseph stood in the center of the courtyard and used his powers to set fire to the big, beautiful French-style home.

CHAPTER 17

Heavy Is The Head That Wears The Crown & Mighty Is The Hand That Holds The Cane!

The time was *FINALLY HERE*! With Julian stepping down from his birthright, it was time for Joseph to claim Silky's throne. When he returned to Cleveland, the commission asked many questions about Silky. Especially after seeing Joseph sporting Silky's gold snake cane sword with ruby eyes. So the commission called a meeting in Little Italy with Joseph, and Joseph alone for him to explain what exactly what happened to Silky.

"Joseph, we have not heard from your uncle or cousin in almost three days now. And you return to Cleveland with Silky's cane? What do you make of this," Johnny Santino asked Joseph.

"Well, Silky attacked me. High off cocaine. You all know he had a habit. I killed him surely in self-defense, I swear. As for Julian, he has stepped away from the business. He got sick of the violence and had no desire to avenge his father. Therefore, there is no one else except for me to run the business. So, from here on out, we are all partners. If you all still want to continue our business that is."

"You mean, you work for us, right," Johnny Santino Junior said.

"Sure, John Junior," Joseph said while gritting his teeth.

"The commission thinks that it will be in the best interest of all families to continue our business with you. You know everything there is to know about all of our businesses. And if you could earn more money in one city than your uncle could in multiple cities? You'll do great running it all by yourself," Johnny Santino said as his son rolled his eyes.

Joseph nodded his head, and all commission members stood up and embraced Joseph with a handshake and "congratulations." After the meeting, Joseph walked out to the car where his brother, Scat, was waiting for him in a green suit, standing by a Cadillac, smiling. He hugged his baby brother and said, "The *KING* has taken his *THRONE*! NOW WE CELEBRATE!" The two hopped in Scat's car and drove to Dearings to celebrate. As soon as Joseph walked in the door, he was greeted by Mary Ann and Abdul with hugs and kisses. Every black gang leader and criminal in Cleveland was in that building that night. Everyone chanted, "SPEECH, SPEECH, SPEECH, SPEECH, SPEECH!"

"ALRIGHT! ALRIGHT! Just calm down, everyone. We're getting closer and closer to our goal, where we will own this city. Where those fucking Italians will no longer own us and we will gain our freedom and independence. I know you all have been patient. But I ask that you all give me a little more time before we move forward. I want to assemble all of our other crews in the other cities and states first. Because we are going to need as much fire power and man power as possible. We're talking about Costa Nostra! So we have to think big! We have to think sharp! We have to be strategic! And most importantly, WE HAVE TO STICK TOGETHER ALWAYS! WE MUST NEVER WAR AGAINST ONE ANOTHER! EVER! AND NEVER LET ANYONE,

ESPECIALLY THE WHITE MAN, COME BETWEEN US. DO Y'ALL HEAR ME?!"

Everyone in the room went wild cheering Joseph on after his speech. And then they partied harder than hard. But while everyone else partied, Joseph walked outside to smoke a cigarette. He stared at the stars and his brother Scat, Mary Ann, and Abdul joined him.

"You did it, Joseph, now what," Mary Ann said.

"We will take everything over. Those fucking wops have no idea what's coming," Joseph said.

"Just like Silky didn't," said Abdul.

The four of them laughed and then Mary asked if everyone could leave her and Joseph alone to speak in private. When they were left alone. Mary held Josephs face in both of her hands and humbly spoke to him about Scat.

"I am so glad that you and your brother Scat have formed a bond. And I am so proud of all of your accomplishments in this past year. But I want to ask you a favor."

"Anything for you Mary."

"Scat is my son Joseph, and I love him dearly. I don't want anything to happen to my baby. He has a terrible temper and can get into trouble sometimes. Please don't add to it."

"I love Scat. I would never let anyone bring harm to my brothers."

"Speaking of *brothers*. The *three* of you *need* to come together. Scat has never met Junior. And you and Junior need one another. You all do. I am not going to be here for long. And it would be nice to know that Scat has you two to fall back on."

"I will make peace with my brother. I promise."

The two hugged one another, and Mary said, "I know where you want to go. Go to her. She has been asking about you for the past few days. She misses you. And I know you have been holding on to that ring forever." Joseph got up and walked up to Wade Park, where his beautiful Jean Taper resided. He knocked on her door. When he arrived at her door, he was greeted by Jean's father, Mr. Taper. Mr. Taper was a six-foot-two, dark-skinned, sophisticated man who was very gentle but stern when it came to his daughters.

"Why are you wearing that ridiculous suit boy? You look like a pimp," Mr. Taper said.

"Sir, I have to see your daughter. "

"She's asleep."

"Is that Joseph, daddy," Jean screamed from inside the house while Mr. Taper rolled his eyes.

Jean ran to the door and said, "Father, can you give us some time alone, please?" Mr. Taper reluctantly walked away from the door. Jean and Joseph hugged and kissed one another. After they were finished, Joseph said, "I have something for you." He went into his suit jacket pocket and pulled out a small ring box. When he opened the box it was a humongous diamond engagement ring.

"Woman, I love you. And I want you, and I need you. I have never met anyone like you in my life. And these past few days, a lot has happened, but I am on top now, baby. I am the king now. Now, I will not lie. I have had to do some things that I will one day regret. But my regrets are my regrets. And my regrets will not come back on you or our family in the future. So, woman, I am asking you. No! I am begging you to be my wife. In this life and the next. Be the light to my darkness. And let me be the shadow to cast away any demon that comes near you. Let me be your protector and your provider until our days end. Please, Jean?"

"Joseph, I love you so much. I will only accept this ring if you accept God in your heart. And make peace with your brother, Junior."

Joseph looked down at the ground and said, "I will try, honey. I will try." Jean kissed Joseph on the cheek and said, "That's a start. Now give me my ring!" Joseph kissed Jean on the lips and screamed, "We're getting married! We're GETTING MARRIED!" Jean's mother, father, and older sister came to the front window to see what all of the excitement was about. When they discovered the young couple were engaged,

Jean's parents did not seem enthused. But what everyone else thought didn't matter to them. They were in *loooooove* and shit. I didn't give a shit about their love. All I wanted was for them to start making babies so I could have my offsprings take every fucking thing over that God created.

But the night of their engagement, the two made love for the first time at Joseph's home. Joseph said after they finished making love, "How soon do you want to have the wedding?" Jean looked at Joseph and smiled while they laid in bed. "How about tonight," Jean asked in a joking manner.

"I can get a judge tonight to marry us now. They're all on my payroll."

"I was kidding, Joseph. I want a wedding. I want our family and friends to be there. Let's wait a few months. Actually, plan the wedding."

"Honey, I think that is a great idea. Plus, I need to get some things in order before we get married. Now that Silky is gone...."

"Silky is gone," Jean asked with an expression of surprise.

"Silky is gone, and now I am running things. So I have to get everything in order with the businesses. Get my soldiers in line. Get you, your family, and my family all around-the-clock security."

"I guess what they say is true, Joseph."

"What's that?"

"Heavy is the head that wears the crown. But in your case, mighty is the hand that holds the cane. Just make sure that Silky's spirit doesn't rub off on you."

After their conversation, Jean went to sleep, and Joseph stayed up all night. To this day, I couldn't tell you what was on his mind. But I can say that a lot was about to change after that night. So just keep reading this shit.

CHAPTER 18

Holy Matrimony & Unholy Murder

Two months after the engagement, Joseph and Jean had the wedding of their dreams. All of their family, friends, and *colleagues* were there. Joseph spared no expense for the wedding at all. All he wanted was to make his wife and now mother of his *first* born happy. Yes, Jean was pregnant by the time the two had married.

At the wedding reception, while everyone partied their asses off and ate food. Scat, the best man to the groom, collected all of the envelopes for the bride and groom. And them mothafuckas were fat as hell, filled with cash! While Scat was collecting all of the envelopes, a man walked up wearing Islamic clothing and an envelope. "I don't believe we've met big brother." Scat looked at the man closely and said, "Junior? Willie Joseph Junior?" With a smile on his face, Scat hugged his brother Junior. "I have waited so long to meet you. JOSEPH! LOOK WHO IS HERE," Scat shouted from a distance. Joseph looked and saw Junior. He could not hide his happiness. Joseph smiled so hard I thought his fucking teeth were going to crack. He took his wife by the hand and dragged her over to see his brother, Junior. Then he called for his sister-in-law and parent-in-laws to meet his brother. The families hit it off well. After a friendly conversation, Junior leaned over to whisper in Joseph's ear. "You and I have to talk," Junior said. Joseph did not give

Junior any back talk, he obliged his request, and the two went outside. Joseph lit a cigarette and smiled again.

"Been a while, Junior. But I've never been happier to see you."

"I'm happy to see you too little brother. And I am glad to see that you're a married man now. She's a beautiful bride. And I can tell she is going to make a great mother. You know she is a member of one of my temples, right?"

"I'm aware. So?"

"She is a light, Joseph."

"That's why I married her. And although I am glad to see you. I have to ask, why are you really here? The last time we saw one another, I had Silky's beating heart in my hand in our childhood home."

"Which is an image that I can never get rid of in my head. But I wanted to see you and talk to you because you and I have been through a lot over the past year. We've battled, we've argued, etc. But now I feel that we should move forward in peace and heal. Especially with you starting new chapters in your life. I want to get closer to you and our brother, Scat. I want us to be a family. And I will tell you now. I will not try to force you to do anything anymore when it comes down to who you follow. If you want to follow Lucifer, you do that. I just ask you of one thing."

"Sure, what is it?"

"I would like to invite you to my new temple this Friday. Abdul comes all the time. You, your wife, Scat. I'd love for you to come. I will be at Temple #18 on Euclid."

"We will be there, Junior," Joseph said hesitantly.

"My boy. I love you. Despite everything we've been through. You will always be my lil trouble maka. Until our days end...."

"And even in the afterlife," Joseph said as he cut Junior off mid-sentence.

The two brothers hugged one another, and Junior walked back into the reception hall to say goodbye to their eldest brother, Scat. Afterward, Joseph returned to the reception hall and danced the night away with beautiful wife. At this moment, Joseph had everything he'd wanted. His wife, his two brothers, and a thriving criminal empire. But there was one thing that was missing. He didn't own Cleveland yet because he was still operating under the Italians.

Days after the wedding, Joseph met with his core crew to discuss their moves against the Italians at Scat's home on Olivet. Because things were getting heated between the black gangs and the Italians now that there were changes to their agreement.

"You mean to tell me these sons of bitches are going up on the price of smack again?! Y'all FUCKING SERIOUS," Scat exclaimed while pouring a drink.

"Calm down, you know your temper can get the best of you, Scat. You definitely get that from your uncle, Knight," Mary Ann said.

"Ain't that the truth," Joseph said as he sipped whiskey.

"Mama Mary, I have every right to be angry about this. The more they go up on the dope, the less of a profit we make," Scat exclaimed.

"We know this, boy. Now with all this damn yelling you doing, have you got a solution for the problem. And not just gathering soldiers to kill the commission and their soldiers," Abdul said.

"No," Scat said as he plopped in his chair.

"Well, listen, I have a solution. We're going to buy double the amount that we usually would. And instead of selling it to our people, we will sell it to the Italians. Get their people hooked on the shit. It'll weaken them," Joseph said.

"What?! How the fuck are we going to do that," Scat asked.

"I have a plan, I will tell you all about it when we leave the mosque. Abdul, you going with us," Joseph said as he got up and put on his suit jacket.

"Not today. I want you two to see your brother, spend time with him, and enjoy one another's company," Abdul said.

"Whatever, listen before we leave, let me go back and get my cigarettes out of my car and we can get the fuck out of here," Scat said.

Scat walked out to his car to get his cigarettes. As soon as he opened his car door, his car exploded. The explosion was so impactful it blew the windows out of the back of the house. Joseph, Mary Ann, and Abdul ran out to the backyard to find Scat lying in the backyard, burned to a crisp, dead. Mary Ann dropped to her knees and screamed, "My baby, God, why'd you take HIM!?" Abdul and Joseph stood there in shock, with tears rolling down their faces. They were in so much shock they could not even console Mary Ann.

Neighbors called the fire department and police. Once they arrived, everyone was questioned, and the ambulance and coroner were called to the scene. Mary Ann was too distraught to answer any questions. When the police, ambulance, and corners left with Scat's body, Mary Ann broke down and cried again. Joseph showed anger and hurt on his face.

"The Italians did this. I know they did," Joseph said.

"But why? Why him? Everyone else got into their cars today, and there was no car bombs. No explosions," Abdul said.

"I don't know. But I know this much. They are not going to get away with killing my brother."

"You've got that right. I swear all of their fucking HEADS WILL ROLL FOR KILLING MY SON," Mary Ann exclaimed.

Joseph walked over and hugged Mary Ann. They both cried together, and Joseph said, "I am so sorry, Mary." After a while of crying and consoling, Joseph left Scat's home and drove to the masjid temple. Service was over, but his wife and Junior were in Junior's office. Joseph walked into the temple, took his shoes off as instructed by the signs on the wall, and walked inside the prayer room. He dropped to his knees, and he tearfully screamed.

"GOD! WHY DO YOU TAKE EVERYONE THAT I LOVE?! WHY DO YOU HATE ME SO MUCH THAT YOU WOULD TAKE MY BROTHER FROM ME?! SHOW YOURSELF, AS YOUR SON HAS! SPEAK TO ME! OR ARE

YOU TOO MUCH OF A COWARD TO FACE ME?! WHY WON'T YOU SHOW YOURSELF TO ME?! AM I NOT SPECIAL ENOUGH?! DO YOU NOT CARE?! WHAT IS WRONG WITH ME WHERE YOU WILL SHOW YOURSELF TO JUNIOR AND NOT I?! I SHARE THE SAME BLOOD AS YOU DO! GOD PLEASE! SHOW YOUR SELF!"

Junior and Jean could hear Joseph from a distance and entered the prayer room. They found Joseph lying on the floor in a puddle of tears. Junior and Jean both embraced him and asked him what was wrong. Before he could answer, God appeared before them in a gold robe and jewels.

"You think I have forsaken you. But I have not my son. I have given you all that you need to soften your heart, but my son's influence is very powerful. I gave you a wife who is truly your helpmate and soulmate. She has love in her heart, and she carries your child. Tending to your wife and children, standing side by side with your brother, will truly change your story's narrative, my child. Lucifer has had an influence on you for years. And I apologize for that. But I am here now, and I will forgive all of your sins. But I ask you to do one thing."

"Repent, right," I asked as I appeared before everyone.

"Yes. Repent," God said. "Just like I asked you to do, Lucifer."

"What about my businesses? The war that is about to begin. How will I walk away from everything without my family or myself having to pay the price," Joseph asked.

"YOU FUCKING SERIOUS? YOU'RE ACTUALLY CONSIDERING THIS?! YOU SAID YOURSELF THAT NO ONE WAS THERE FOR YOU BUT ME! YOU DAMNED GOD AND YOUR BROTHER! NOW YOU WANT TO CHANGE THAT," I exclaimed to Joseph.

"That all will work itself out because it is in my hands now," God said.

Joseph looked at his wife and brother, stood up, walked up to God, kneeled before him, and said, "I repent for all of my sins." When he said that, my fucking feelings were hurt. This son of a bitch chose God over me. Then God had the fucking nerve to say to me, "I think that it would be in your best interest to leave my son," as his eyes turned the color bright gold. I knew I didn't want that smoke, so I got the fuck away fast. After that day, I left Joseph alone. But just remember, this story ain't over yet. So keep fucking reading.

CHAPTER 19

Ten Years Later And Armageddon Is NEAR!

Ten years had passed, and I still had all of these evildoers doing my bidding. But my advocate was walking in the sands with God and his brother Junior. Leaving their footprints everywhere they went. It was fucking disgusting. Joseph left his family's business over to Mary Ann and Abdul. When the business fell into their hands, they started a war with the Italians out of revenge. A lot of blood was shed. Innocent civilians were killed in the African American, Italian, and Jewish communities. Considering that there were a lot of Jewish businesses in Cleveland, they suffered the Italian's wrath because of their association with "*the blacks*." But despite everything that was going on, God kept his word. He kept Joseph and his family shielded from all of the chaos. Joseph's wife had just given birth to their second child. A little girl named Ola. Their firstborn was named after Joseph's oldest brother, Scat. His name was Ezekiel Andre Williams. And at the age of ten years old, the boy was stronger than I thought anyone could've been at his age. Joseph and Junior trained Ezekiel to control his powers so he would not become destructive. Ezekiel was a brilliant young man raised in the mosque since Joseph converted to Islam after his encounter with God.

Now you all can call me a piece of shit, but I wanted to corrupt that boy so fucking bad, but at this point in Joseph's life, I knew what he was capable of. And the last thing I wanted was to fuck with him on any level where he could possibly send me to that place that Junior almost did when he and I fought him ten years ago. I am not too macho to say I didn't fear him or Junior. Especially considering how strong they'd become over the years. But regardless, I always tried to figure out a way to get to Joseph and get him back on my team. And in between those ten years, I would visit him every now and then and talk to him. He never rejected me, but he never embraced me either. He said to me once that he chose God over me because he saw no benefit in serving my purpose because he was losing the ones he loved the most. And following me wouldn't give him what he wanted. Which was *family*. When the truth is, I was all the family he fucking needed.

So, the boy was no longer in my grasp. There was no more of him leading my ill repute. Instead, he was out feeding the homeless, building homes for the homeless, and using all the money he earned to build legitimate businesses and holy temples that benefited the community. He did everything he could to right all of his wrongs in the communities. He even made a deal with the black gangsters where they would keep their drugs and violence out of their own communities. Which the black gangsters did out of respect for who he was. But like I said, the Italians brought war to their communities, leaving them to defend it.

Throughout the years, Joseph remained close to Abdul and Mary Ann. He never tried to change them, and they never crossed boundaries with one another because, as far as they were concerned, they were a family. When Joseph left the organization, he made sure he left them with a multimillion-dollar empire because he knew they were not leaving that lifestyle unless it was in a body bag, especially Mary.

One summer day in 1964, Mary visited Joseph and Jean because she had not seen her baby goddaughter Ola since she'd been born. The beautiful woman sat in Joseph's backyard, held the child, and played with her until the child fell asleep. Jean took the baby inside the house and put her to bed, leaving the former business partners alone.

"Who would've thought that you would grow up and wanna save the damn world, Joseph," Mary said with a smile on her face.

"What can I say, Mary? It was time. After losing Scat.... I just didn't know what to do. I didn't know where else to turn to. And I'm sorry that I lef....

"Don't you dare apologize. Scat was my son, I raised him as my own. I knew it was a matter of time before they got to him. He had so much anger in his heart because of how he was brought into this world. There is no telling what he did behind our backs to the Italians out of hate. But honestly, I am glad you're out. You look happy, and healthy, and you're taking care of your family and your people. I am not mad that you left, Joseph."

"I worry about you, Mary. You more than Abdul. Abdul knows when to back off. You on the other hand, you'll never get over what they did to Scat until everyone is dead."

"I am going to tell you something, and then I am going to head out. When your mother first gave birth to Scat, she handed him to my husband and me. When I first held that boy, I knew I would love and protect him. But as he got older, he did a lot of crazy things. He was a natural-born killer. He was all over the place, which is why we called him Scatter Brain, Scat, for short. Deep down, I knew he would leave this earth before me. But not like that. Not from an explosion. So you're right. I will not rest until my baby is avenged. But I have to get going now, and I love you dearly, Joseph."

Mary Ann stood up from her chair, gave Joseph the biggest hug and kiss on the forehead, and left. That was the last time that Joseph saw his dear friend alive because days later, Mary Ann was gunned down in front of her house on Hampden in broad daylight. Joseph was at Temple #18 with his family, breaking fast and watching Malcolm X on television when it happened. The phone in the kitchen rang, and Junior answered it. When he answered, Abdul was on the other end of the line. He was crying. Joseph looked at Junior's facial expression, walked into the kitchen, and took the phone from Junior. When he got on the phone, he could hear Abdul crying.

"Say it, Abdul," Joseph said as he began to cry.

"I can't say it, Joseph. I cannot form my mouth to say the words."

"When... did it happen?"

"A few hours ago. In front of her house. Driveby," Abdul said.

Joseph dropped the phone, fell into his brother's arms, and cried. He looked at his brother Junior and asked, "Did I do the right thing by leaving? I mean if I had not left, Mary would probably still be alive." Junior looked at Joseph, and his response was, "You did the right thing, Joseph. You did what was best for your wife and your children. Mary wanted that for you. She was proud of you." Despite the comforting words from his big brother, Joseph still felt a sense of guilt.

So he left the temple and teleported to Little Italy. He saw all of the dons in the commission's cars parked outside a pizza shop on Mayfield. He teleported into the pizza shop's dining room, where the commission ate. All of the dons looked at Joseph, wondering how he got past security. Johnny Santino angrily asked, "How the fuck did you get in here, you fucking nigger." Joseph's eyes lit up a bright red, and every don in the city of Cleveland combusted. Once they'd all turned to ashes, Joseph said, "This is for Mary, Scat, and all of the innocent people you all have killed."

After hearing the screams from the outside, all of their guards ran into the dining area. As soon as they saw their bosses burned to a fucking crisp, they pulled their guns and opened fire. The bullets hit Joseph but did not penetrate his skin. Joseph stood there and took the bullets until everyone had exhausted their clips. Then he looked down and telekinetically made the fallen bullets rise. The guards looked dumbfounded. Joseph said, "I will cleanse this world of pure evils," and pointed his index finger at the guards. When he did, the bullets that did not penetrate him penetrated the guards. Joseph killed everyone in the room. Then he walked out of the pizza shop and snapped his fingers, causing a fire to spread wildly throughout Little Italy.

Then Joseph looked to the sky, spread his wings, and flew above Little Italy, looking down at everyone. He watched everyone run out of their buildings. I wanted to make myself visible to the young man, but someone else met him in the sky before I could. And it was Cain.

"Now, now, now! God would not like this at all!"

"Who are you?"

"Son of Lucifer and Eve," Cain said with a sinister smile

"Cain."

"Indeed. Now tell me something. Why'd you do this? I mean all this time you've been with God and your brother. And now you decide to kill after ten years? You've repented for your sins. All that shit. What was the point of this?"

"I don't know why I did what I just did. I felt compelled to do it, I guess..... I wanted revenge."

"What about God?"

"What about him? I keep losing family no matter who I follow. Whether it be God or Lucifer. I am tired Cane."

"I understand. I do. You are a lot like me my friend."

"How so?"

"You never had a choice. Your decisions were always made for you. So what now? You can't go back to God now. Not after this shit. Lucifer will probably accept you, but do you really want to go back to the bitch who has deceived you all of these years? But shit, I don't know. At least he fought to stay in your life."

"What do you mean? Lucifer may have his ways. But he never deceived me. He always told me the truth."

I knew where Cane was going with this bullshit. And I made myself visible as soon as I could. God and Junior appeared and screamed, "CANE, DON'T DO IT," before I could do or say anything. Cane put his hand over Joseph's face and said, "Let me show you the truth!" Cane showed him everything about his parent's death, and once the vision was over. Joseph levitated over Little Italy in the sky in shock.

"I.... killed... my parents.... I killed my uncle for killing my parents. And all the time, it was me?"

"Joseph, it was Lucifer making you do those things. He possessed you. It's not your fault," Junior said tearfully.

"IT IS MY FAULT! IT'S ALL OF OUR FAULTS! WHY?! WHY WOULD YOU DO THIS TO ME LUCIFER?!"

"Because I needed you," I said with little to no emotion.

"AND YOU TWO?! WHY DIDN'T EITHER OF YOU TELL ME," Joseph asked Junior and God as he directed his attention towards them.

"My child. If you had known, it would've destroyed you. It was better this way. We tried to protect you," God said.

"THAT'S IT! I'VE HAD IT! NO LONGER WILL I BE THE MEANS TO JUSTIFY ANYONE ELSE ENDS! NO LONGER WILL I BE THE THE PAWN ON YOU ALLS CHESS BOARDS! I WILL TAKE BACK ALL OF MY POWER AND CONTROL MY OWN DESTINY! AND AS FOR THE REST OF YOU?! YOU WILL ALL PERISH!"

Joseph raised his hands in the air and threw them down, causing a fire to rip through Little Italy. Burning every single house and building down. His eyes turned red, and he took on the form of the man/beast form. The sky turned black, and he stood before us and said, "Now, which of you should I kill first?!"

CHAPTER 20

Final Chapter of The End of The Beginning!

Joseph looked at me first and charged at me. I tried my best to dodge his attack, but he was too fast. He hit me so hard that he knocked be into another universe. I mean... He literally knocked me into another universe. In this universe, the timeline was even different. I landed inside a mansion where a man that resembled Joseph was talking to his family about expanding a book publishing business and shit. And a woman who sat beside him. It had to be Jean in a parallel universe. I snapped my fingers and returned to my universe and timeline. When I returned, I saw my brother Jesus and God trying to take on Cane. But Cane was getting the best of them. So, I figured this would be my time to strike and get rid of them both. So, while Joseph and his brother Junior fought, I attacked God first, I punched him in his face while he was distracted. God looked at me and grabbed me by my dreadlocks and threw me so hard he threw me back into the same universe I had just left. I landed in a hotel room on the floor. I looked over to my left and saw Cupid sitting there with his bitch ass. I could not stand Cupid and that funky ass New York accent he had. Anyway, I snapped my fingers and was back in my universe, and when I returned, God punched me in the face.

The next thing I knew, Jesus was charging at me, and he hit me multiple times in the body. Then he hit me so hard he knocked me into another universe. Except this time, it was a different one from the last. This one had Carma in it, Cupid's twin sister. Which... she was a nice piece of ass at one point and time. She is another one of God's Rejects, but that's another story for another book (hint hint). Yet again, I snapped my fingers and returned to my battle in my universe. When I returned this time, Cane was fighting Jesus, and God was waiting on me so he could kick my ass some more. And trust and believe, he kicked my ass worse than he did in our first battle.

While I was getting my ass kicked, Joseph and Junior fought to the death. They did not hold back. Joseph and Junior transformed into their most powerful forms, and each punch they landed on one another was fist to fist. This caused a ripple between the multiple universes that God had created. Finally, Junior landed the first punch in Joseph's stomach. Before Joseph could recover from the punch, Junior said, "Think about your wife and two children before you make matters worse!" Joseph looked at Junior and said, "Do not bring up my family ever again in your life!" Joseph went to attack Junior, but Junior dodged his attack and grabbed Joseph by his wings. Joseph had a hard time breaking loose, and before we knew it, Junior had broken his brother's wings.

Junior released Joseph's broken wings. Causing him to fall from the sky while screaming in pain and agony. Once Joseph fell to the ground, Junior assisted Jesus in fighting Cane. Cane was having a hard time fighting them both, so before we knew it, Cane had just vanished. While Jesus and Joseph were trying to figure out where the hell Cane went, God was still whooping my ass. But after a while, I finally was able to block one of his attacks, and I landed a punch in his gut. God looked at me and said, "You know that was a big mistake, right?" Then God began to speak Enochian while Jesus and Junior were heading to attack me. But before they could attack me, Joseph's wings healed, and he attacked me first.

Joseph looked at Jesus and his brother and said, "Lucifer's ass is MINE!" Joseph came at me with everything he had and tackled me.

While flying around with me in the air, punching me, we went through multiple universes and timelines. He was kicking my ass in every one of them. After a while, we finally returned to our universe, and when we did, Joseph slowly was transforming back into his regular self. Once he reached his original form. Joseph fell from the sky again and onto the ground. No one tried to catch him. Instead, everyone's attention was set on me.

God continued to speak Enochian, and Joseph and Jesus got to me as fast as they could and they held me down. God then levitated towards me and placed his hand on my chest, burning me from the inside out. Then he waved his hand and opened a portal to a firey pit of souls falling from the sky. I broke away from Jesus and Joseph and attacked God. He caught my hand and teleported us to his throne room. And there we were, standing across from one another. Just the two of us.

"Let's end this here. Just the two of us," God said as he got into his fighting stance.

"You won't win this time."

"I really wish that things would've been different between us. I loved you so much. You were the greatest and the worst thing I have ever created. You are an abomination, and so are your children. The greatest thing that came from you is Senior and Junior. I hate you, Lucifer. You are not my son."

When God said that to me, it really hurt my fucking feelings. Because I didn't hate God. I just didn't like his ass. But hate him? I still loved him. He was my father. But at that moment, I knew that I would kill my father before he locked me away in that prison. So we fought to the death. And it was the bloodiest battle I'd ever been in. But as we fought, God grew stronger and stronger. And the stronger he got, the more impact his blows had. His last blow made me drop to my knees. I was so weak I had no more strength to fight anymore. The next thing I knew I looked up, and Jesus, Junior, Michael, and God stood over me. I don't know where the fuck they came from, but there they were. I looked to my right, and Joseph was lying next to me on the ground, passed out.

"Look at all you bitches. ALL YOU PUNK MOTHA-FUCKAS! CAN'T TAKE ME ON SINGLE HANDLEY, SO Y'ALL ALL GOTTA TEAM UP! AIN'T THAT A BITCH?! SO WHAT'S NEXT?! Y'ALL GONE KICK A MAN WHILE HE'S DOWN?! TAKE ADVANTAGE OF ME BECAUSE I DON'T HAVE THE STRENGTH TO FIGHT ANYMORE?! HUH?! ALL OF YOU BITCHES CAN SUCK MY UNHOLY DICK! THIS IS Y'ALL FAULT! IF YOU ALL DID NOT DECEIVE MY SON IN THE WAY THAT YOU ALL DID, THIS WOULD NOT BE HAPPENING!"

They all just stood there and stared at me like I was insane. God opened up the portal to my prison again, and I stood up, holding my ribcage. I tried to attack God one last time, but before I could, Joseph woke up and called for me. He stood up, looked me dead in my eyes, and said, "GO TO HELL!" He punched me in the ribcage, ripped one of my ribs out of my body, and stabbed me in my chest with it. Then he grabbed me by my throat and threw me into the portal.

Afterward, Joseph looked at Michael, Jesus, Junior, and God. He cried tears of sadness and expressed his feelings.

"I killed my parents. I killed Timothy because I was deceived. No one saved me from him. But you are the most powerful, right, *God*?"

"My child, it is complicated," God said.

"What I find to be complicated is that you are the only thing that exists that is supposed to be perfect. But everything that is a product of you is not. Why is that? I mean, Lucifer came from you, right? From Lucifer came Cane. From Cane came the rest of us. So maybe you're not so perfect after all. Because anyone who can create the devil is not perfect. I will never forgive any of you for letting any of this happen. You all let me walk through this earth blind. When I did nothing but be born. You don't care about me. You only care about the fact that me and my offsprings can wreak havoc into this world. Well just know this precious God. This shit ain't over. And if Lucifer is not dead in that prison of yours, I will find a way to kill him. Like I will find a way to kill you all."

After Joseph said his final words, he disappeared from everyone's eyes. Amid everything going on, the city of Cleveland was in an uproar. Race riots were happening, looting was happening, and buildings were burning everywhere. The city had gone mad. And as far as I was concerned, I was healing from all of my injuries in the prison God had made for me. The hell he made for me was something egregious. This mothafucka put me in the hottest, firey pit. There was nothing except fire, brimstone, and lost souls falling from the sky into the fiery pit! But that wasn't the worst part! This mothafucka cursed me with empathy! For me, that's terrible because I am omnipresent. So, even in my prison, I could still see and feel people's joy, pride, and most of all, pain! IT HURT! IT FUCKING HURT SO BAD!

Death would've been sweeter than being in that pit. But after a while of being in that pit, I saw a lot of people from my past just popping up all in my fucking face. The first person I saw was Timothy. He was wearing a suit, with a bullet hole in his head and he was angry. He did not speak, but his facial expression showed his anger. As I walked some more, I saw Silky. He was also angry. He walked up to me, stared me in my eyes, and screamed, while holding his heart in his hand and a hole in his chest. I continued my walk and found a dark tunnel. In that tunnel, I could see a silhouette of a woman with a figure out of this world. She called for me softly, "Lucifer. Lucifer, Lucifer. I miss your touch." The silhouette of the woman began to walk towards me. When she came to the front of the tunnel, it was her. It was her. It was my beautiful Eve, standing in front of me with her body fully exposed. I looked at her and said, "You're not real, you're dead." I began to back away from her, but she walked toward me.

"My love, God never killed me. He punished me. He removed me from the earth to keep me away from our family. He wanted for you and Cain to think I was dead. But here I am. In the flesh. And I want yours so bad. I think of how it felt when you were inside of me the day we conceived Cain. It was the most beautiful experience in the world. So come. Embrace me as you once did. We may be stuck in this hell. But at least we're together."

I walked towards her and reached my hand to touch her soft, round, and brown derriere. As soon as we made skin-to-skin contact, our skin began to boil. It was the most painful thing I'd ever experienced to this day. We both screamed in agony! Once I removed my hand from her body, the pain went away. We both cried, and I said, "I just want to feel you! I love you! I LOVE YOU EVE! CURSE YOU GOD!"

TO BE CONTINUED.......

Fun Fact About God's Reject

So here are a few fun facts about the first installment of the Welcome to 10-5 (Hell) Book Series, "God's Reject." So, first things first. God's Reject was originally titled "The Devil's Memoirs" and was released for free online, and no one ever viewed it. How unfortunate, right? However, when I saw that no one ever viewed the story, I decided to release the short story for a profit. Once I released the short story, I only released a portion of it. There was a second part of the story that I did not include simply because I hated the storyline, and it would not fit into how I wanted to expand on the short story and turn it into a series. Therefore, you all are about to witness a draft of that second part of "God's Reject," aka "The Devil's Memoirs." Also, keep in mind that I wrote this second part and never touched it again when I was only a sophomore in undergrad. Therefore, I knew how to tell a story, but not the proper way, and the formatting was WAY OFF! So I hope you all enjoy it!

Continuation of God's Reject PT.1

When you've been on this earth from the time there was no life, you've seen a lot of shit, and you've especially met a whole lot of fucked up people. As crazy as this may sound, I met the craziest motherfuckers in Cleveland than I have any other place, they were even the most evil and greedy. They was all fucked up. It sometimes scared me, and I'm the Devil. It was one family that really fucked me up, and that was the Jackson family. The Jackson family was truly a success story. They came up off of Superior Avenue. It began with William and Jean Jackson, along with their son Delmar and their daughter Van. William and Jean had just moved from the south with their two children. William and Jean didn't have no more than a 6th grade education, but they made sure their children took advantage of all of the opportunities they didn't have growing up. They made sure their children went to school every day. Both of them worked very hard to make ends meet. Most of all they kept their faith in God, and instilled religion in their children as well. Delmar and Van were very smart kids, they specialized in numbers. They were math geniuses. I would sometimes sleep in the alley behind their home and they all would feed me from time to time. They even would give me clothes and let me wash up in their backyard. Their faith was too strong to break, and I actually grew to love that family. They didn't have much but they were givers.

The kids taught themselves how to invest in the stock market, they knew what companies were going to rise and what companies were going to fall. Every time you seen them, they had their heads in the business section of the Cleveland Plain Dealer. They were amazing. They taught their parents how to do the same thing. William and Jean started small. They both took 500 dollars out of their personal checking account and invested it in a company called "Stacy Adams." It was a very popular shoe company. By the end of the week, that money tripled. They each made about 1,500 dollars.

William and Jean each put 1,000 dollars of their earnings in their joint savings account. This left them with 500 dollars each. They both went in together to buy the kids new clothes, and school supplies. They also got some work done to the house. Lastly they each gave me 50 dollars, and some boots, and winter coat. They were beautiful people. I never knew that anyone on this earth could be so caring, so giving until I met these two people and their children.

The years are flying by and the stock market is going up, and up, and up, and up, and up. The more the Jackson invested, the more money they made, by the time Delmar was on his way to college, the Jackson family were worth a little than 12 million dollars. All the money they had they never left their neighborhood. Superior Avenue was and still is considered the "hood" or low class because, majority of the people that lived in this neighborhood had very low income. I was yet again shocked. All of the fortune they had they, looked down on no one. Instead they helped the people that lived in their neighborhood. They started up small businesses that provided jobs for the people in the neighborhood. They restored condemned homes and buildings, turning them into shelters for the homeless. They took care of everyone, especially me. I don't know what they saw in me, but they did a lot for me. The first thing they did for me was cleaned me up. I was so drunk and high I couldn't move out of my cardboard box. William walked out in that alley and picked me up and threw me over his shoulder. He carried me into one of the homes that him and his wife restored and threw men in the shower with all of my clothes on. He ran cold water on my face to wake me up. When I woke up William was standing over me with a towel and soap, he told me to clean myself up, and that today was going to be a new day for me. He walked out of the bathroom and I cleaned myself up. I couldn't help but to think if God was disguised as these two beautiful people. Even if he was why the hell would God want to do anything for me after all the shit I've done. These people knew nothing about me being the Devil, hell they probably wouldn't have even cared. They treated everyone so well, like God would want them to.

After I was done cleaning my body, William had clean clothes waiting for me he told me when I was finished getting dressed to meet him outside, and that there would be a limousine waiting. When I went outside and got into the limo, William gave me a pamphlet, about rehab. He said that he wanted me to get my life together and work for him when I did. I agreed to do so. When the limo stopped we were at a barbershop. William paid for me to get a haircut and a clean shave. After that he took me straight to the rehabilitation center, and left me there for a year.

I actually went through with this rehabilitation bullshit for a whole year. I would just sit in my room and think, "I can fucking teleport right out of this room if I wanted to. I could make all of these people forget about the homeless, drunken, drug addict bum." But I did this shit for a whole year. After my year in rehab was up, William, Jean and their daughter Van came to pick up. William had a custom made suit waiting for me and an expense account. When I got changed into my suit, I walked out to a pearly white stretch Rolls Royce limousine with the Jacksons. When we arrived back to the neighborhood, it was beautiful. They had completely turned the neighborhood around, it was like I was in Hollywood, or some shit. It was amazing. The same house that I got cleaned up in the day I went to rehab was the same house that the Jacksons was giving me. It was something how everything had changed in a whole year. I caught a glimpse of the "Plain Dealer" when I walked into the house. There was an article on the Jackson family. The title said "Jackson Family Worth 100 Million, Thanks To Smart Investments." All of this in a year. They got rich so fast without making a deal with me. They never sold their souls.

Continuation of God's Reject PT. 2

The year is now 1989, and William and Jean are beginning to get older, and passed down a lot of their responsibilities to their children who have been out of college for a while now. Delmar graduated from Ohio State University with a degree in Business Management. Van on the other hand graduated from Kent State with a degree in Advertising. The two siblings were great together, they had a close friendship and a great partnership. They were like peanut butter and jelly, a great combination. As far as I was concerned, William and Jean gave me a very high ranking position in their company "Jackson Corp." I was Vice President of their company. This company, and small businesses. William and Jean sat at the top of the food chain as CEO (Corporate Executive Officer), while their children sat second in command with positions as COO's (Corporate Operating Officer). "Jackson Corp." was an Investment firm that made billions of dollars every year.

William and Jean didn't give up complete control to their kids. They were only in their late mid 50's or so, but they wanted to enjoy life, and most of all they wanted to enjoy their grandchildren. Delmar had 4 children and so did Van. Delmar had 3 daughters and a son, and Van had 4 sons. Both of the siblings did the best they could to raise their kids, and some of them turned out just fine and then some of them were so evil, they could've been my children. Even though I was evil and hated almost everything good I grew to love William, Jean, Delmar and Van, but I was beginning to see something that I liked but didn't like with the new generation of Jacksons. When they became teenagers some of them were completely off the chain. All of them weren't bad, but the ones that were, their actions were indescribable. I couldn't believe they were even Jacksons. It was almost sad, but who am I to talk, because the ones that were doing badly were the ones that I would eventually use for my soldiers, I knew they would sell their souls.

Continuation of God's Reject PT. 3

The year is 2004, and by now all of the grandchildren are grown up. Educationally they have followed in their parents footsteps, but otherwise some of them went down my road. Delmar's children all went to Ohio State University just like him and majored in Business Administration. Vans four sons majored in Advertising and Marketing and attended Kent State University. All of them were highly educated, and of course they worked for their families companies. Sheryl, Christine, Kaysha and Hill were Delmar's children. Sheryl was the first born, and she was very greedy and evil and selfish as hell. She was the true definition of a bitch. She cared about no one but herself. She was power hungry and wanted everything for herself. She would do anything for the money and the power. Even if she had to kill for it. Kaysha was the second child of Delmar's, she was a kind spirit, and she was just like her grandparents and aunt Van. Hill was Delmar's only son, and he was a punk ass, he could never stand up on his own two feet as a man. He was a cry baby, but he wasn't a bad person. Christine was Delmar's baby girl. She wasn't what you would call evil, but she was a dumbass, and she was easily led by her sister Sheryl. Whatever Sheryl told her to do, she did it. No matter what it was, she did it. If you ask me the girl was a fucking retard.

Then there were Van's four sons Sylvester, Wardell, Kingsley, and Montez. Sylvester was the oldest and the bossiest, he always looked out for his younger brothers. Wardell was a sneaky bastard, and slept with anything with a vagina. Kingsley was a coke head and a terrible alcoholic. The boy could never keep a straight head. He was fucking insane. He had even killed a few people before. Montez was the youngest son of Van, and he was a genius. He was always alone, he never had many friends. He was always reading books trying to figure out how to build his own empire so that he would not have to live off of the family name forever. He was different.

Continuation of God's Reject PT. 4

As I said earlier, I was the Vice President of the corporation, and after 40 something years of not showing my true form as the Devil himself, I practically lived in an office. I was living the life of an ordinary business person. I myself was not causing destruction, but others were still doing it for me, and I still remained powerful. I didn't have a connection with William and Jean's grandchildren, they never even met me, but from the day they were born I knew everything about them. I watched every single thing they did. I watched how some of them were beginning to lose their faith in God, all of the terrible things they had done to each other. I knew for a fact that Sheryl never had faith at all.

William and Jean are now in their 70's, and they have a lot of health issues. So they decided to give everything up to Delmar and Van. Delmar and Van were now the CEO's of everything. I kept my position as Vice President, and by now the grandchildren have been promoted as the COO's (Corporate Office Operators).

For some the position was enough, but for others like Sheryl, it wasn't enough at all. Sheryl wanted to be President and CEO. She wanted to be the ruler. So she began dealing with a lot of criminals, making them offers they couldn't refuse. She wrote out a whole hit list of family members she would kill to make it to the top. She used her baby sister Christine to get close to some of the family members on the hit list. The first one to go was their sister Kaysha. Sheryl knew that Kaysha was nothing to fuck with and wasn't stupid. So Sheryl told Christine to call Kaysha and tell her to she wanted to meet up at their restaurant to discuss starting a new business. Christine followed orders and called Kaysha. Kaysha was suspicious but she went. Before she left for the meeting, she packed her gun, she was ready for whatever. Christine never called Kaysha on the phone before, and for some reason Kaysha had a feeling that something wasn't right. When Kaysha was on her way to meet with her sister Christine, one of the hit men that Sheryl hired was on motorcycle, he road right up on the side of Kaysha's car. They both looked each other in the eyes as if they were trying to time when they were going to draw their guns on each other, but neither of them did. Kaysha then went to their restaurant, and when she got there her sister was already seated at a table. Christine was acting very nervous. There was no one else in the restaurant because they met before opening hours. Kaysha noticed how nervous Christine was acting, so she was ready. Kaysha sat down at the table and gave Christine a blank stare. Christine got up out of her seat and walked across the table and hugged and kissed her big sister. After this Kaysha went for her gun, but it was too late. There were two hit men in the kitchen waiting for Kaysha to pull her gun so they could kill her. After they killed Kaysha, Christine left the building and met with Sheryl at her office. She was in tears. Sheryl told her to stop crying, if she wanted her share of the company when everyone was gone. Christine asked what the men were going to do with Kaysha's body. Sheryl told her they would burn it along with the building.

Kaysha's death took a toll on the family, she was everyone's favorite. When Kaysha died, William and Jean's health began to decline even more, and Delmar completely lost his mind. He wasn't stable enough to take care of any business, not even his daughter's funeral arrangements. So Van helped her brother bury Kaysha. As time passed and Kaysha's death wasn't as fresh, Delmar wanted his only son to take his place as far as the families company went. Hill accepted this position. When he took over his father's position, he never abused his power, but he was fucking up as far as not keeping up with our clients' accounts. His aunt Van was beginning to get sick of his fuck ups and was speaking on what he needed to do better. Every time she gave him constructive criticism, he cried like a bitch and would say "I can't do this, I can't deal with this." It was actually disgusting. Sheryl knew for a fact that she could get him easy. So once again she called on Christine to lure him in. Christine then sent Hill an e-mail telling him to meet her on the family yacht to catch up since they hadn't talked in so long. Hill met Christine on the yacht and they sailed out into Lake Erie. They had a chef, or should I say a hit man in disguise cook them lunch. They sat and enjoyed their food and talked about the future of the company. Later on in conversation, Christine got up from her seat to pour them a glass of champaign. She knew that this would really weaken Hill's defense and awareness. One sip got Hill drunk as a skunk. This is when Sheryl's hired gun walked up behind Hill, and choked him to death with a garrote rope. He then took his body and dumped it into the water.

The next day, everyone questioned Hill's whereabouts, because he had an important meeting with a high priority client, and he never showed up. Delmar was starting to get suspicious, so he put some private investigators out there to find his son. These private investigators searched every piece of property owned by Jackson family, including the yacht. They found nothing. Two days later someone found a dead body that had been washed ashore. It was Hill. When the Jackson family found out that another child in the family was dead, they were devastated. Delmar was completely insane by now. So Sheryl got a power of attorney over her father sent him to a mental illness institution, where he would stay permanently. She then took it upon herself to take her father's position in the company as one of the CEO's, sitting at the top of the food chain with her aunt. You would think this was enough for her, but she wanted more. I swear this girl was so evil, she was too evil for me. I didn't even want any parts of her. From the time she was born she was evil, not an ounce of goodness was in her heart at all. She was just an evil whore. I never thought that there could be anyone more evil than me on this earth. You would think that a child born with so many privileges, would be grateful for the life they had, but not this girl.

Tension was very strong between Sheryl and Van. They hated each other with a fucking passion, and Van's 4 sons weren't that fond of her at all. They all suspected Sheryl of being responsible for her brother and sister's death. They never really liked her to begin with, but they tolerated her. Things only got worse when William and Jean sicker. Sheryl did everything to take over the whole company. She knew that her father could do nothing to stop her, because he was clinically insane, her grandparents were too old and sick to fight, and her aunt Van did everything she could to keep pressure off of her parents. If it had not been for William and Jean, Sheryl would've been dead a long time ago, because Van would've had no problem killing Sheryl, and neither would her sons.

After years of suffering, William and Jean finally passed on. I was actually sad. I was very sad. I grew to love those two so much, almost as much as I use to love God, if not more. They never knew who I really was, or what I really was. They took care of a "demon, beast, and devil." I kept this whole charade up for so long, I was forgetting to do my evil duties, maybe because others were doing it for me. Still though, every lost soul needs a leader, and I had been neglecting these lost souls. My goal was still the same, and that was to over throw God. So when everything was over with William and Jean, and they had been laid to rest, it was time for the reading of the will.

The will said that Sheryl, would get 100% of everything. EVERYTHING. The money, the properties, the many, many businesses they owned, and the corporation. Kingsley was so fucked up on dope he pulled a gun out to kill Sheryl in the lawyer's office. He knew, and everyone else knew something wasn't right. They knew she did something to that will, and she did. Comes to find out she was paying off her grandparent's lawyer to forge a completely different will, and signed her grandparents name to this false piece of shit.

It wasn't a good week before she ran the company, and she fired all of their original staff, including me. She hacked everyone's bank accounts and cleared them completely. A lot of people didn't know what to do, they didn't know how they were going to live, provide for their families. So a lot of them killed themselves, and their families. Van died of a heart attack not to long after Sheryl had done this, and the 4 brothers were left homeless. I too was left homeless. I went right back to living in the alleys off Superior Avenue.

As time went by, the neighborhood began to decline rapidly. Sheryl and her right hand Christine had let all of their businesses in the neighborhood go except for 4 of the McDonald stores they owned. Drugs took the city over completely, and the 4 brothers had completely disappeared. Sheryl even let their family home fall. It went from being a loving family home, to a condemned crack house. The neighborhood that was 100% owned by the Jackson family had now fallen, it was a crying shame, but it is what the fuck it is. Shit really hit the fan when Christine saw what happened to their family home, because it was very rare that she would go near Superior Avenue. She was angry and hurt. She was beginning to regret all of the things she had done. They had all of the money in the world, but they had no family, no friends, no nothing. No one knew where to even start to look for Van's sons, and Sheryl wasn't worth a damn. So Christine later approached her big sister, she felt that they should find their cousins. Sheryl sensed weakness, and she pulled out a gun and killed Christine. She feared that Christine would talk and rat her out to the police about all of the people that she had set up to be killed. Now for a long time Sheryl didn't think to do anything to her cousins, but now that she had all of this power, she had become very paranoid. So she decided to find her cousins, and kill them.

Continuation of God's Reject PT. 5

I was the Superior Slum, a homeless bum with long dirty hair, a long dirty beard, and stinky nasty clothes, which reeked of shit, piss and alcohol..... AGAIN! Ain't that a bitch? I was thinking about just going back to my original form, then I wasn't so sure. I had been in the same form for over 50 years now, and believe it I had actually gotten comfortable being the homeless man, and then the rich clean entrepreneur, and then back to the homeless man again. But one night I decided what I would do. Just one night.

It was a cold night in Cleveland, Ohio. The snowflakes were falling and the streets were very icy and slippery. I was sleeping out in an alley in a cardboard box trying to keep warm. The night was very still and quiet in the beginning, until the sound of sirens and gunshots rang out, echoing in the black sky. Then that is when I saw it. A beautiful black Chevy Camero speeding down Superior Avenue with the top let down and four men laughing. The 2 men in the back seats were shooting at 12 police cars chasing them down this icy, slippery street while the police officers returned fire on them. Then "BOOOOOOOOOOOM" a 12 car pile-up. The back seat passengers of the Chevy Camero shot out the tires of 3 police cars, causing a terrible accident. These 4 men fled the scene and gave each other a celebratory high five. These 4 men finally arrived to an old warehouse that use to be owned by the Jackson family. The 4 gentlemen, got out of the car and opened the trunk, each grabbed a duffle bag full of one hundred dollar bills. I camouflaged myself so that no one would see me, and watched their every move, trying to figure out who the hell these men were. The year is 2012, and I knew I had seen these men before. Then I figured it out, it was Van's 4 sons!!!! I figured that now it was time to come out of retirement and show who I really was again.

Before the 4 brothers caused all of this shooting and car accidents, they had just got done ripping off about 3 different McDonalds that was owned by their cousin Sheryl. Each McDonalds they ripped off they cleared every safe and every cash register in the place. They were very successful with the first two spots that they hit. Everything was going just as planned. It wasn't until the third lick that was about to hit when things went wrong. After they had cleared the last safe in the last spot and were about to get away with no type of attention, Kingsley was so high off of cocaine, he slipped and pulled the fire alarm. This was when all of this bullshit began with the cops.

Those boys sure were lucky that they got out of that situation. This is when they met me, the real me. Not the man in the alley, but the Devil himself. The warehouse, the beginning of the end. They walked in that warehouse with their heads up high and about forty thousand dollars in cash in each duffle bag.

Sylvester said to his brothers "this is a new start, it's time for us to make our comeback. We all agreed that this would be our last lick. Our family took everything away from us when our parents died, we gotta make smart investment to show them we can't be broken".

"I say let's buy some kilos of coke and sell it on the streets" Kingsley said. "

"No way in the hell we're gonna do that. We ain't never had to do that before, we not about to start now. Just because we from the hood doesn't mean we have to meet every stereotype" Wardell said.

"He's right. Besides you would snort it all anyway King. We have too much education and class to do that. We're business men, not some savage ass drug distributors. We will not bring down our neighborhood or any other neighborhood with that poison" said Montez. That's when I walked in. Ha! You should've seen them. They pulled out their guns thinking I was some punk ass pig. That is when they saw the bum that stood before them. The "Superior Ave Slum." They lowed their guns and that is when I said to them, "I've been watching you all ever since you were babies." They didn't speak a word, it was almost as if they were in a state of shock, trying to figure out how I got in the warehouse without them seeing me. I told them that I could make them richer than what they ever were in a life time, but only if they follow me. This is when I revealed the form that was given to me by God. I showed them the perfect human, the former angel that God once knew as Lucifer. They all looked at me in amazement, all except the baby boy. Mr. Montez was not impressed at all with me. He walked up to me without any fear, looked me in my face and said to me "Go back to hell and stay there, I will never follow you." His brothers wanted him to stay with them and follow me, but he told them "haven't we done enough of his work by corrupting ourselves, stealing. I'm not going to sell my soul to the Devil for a dollar. I'm taking my share of the money and I'm out." The other brothers were upset that he wouldn't take the deal with me, but they got over it.

Ten years passed by. Sylvester, Wardell, and Kingsley had become 3 of the richest men in the country. They took my advice, they started a record label that show cased gangster rap only, and a sports agency with their money. When they got their power back, the brothers had access to a lot of people. Bad people, and dangerous people. Their cousin Sheryl had went into hiding for a very long time. After sabotaging the company, letting all of the small business fall and destroying the whole family, she was afraid that the brothers would find her and kill her considering they were the only ones to escape her wrath. She was right. I've done so much dirt in my life time. From Adam and Eve all the way up to now. So many souls I've collected in my life time. The politicians, the lawyers. Look at them, they are some of the most prosperous and prestigious people on earth. They make their money off of the backs of others. A lawyer will know his client is guilty of anything, rape, murder, anything, and these people will work their asses off to get them off. Then charge their dumbasses 600 an hour. It is so terrible and so funny at the same time.

This is a new day and age though. At least the politicians and lawyers went to school to become legitimate criminals. These kids in this new generation want everything the easy way. So they figure if they become a musician, or an athlete, or a video vixen/gold-digger they've made it. Then when they get all that money, all that fame, they don't know how to handle it. These young kids, they look up to the bastards, wanting to be just like them. So I figure why not corrupt the youth they're goners anyway. And the three brothers did exactly that. These young kids signed contracts, not even reading them, not knowing that their souls now belonged to me. When you work for stewards of the Devil, the Devil owns you.

Mr. Montez took his share of the money and donated it all to the Masjid and different charities. He even converted to Islam and turned his life over to "Allah". He even became an Imam and had his own masjid. He even changed his name to Ahmad Azian. He stayed in Cleveland and did everything he could to save everyone he could. He saw my work and knew it was all thanks to his brothers. People idolized the explicit rap lyrics, the tattoos, the ridiculous bulky jewelry the women bouncing around half naked, and these women on reality TV shows doing anything to make their claim to fame. So he flew out to California to see his brothers after all of this time. He figured if he could save his brothers from me he could save more. When he arrived in Cali, he went straight to their office of work. They were very happy to see each other. Azian/Montez asked his brothers to give up the fast life style they lived and come back home. They still refused to leave me. They had become atheist. They felt that God took away their family. They questioned God and his will. This is exactly what I wanted. They worshipped me. They would never go back to the other side. When Azian realized that his brothers would never follow him to the pathway of goodness, he got back on the first plane back to Cleveland. He prayed for his brothers' souls everyday all day.

After Azian left Cali, his brothers just got worse. Kingsley was the first one to die. He was so high off of cocaine, he got behind the wheel of his Maybach and drove it off of a cliff, because he thought his car could fly. Wardell gave his brother bad dope because he wanted the companies for himself. Wardell was the second to go. Wardell was killed by his other brother Sylvester. Wardell was sneaking behind his brothers back sleeping with his wife. One night Sylvester caught them and killed them both. Sylvester was so upset after everything he called his baby brother, telling him that he loved him, he regretted that night he ever had made that deal with me. The last words he said to his brother was "I'm sorry, forgive me for I am about to sin". He then took the same gun to kill his brother and wife and put it to his head. He pulled the trigger while on the phone with Azian.

Tragic story, I know. It is almost sad. Now I know all of my readers are reading my words and are saying, you are one evil bastard. I know, I know. But ask yourself this, am I really the bad guy, am I? I didn't put a gun to anyone's head and tell them to cut a deal with me. Last I remember, God gave us free will. I should know, I was the first one to have it. They were their own worst enemy. Look at Azian, he's doing well for himself. Of course he's hurt behind the death of his brothers, but let's think here, he had the courage and faith in God to face me, stare me down, and walk away from me. Ha! Its amazing how four people can start out on the same path together, and don't make it to the finish line together. I hate to say it but that little bastard had some guts. Now he's the last one standing, with a happy life. He's doing what God sent me on earth to do, and he's doing his job well. Montez or shall I say Azian is the real MVP....... For now.

Continuation of God's Reject PT. 6

A lot of people might think after all the shit that went down with the Johnson family I would be done with them, well people thought wrong. I was far from done. Azian still lives and as long as there is breath in his body, I will always torture that family until he breaks. He walked away from one of my deals. MY DEALS!!!!! All of these years I've walked the earth and never has anyone walked away from a deal I've laid out on the table. Well, except for my little brother, the messiah of course. I almost had my little brother but he was too strong. He wouldn't break, and that still angers me. I remember when Jesus was first born. It was the most peaceful night I've ever seen. All of the stars were out, there was no evil deeds going on at all. That night even I was at peace within myself. I know that shit might sound crazy, but it is true. Even though I was angry with God, I had to go see Jesus myself. When I went to go see him I came bearing a silk swaddle and gold but I could only see him from a distance at first. He was beautiful, he was perfect. I couldn't hate him just because me and God wasn't getting along, we shared the same blood, he was my little brother. I couldn't even get close to Jesus or Mary and Joseph because the three wise men and Gods angels were surrounding them waiting for me. You should've seen them, If looks could kill, I would've been a dead motherfucker. They had weapons in their hands blessed by God himself, just in case I tried to kill the so called true son of God. Ha ain't that some shit? With the permission of Mary, I was able to get by the guards and provide my gifts to the newborn king. She knew I would do no harm to her son, I was even able to hold him. I felt happy for the first time in a long time when I held him. I think that it was because I felt that I was no longer alone in this world. I may have lost my son, but I now have a little brother. Someone that I knew would love me regardless. I never felt that God truly loved me, especially when he took my family away from me. God is suppose to be forgiving, instead he punished me for going down my own path. Besides I knew that it would only be a matter of time before I had my brother right where I wanted him, which was on the dark side with me. I couldn't bear to kill him along with our father, when I took over everything. So I would hope that he won't try being a hero sacrificing himself again.

I'm sorry I got a little bit off of topic, back on Azian. Azian would break but it would have to be through something else. A loved one, such as his children. Azian had a wife and children. His wife was fine as hell she had a beautiful body and a smile that will make you go insane, but she was no Eve. Her name was Ameera. She was an Arabian goddess. She had beautiful brown skin with thick long hair and a nice ass body. Bitch was bad. I thought about hitting that but I was in the middle re-building the Johnson families empire to completely make it my own. I didn't have time to be fucking around with none of these women. The sports management company was still going strong and the.......

(I NEVER FINISHED THE STORY BECAUSE I HATED IT THAT MUCH!)

What's Next?

OKAY! So, you all have had the experience of reading my most egregious work from the past. Now, let me bring you all up to date with some new content. Now not to brag on myself, but I have RANGE! I can write anything. Not just tragedies and crime fiction. Therefore, I would like to share the first few chapters of my romantic comedy, titled Cupid's Love & Sex Chronicles: Pen's Journey. A story about a young author, Ahmad Pen is looking to branch away from his family's billion-dollar book publishing company to publish the authors he wants to publish and focus on writing his romance and erotic book, "Love, Sex & Heartbreak." On his journey to becoming an independent author and publisher, he returns to the dating world after a breakup to get inspiration for his book and to find true love. I hope you all enjoy the first few chapters!

Merriam Webster's Definition of Love, Sex, And Heartbreak

Love (noun):

- "an intense feeling or emotion" or "warm attachment, enthusiasm, or devotion."

Sex (verb):

- "to arouse the sexual desires of."

Heartbreak (noun):

- "crushing grief, anguish, or distress."

Chapter 1: Writer's Block & Family Business

"Man, this shit will *never* work," said Pen as he balled up another poem he'd just written and threw it across the living room of his penthouse apartment out of frustration. This had to be the tenth time he had done this in writing the first poem titled "*You*" for his book of poetry that had yet to be titled. His five foot eight caucasian, redhead, former college roommate Lee walked out of the kitchen with a piece of fried chicken, wearing a wife beater and a pair of basketball shorts. He picked up the last balled-up poem that Pen had written and said, "Dude, this is probably the best one you wrote. Like, bro, bro, bro. This poem might actually get you some serious ass, man. Like seriously, you should publish that shit. Fuck it, just publish it." Pen looked at Lee with so much frustration and disgust because, for every poem that Pen wrote, Lee always said the same exact thing, "Publish it."

"Lee, you don't get it, man. This has to be perfect. This is going to be the first book that I will publish independently, and it has to be the fucking best," Pen said as he laid his head down on his desk in the living room.

"Well, Ahmad motherfucking Pen, I think you're just being hard on yourself. Maybe a little too hard. I mean, come ooooon, You've got the talent, dude. You just need some inspiration."

"Like what?"

"Food and pussy..... Extra on the pussy," Lee said while laughing.

Pen jumped from the desk, snatched his pad and ink pen, and was about to leave his apartment. Lee stopped laughing because he saw that Pen was only becoming more frustrated by his jokes. He ran up to Pen and said,

"Okay, look, bro (chews on fried chicken) in all seriousness. This new shit that you're writing isn't bad. I think you just need to experience more before you write a book like this. Your ex was your first, your one and only. And after she cheated on you with that football player, dude, she fucked you up. You lost confidence in yourself. You need to get your confidence back, man. And you should get out more, date chicks and hot ones. Shit, I don't know, man. Maybe you should give it a year or two, or even three, of just dating, fucking, traveling, and finding yourself. You have written so many books since our freshman year in college, and everything has been a best seller. You've got enough money that you don't have to run to your billionaire family for anything. Take a break and experience some shit before you write some shit about love and all this other shit. Shit, be like me. I always take a break."

"First off, Lee, how much longer will it take for your house to be built? I really am tired of my writing penthouse smelling like fried chicken. I come here to write, not smell chicken. Second, why do you say some of the realest shit after saying a bunch of dumb shit?"

"I dunno, bro (laughing). It's the fucking chicken man. It gives me brain power. You've gotta love this shit from KFC. It's addicting. And I've got one more month before my house is complete, and once it's finished, trust me, it is going to be bitches and parties."

The two friends shared a laugh and then said in unison, "Extra on the bitches." Pen gave his friend Lee dap and a hug and said, "Thanks, man. I really needed to hear that, I guess." Afterward, Pen walked out the door and went to the garage of his penthouse, where he had an entire fleet of old-school cars. And since it was a beautiful summer day in Cleveland, Pen drove his customized 2004 black-on-black drop-top Chevrolet Monte Carlo. He drove around the city briefly before heading to his family's estate, thinking about how he would tell them he was about to start his own publishing company and write in a different genre. After almost four hours of driving and a gas station trip later, Pen finally decided to make his way to his family's estate in Bratenahl. As soon as he pulled up to the gate of the estate, the only thing that everyone could hear was Ice Cube's "Good Day" blaring through the speakers. Pen loved making an entrance with his music, but his mother and grandmother hated it.

Once he pulled through the gates, he saw all of his cousin's cars and his aunt and uncle's car in front of the house. Pen began to sweat because his anxiety was starting to rise. He was not ready to reveal to the entire family yet that he was ready to branch off on his own. He would have felt more comfortable just telling his mother and grandparents. He sat in his car in a trance, breathing heavily. It wasn't until a six-foot-four, burly, brown-complexioned, bald man walked up, placed his hand on Pen's round bald head, and said, "You know that anxiety is gonna be the death of you, right." Pen looked up, and it was his uncle, Andre Pen. His uncle wrote books based on his fishing adventures, and they were the top-selling books in their family's book publishing company, "*Pen2Paper Publishing.*" Pen smiled and began to breathe slower, and he hopped out of the car, shook his uncle's hand, and said, "I wasn't expecting the entire family to be here." His uncle Andre chuckled and said, "Nephew, you're the last one to arrive, so now we can get this party started," Andre said with a smirk on his face. Pen looked at his uncle with a confused expression on his face and proceeded to walk into the house with his uncle.

As soon as they walked through the solid gold front doors, Pen's mother, Lola, greeted him with a hug and a kiss. Pen's mother shared the same sense of humor as his uncle. So she looked at her son, then at her brother, then back at her son, and displayed a goofy smirk. Pen looked down at his short, heavy-set, freckled face mother and said, "Mommy, what are y'all up to?" Lola looked at her brother and asked if he could go into the grand room with the rest of the family while she spoke with Pen. Andre nodded to his sister, Lola, and entered the grand room. Lola put her hands on Pen's chest to smooth the wrinkles in his polo shirt and straighten his collar. She grabbed her son by the face, looked deep into his eyes, and smiled with no words.

"Mommy, why are you acting so weird? You and Unc? What is going on?"

"Baby boy, you remember when I told you years ago that you would go many places by sticking with Pen2Paper Publishing because of your writing?"

"Yeah, but....."

"Sweetie, your books are doing so great that you have surpassed your uncle's sales. No one has done that in this company."

"Okay, but..."

"Boy, shut up and listen. You and your cousins are about to get the opportunity of a lifetime. Just go inside and look happy," Lola said as she pulled her son Pen by the arm and opened the doors to the grand room.

As they entered the grand room, everyone was sitting at a long gold table, in gold throne dining chairs, with the company's logo (pen balanced on a sheet of paper). Pen's grandfather, Raheem Pen, stood up, hugged his grandson, and told him to have a seat. Before Pen followed instructions, he hugged and kissed his grandmother, Queen, and proceeded to go to the last available seat at the table. Raheem stood up at the head of the table and looked at his two children and his five grandchildren for a good two minutes in silence with a smile. "Honey, I think you should snap out of it and just tell them all the news already," said Queen. Raheem looked at his wife and then looked back at his children. With his strong and deep voice, he said:

"I am so glad to have you all here today. It has been a very long time since I have had the privilege of having all of my grandchildren here with me at the same time, in the same room. I have some very great news. Pen2Paper Publishing has not made this family not millions but billions of dollars for many years. And we are the first black family to ever do this in the history of the book publishing industry. But now, it is time for us to make more money from these billions. So I would like everyone to open up the portfolios before you."

Once everyone opened up the portfolio binders sitting on the table, the first thing that everyone saw was a check with their names on it. Everyone except for Pen smiled, hooped, and hollered. Everyone received a check for one hundred million dollars. And while everyone else was happy, only Pen and his cousin Markeisha were reading the documents that the check came with. The documents stated in the first paragraph:

> "As of June 3rd, 2016, Pen2Paper Publishing will be expanding into other industries, which include sports/athletics, bars and restaurants, clubs, movie and television studios, barbershops and beauty salons, car repair and customization garages, clothing/fashion brand and stores, cigar manufacturing and distribution, and whiskey and wine distribution."

Pen and Markeisha looked at one another while everyone else cheered, and they continued to read the documents. While Markeisha didn't seem to have any issues with the documents after reading them, Pen did. The reason was that after reading the documents, he also saw a non-compete clause. Therefore, Pen could not follow his dream of being an independent book publisher and escaping his family's billion-dollar shadow. Finally, the excitement wore down, and everyone was back in their seats. The grandchildren signed the contracts to obtain their responsibilities and money in their family's business. Once they signed their contracts, they slid them across the table to Lola and Andre.

Pen still held on to his contract. His grandmother, Queen, stood up and walked around the table, leaned over and wrapped her arms around her grandson's neck, kissed him, and said, "Baby, you didn't sign your contract." Pen let out a deep sigh and bit his lip. Tears began to roll down his cheek. He looked his grandmother deep in the eyes, kissed her on the cheek, and stood up at the table.

"I have some concerns," Pen said.

"Speak your mind," said Andre.

"I noticed that for us to receive this money and access to all of these other business ventures. We have to sign a non-compete clause," Pen said, letting out another deep sigh.

"Well, son, your mother wanted that in the contract," said Raheem.

"Seriously? You knew I wanted to start my own book publishing company and eventually become independent. You also know that I have invested in other companies that will be a conflict of interest for the family's business. You did this on purpose," said Pen with anger in his voice.

"Boy, do you realize that we are the first black privately owned book publishing company ever to surpass these giants that have ever gone public?! Today, we are worth more than 19.4 billion dollars as an organization. And we did it on our own. And you just want to walk away from that," Lola said angrily.

"No, Mother, that is not what I am saying. I'm just saying that whenever I talk about writing something different, you tell me to stick to what I am already writing because it sells. I want to branch out as a writer. I can still write the genre I have written for years, but I want to write love stories and poetry. I can do it under a pseudonym. You even make a big deal about the authors I want to sign. You won't let me sign them because you feel their writing doesn't fit our standards. All I am saying is that I want to help the family, but I also want to do my own thing as well," Pen said.

"Well, nephew, I will ask you this right here and right now. What can we do to get you to sign this contract and accept what is rightfully yours?" Andre said with a look of concern.

"I already own the trademark to my company name, *KingPen Publishing*. If you, my mother, and grandparents are willing to let me use what I have already started as an imprint, not only would I be able to use this imprint to sell books, sign and manage authors. I could also help with writing, filming, and distributing the movies and television shows we will produce for the family company," Pen said.

Pen's uncle and grandparents smiled. The three of them looked at one another and gave each other a nod. Then Andre, Queen, and Raheem looked at Lola, and it was safe to say that Lola had a look of discernment and disgust.

"You all are for this," Lola asked her parents and brother.

"Yes Lola, why wouldn't we be? I don't think what he is asking for is bad. I think that Pen is more than capable of running an entire company division independently. He is young, smart, and very talented," Queen said to her daughter.

"He's not ready," Lola screamed.

"Auntiiiie, I think Pen will be cool running his imprint. And he'll be the first to do it in the family. Give him a chance," said Pen's cousin, DeMarcus.

"The last time that I checked, only four of us ran this damn company. And the decisions are made unanimously between Me, my parents, and my brother, *nephew*," Lola said.

"Well, if this is the case, I'm not signing that contract. Also, I refuse to sit here and be told that I am not ready to do something like this when I have been doing it my entire life. I have worked daily for this company, following the rules and ensuring I did what you wanted, mother. I love y'all, but I think it is time for me to step away from the day-to-day operations," Pen said sadly.

"Woah, wait a minute, Lola. Let's rethink this. We cannot afford for this boy to leave his empire like this," Andre said to his sister Lola.

"*Let. Him. Go.* See, his goal is to sign these urban and erotic writers. This hood, ghetto shit he always speaks of. That's what he wants. We don't publish books about drug dealers, prostitutes, pimps, hoes, sex, and all of that other ghetto trash. No! We publish what people actually want to read. And I will be damned if my son risks ruining the reputation of this company with that trash! So no, if he wants to leave, he can leave. He just won't gain more shares in the company like the rest of the grandchildren because he's not signing the contract. But just remember one thing, son," Lola said to Pen while giving her son a very cold stare.

"What is that, mother?"

"Your author contract states that you owe us another book within the next two years to finalize the last part of your "*Dark & Dirty Spirits*" book series. So we will expect that in your *little venture* as an independent publisher," Lola said.

Pen stared at his mother and nodded to assure her he would produce that book. He looked at his grandparents and his uncle, bit his lip, and said, "Well, I guess this is where we part ways. Just know that it was never a competition thing. I just wanted to do something different. Queen looked away from her grandson with tears in her eyes. Pen walked over to his grandmother and hugged and kissed her. Queen said to Pen, "I will talk to your mother. I want to see this imprint happen. You have no business away from your empire like this." He looked at her with tears in his eyes and he looked at the rest of his family, silently nodded his head, and walked out of the grand room, leaving his family in silence.

Pen went straight to his car, and before he pulled off, he heard, "WAIT!" His cousin, Markeisha, was behind him, trying to get his attention.

"Listen, I think that what you are doing is great! If you need any help, little cousin, all you have to do is call me."

"I appreciate that, but honestly, I think it is best to do this all alone. I have my own money, and everything that I have now, I brought it myself. The family doesn't own me. The company doesn't own me. My mother doesn't own me. So I will be just fine. I will contact you soon to see how you want me to resign as the company's Chief of Marketing & Artist Management and a fellow author. You know, how it will be delivered to the press and all.

"I know you will write your last book for the company and end your contract as an author. And I know you're about to start your own business, but do you really want to publicly resign from your position so fast like that?" Markeisha asked.

"Yes, people are going to find out anyway. Once I announce my company, then it is out there. It is best to formally deliver the news to the public rather than trying to do everything on the low," Pen said.

"Well, I will get one of our PR people to draft a press release, and you and I will get together in the next few weeks to schedule a press conference. Of course, I will follow protocol and take up with our grandparents and our parents."

"I wouldn't expect you to do anything less. I love you, cuzzo."

"I love you more. Now, where are you off to on this beautiful day?"

"I'm going over on 105 with the guys. You know, play some dominos, relax, and talk shit," Pen said.

"You enjoy yourself, be careful, and tell our family and your friends I said hi."

"Will do."

Chapter 2: And Then There Was Cue?

As Pen pulled out of the gates of his family's estate, he sent his friends a group text message saying, "Meet me at the spot at 9 pm." While driving through Bratenahl, casually, a man wearing a pink double-breasted Tom Ford Suit with a red, white collar French cuffed shirt with the top button unbuttoned, red sunglasses, and a pair of bright red studded loafers with no socks appeared in Pen's back seat. The man had dark skin, sponge curls, and a neatly shaped beard. The man said to Pen, "Well, you're the man that God sent me to huh?" Pen was startled by the unexpected voice and pulled over to the side of the road as fast as he could. He jumped out of the car once he pulled over and looked at the man sitting in his back seat with fear and surprise on his face.

"Yo, who the fuck are you, and how the hell did you get back there," Pen frantically asked.

"You would not believe me if I told you, young man," said the man who appeared from nowhere.

"Look, money ain't an issue. I can give you plenty of money if that is what you want. Just don't kill me, man. I am only twenty-one. I've only slept with one girl, and I am trying to have as much sex as I can before I die, and now I am just rambling because I'm scared, and I don't know where you came from! Where did you come from, dawg?! Aw, LAWD, Jesus, this is for that time I broke my mother's vase and lied and said it was Rich, wasn't it? Now you done sent somebody to ice me! I'm sorry I lied on my cousin, God! I'll never lie again," Pen said while crying and getting down on his knees, pleading for God's mercy on the sidewalk next to his car.

The man stepped out of the car's back seat and stood before the crying, frantic young man, Pen. He smiled at Pen with his pearly white teeth, extended his hand, and said, "You are innocent. Just like my father said, you were. Get up, son. I ain't here to hurt you." Pen allowed the strange man to help him off the ground while staring at him in amazement.

"You said I wouldn't believe you if you told me who you were. But I am pretty open-minded. So just hit me with it, bruh. Who the hell are you, and how did you just appear in my car like that? Did you sneak in while I was at my family's home? You supposed to be my security," asked Pen

"Well, I am here to protect you, but not in the way that you expect me to. I am also here to guide you," the man said while smiling.

"Stop being cryptic, dawg."

"I am an angel sent by God from Heaven."

Pen looked at the man and laughed. He laughed so hard he almost fell to the ground while holding his rib cage. The man stood there staring at him with a look of confusion on his face.

"You must be one of my family's security details," Pen said while still laughing. "Because that is some bully bull bullshit!"

"I'm serious, son."

"So what you saying, you Cupid or some shit?!"

The man gave Pen a severe stare and was silent.

"Yo, no way! You're not a pudgy little white dude with a diaper on and curly blond hair, and wings, and a harp mandoline! And since when did Cupid dress this fly and have a New York Accent? Man, I have got to be losing my mind now. I can't wait to tell my therapist about this. Well, I will tell you what. Since you found your way in my car without me knowing, you can find your way to where ever you came from because that? That is some bully bull bullshit," Pen said while opening the driver's door to the car.

"Nah, I'm Cupid son. But you can call me Cue. And you have a great ear for accents. Because actually, I'm from Staten Island," Cupid said as he stood and watched Pen get into the car.

"How do I know you're not lying to me about being Cupid," asked Pen while looking suspicious.

"Well, let's see here. I have some notes about you on my phone. God gave me your portfolio," Cupid said as he went to the notes on his iPhone. "Ah, here we go. You and your girlfriend just broke up."

"She's a famous rapper and singer, and I am a famous writer. That's public knowledge," Pen said sarcastically.

"You love to sing 90's R&B in the shower."

"Bruh, who doesn't?!"

"Meh, got a point there, kid," Cupid said while nodding in agreement. "You like mint chocolate chip ice cream. It is your favorite."

"Dawg, that's common as hell!"

"That ain't common, son. I don't think that is even natural. Might as well put toothpaste on a Hershey's bar and freeze it!"

"Well, from what I can see, you've got nothing to prove that you were sent here to look after me, so I'm about to roll out and meet my boys," Pen said as he started his car.

"When you first saw your ex, you were in kindergarten. You couldn't comprehend your feelings but knew you liked something about her. As you two got older, you grew closer. You two shared your first kiss on the first day of high school, and you fainted. The first time you had sex with her was during your freshman year in college. You had sex in her room because her roommate wasn't there. You had a hard time putting the condom on because you didn't know how to. Once you finally got it on, you got on top. You kissed her gently and asked her what you should do. She took her hand and stroked your penis for a moment, and inserted you inside of her. You both let out a gasp as you proceeded to stroke her body slowly and gently. She wrapped her arms around your neck and moaned softly. She asked you to never stop loving her the way you do. You replied, "I will always love you. I have loved you since we were five." She could feel herself about to climax and asked you to keep the same pace. She then grabbed your face and kissed your lips while you continued to stroke her until you both let out a loud moan from climaxing together as one. Is that enough to prove to you that I am Cupid?"

Pen sat in a trance. Tears began to roll down his face as he cried in silence. He turned the car off and stepped out.

"Man, no one knows about that except for her and I. Not my friends, cousins, nobody."

"Like I said, I'm Cupid, but you can call me Cue. And Cue is here to help you. So what it DO, son!!!"

"Let's say I believe you. How are you going to help me? Protect me?"

"Well, let me put it like this kid. Forget all the shit you've seen on tv, where the little chubby white dude shoots an arrow and BOOM! You are in love. Nah, son, that ain't it. See, you can't force love. You also can't just get rid of it so easily. And you have to be careful with it. Now, you, my friend, are in a very odd place in your life. And that is what I am here for. First off, you just graduated from undergrad. You lost who you thought was the love of your life. You're walking away from your comfort zone, which is your family's book publishing empire. And now you are about to start a new journey in life with your writing and your business. You're going back to school. And on top of that, you want to be active in the community? Kid, you've got a lot of things going on. Three things will take place while having all of these things happening in your life," said Cupid.

"What's that?"

"Love, sex, and some heartbreak. It is inevitable. We all go through it. But sometimes, all three can consume us if we let it. I'm not God, so only God knows his plans for you. But I do know how to guide you on your journey. I've done it for years now. Too damn long, son. I think after you, Ima have to retire, you feel me?"

"So you can't tell me what my future holds or the outcomes. You can only tell me how to get through it all, and that's it?"

"Not tell, but guide you."

Pen had a look of confusion on his face and said, "Alright, well, that's cool. I guess. Sooooo you getting back in the car or nah?" Cupid laughed at Pen and responded, "Nah, kid, I got wings, and I ain't drink no Red Bull to get 'em. Deuces. Catch you on the flip side."

Cupid spread his wings and disappeared, leaving a gush of wind behind him. Pen looked around him and said aloud, "So nobody saw that big, black-ass angel spread his wings and fly, huh? Just me? Okay, I'm crazy as hell. I'm just losing it now." The young, confused man returned to his car and drove to his childhood home on Hathaway Avenue. When he arrived at his childhood home, he walked in the door, and the first thing he looked at was a picture of him and his ex on the mantel. Tears began to swell up in his eyes, but before they could roll down his face, he could hear and feel a heavy bass coming from a car outside. He looked out the front door and saw it was his friend Manny in an old-school Chevy Camero that he had rebuilt himself. Manny walked into the house, hugged Pen, and said, "Long time no see, Marlisia." Pen responded, "Yeah, I've missed you, Princess." The two laughed because they'd joked like this since they were in the second grade.

"When is Big T getting here," the light-skinned, freckled face, five-foot-eleven Manny asked.

"Soon, man, very soon. But since it's just the two of us what's up with you, man?"

"Nothing, man, I'm just still doing my thing with the cars. I've got six auto repair and car customizing garages and shops,"

Manny said as he grabbed a glass from the bar shelf in the dining room to pour him a shot of Hennesy.

"That's what's up, bruh. I didn't know you had expanded your business like that!"

"Because you shut down after you and Iesha broke up. For an entire year at that. I'm surprised you even kept up with your online classes and are able to graduate," Manny said while sipping on his Hennesy.

"I know, man. I just.... Iesha was my everything, dawg. I never thought we would break up like this. I mean, she didn't just cheat on me and leave me for any ole football player. She left me for a dude I once called my friend, my family, since we were babies. I remember when that mothafucka was afraid of the dark and wetting the bed!"

"You, me, and Big T remember. He literally peed the bed until he was fifteen. And don't get me wrong, I feel where you're coming from. But Pen, she didn't deserve you. She couldn't appreciate you being the good dude you are. So forget her man."

Pen nodded his head in agreement with sadness displayed on his face, and then Manny and Pen could hear "Wu-Tang Forever by Drake" blaring out of someone's car speakers. Without looking out the door or trying to guess who was pulling up to the house. The two young men looked at one another and said, "Big T and that damn Tahoe." The music stopped, and a loud, deep, raspy voice said, "Big T ALL UP IN THIS MOTHAFUCKA!" Pen stepped to the porch and greeted the five-foot-ten, heavy-set, dark-skinned man with deep waves and a beard with a hug. Tyson, also known as Big T and Pen, had been best friends since kindergarten at Joseph F. Landis. All three young men walked to the backyard and began to play poker. Pen lit his cigar while the other two lit a joint. It was a long and awkward silence until Big T broke it.

"So, you just called us, huh? You ain't call your other homies," Big T asked.

"Nah. I needed to be with my day ones. The ones who know me better than anyone."

“I feel it, man. You know I’m here for you, bruh, especially with Iesha getting engaged.”

Manny gave Big T a cold stare, and Big T looked at Manny and then back at Pen. Pen had an expression of anguish on his face. Pen slammed his cards on the table, fell back in his chair, and took a large puff of his cigar as he looked to the sky.

“Wow. And you knew the whole time, Manny, and wasn’t going to say shit,” Pen asked as he exhaled the smoke.

“I didn’t want to bring it up. But apparently, some people just don’t know how to keep they mouth shut!”

“I’m sorry, man, but you’re not going to miss it, considering it is all over social media and the news. On top of that, you know she did an interview with your homegirl from college. That slim girl with the eyes, What’s the name of her talk show again,” Big T said.

“Sipping the Tea with TEE,” said Pen.

“Well, it has gone viral. So I just wanted to give you a heads up,” Big T said.

After hearing the hurtful news about his ex, Pen changed the subject, and the three finished their card game and discussed their plans and goals for a couple more hours until Manny and Big T got tired and went home. Now that Pen was alone, he went upstairs to his office and to his computer to open up the unfinished poetry he’d started typing for his new book. Taking a deep sigh and falling back in his chair, Pen put his hand on his forehead and said, “Alright, Pen. You’re going to be okay. You’re going to be just fine. Stay focused.” But he did not stay focused. Pen couldn’t begin to edit or write anything due to being so distracted by the thought of the viral interview that his ex had done. So Pen shut down the computer, went straight to his den in the basement, turned on his TV, and went to the “YouTube” app. The first thing that popped up under suggested was the interview that he was so desperate yet reluctant to see. He took a deep sigh and turned on the interview.

Chapter 3: Sippin Tea With TEE Interview

The interview is starting, and Pen's college friend Tiana, also known as "TEE," shows up on the screen with a big smile on her face, wearing glasses, a bun tied in her hair, and a skin-tight green dress hugging every curve on her slim, brown skin body. With so much enthusiasm, Tiana squeals in a high-pitched voice, "HI! THANK YOU ALL FOR JOINING US TODAY! MY NAME IS TEE, AND YOU ARE NOW TUNED IN TO SIPPIN TEA WITH TEE!" Her live audience clapped for her and screamed, "WE LOVE YOU TEE!" Tiana waited for the crowd to settle down and then said, "We all have a very special guest today. She is one of the world's biggest female rappers and singers, a dear friend of mine, and the future wife of NFL star quarterback Jay Stansfield. Please GIVE IT UP FOR IESHA!" The crowd went crazy, and Iesha walked out from backstage to The five foot two thick, curvy, light-skinned woman with green eyes and long jet-black hair who was sporting a red dress with red high heels and waved to the crowd while displaying her beautiful smile. She walked up to Tiana and gave her a great big hug and kiss on the cheek before the two sat down. Once the two sat down and the crowd settled down, the "Tea" with "Tee" began.

"OMG! Girly look at you?! You are just so gorgeous, isn't she gorgeous, guys?! YEEEEAAAAAH," Tiana said as the crowd went wild.

"Thank you so much, Tee, you as well, you as well," Iesha responded softly and calmly.

"Thank YOU! Okay, so you know here we are all about the tea, and hunty it is pippin hot girl. And you already know I have my Executive Producer in my ear with some hot topics. Shout out to my girl Robin! So tell me, you have a new album coming out, do you not?"

"I definitely do. The name of my new album is "*My Love Is Not For Sale.*" It will be available on all streaming platforms, with fourteen tracks, and will feature some of the greatest artists," Iesha said as she smiled and the crowd clapped for her.

"Good for you, girl I am so proud of you! Now, what inspired the title of your album," Tiana said as Iesha expressed sadness on her face.

"Well, I started writing this album about a year ago. And if anyone knows me, they know that my love has always been music. At the time, I was going through some issues with my record label. They wanted someone else to record and perform the songs I wrote for this album. And because of my contract, they tried to make me hand over the songs. So I went home, and I called my boyfriend........"

"You mean your ex-boyfriend Ahmad Pen? He's a famous author and prince to the world's largest black-run book publishing company," Tiana said, cutting Iesha off mid-conversation.

"Yes," Iesha reluctantly said. "I went home to Ahmad, and we were conversing about it, and he looked at me and said, "Baby, you are beautiful and talented, and you seem confident about this project. Your love is your music and is not for sale." When he said that, he really made me believe that, and I was trying to figure out how I could get out of this bogus contract I was in. Two days later, Ahmad had a team of lawyers go to my record label, and I was out of my contract. Don't know what he did, don't know how he did it, but he did it. And he told me that same day, "Now you're an independent artist, do what you will with your project." And it was his words and actions that birthed my album's title."

The crowd let out a big "AAAAAAWWWW," and Tiana looked at Iesha with tears in her eyes and said, "Wow! That man really loved you! Like he really loved you to do all of that. GIRL!" Iesha sat there and displayed discomfort in the conversation.

"Yeah, he helped me a lot on my journey. He's a great guy. But that is the past. It has been well over a year since he and I have been together. Now it is time for us to focus on the future."

"Right! Let's talk about the big black GAWD of the NFL, Mr. Stansfield. How'd you two meet?!"

"Well, we have known one another since the second grade, and we've been friends for a really long time, and a year ago, we just. We just. We just..."

"You two just fucked and you fell in love?"

"No, to be honest, I always loved him. He was fun, funny and exciting, and tall, and dark and, OH MY GOD! He was just a dream!"

"So you were in love with this man even when you were in a relationship?"

"I was. I tried to fight the urge, but I mean, look at this man. Do you not see him," Iesha said as she bounced with joy in her eyes and looked at the picture pulled up on the stage of her and her fiance.

"So, is he the reason why you and your ex broke up?"

"I wouldn't say that," Iesha said hesitantly. "Listen, I didn't get on here to talk about my ex Tiana."

"SWEETIE! You brought him up first, not us. Everyone knows you two have been in each other's lives since you were five. And let's not forget I was there when you two first like, REALLY hooked up."

"Sure you were, honey," Iesha said with an attitude.

"Honey, I was your RA, I was the one knocking on your door to tell you to keep the noise down the day you two moved into your dorms. Now, I told you the tea is hot on this show, so let's go!"

"Listen, honey. I love you and everything you're doing, but I refuse to feel attacked or disrespected," Iesha said angrily, crossing her legs, while sitting back in her chair.

"I apologize. But you realize that this is your first interview and project you've released since your last relationship. Second, the last time you were here, you and your ex were together to promote your joint project because you did the soundtrack to his last book. And with me knowing you both personally. I could tell he really loved you. And you *seemed* like you loved him. But I guess that love isn't always reciprocated like we think it is," Tiana said seriously as she stared Iesha deep in her eyes.

"Sometimes people are just placeholders until you get what you really want. And now that I have what I really want. I'm not letting that go. I love the man I am with and refuse to let him go. He is fine as hell. He gives me what I want when I want. He is exciting, and he's not some corny-ass dude who sits up and writes me lame letters and attempts to write me poetry *AND* buying me flowers all the damn time. He actually celebrates me by taking me out to my favorite places! Who wouldn't want that," said Iesha.

"Um, well, what's wrong with the little things? Everything doesn't have to be grandiose in a relationship. I see nothing wrong with flowers, a home-cooked meal, and intimate quality time. I think it is special. And I think that a man willing to do such a thing is special, especially when they are working hard themselves," Tiana said.

"If that is the case, then have at my ex, but I know one thing. I cannot wait to marry *Mr. Jay Stansfield* and become *Mrs. Jay Stansfield*."

"I see, boo, I can definitely see. Well, congratulations on your new project and your engagement. I hope that all goes well," Tiana said to Iesha with a forced smile.

"Thank you," Iesha responded with a forced smile as well.

"OKAY GUYS AND GALS! WE WILL TAKE A QUICK COMMERCIAL BREAK, AND WE WILL BE RIGHT

BAAAAAACK WITH OUR NEXT GUEST JOINING IESHA AND ME! YEEEEES!"

During ads running between the show being streamed on Pen's TV, he looked at his phone where he had received a text message from his college friend and the executive producer of "SIPPIN TEA WITH TEE," Robinette, aka Robin. The text said, "HEY FRIEND? HOW ARE YA?" Pen looked at the text and said aloud, "I am not in the fucking mood right now to talk," and threw his phone on the table. After the commercials, Tiana returned to the TV screen, showing off her beautiful smile.

"HI EVERYONE! WE ARE BAAAAACK! Now, I know that the tea got a little hot in here earlier, but I just wanted to say that this young lady is my girl, and I just love her! Iesha I am so sorry if I made you feel some type of way but you know how this journalism game is!"

"Mmm Hmm," said Iesha with a forced smile.

"So we actually have a surprise guest today, everyone! I hope you all are ready for "*Stan The Man*" Jay Stansfield!"

The crowd lost their minds, and the women jumped up and down, screaming, "OH MY GOD! HE IS SO FINE! I LOVE YOU JAY!" The six foot five, dark-skinned man with a clean beard and long dredlocks was sporting a white t-shirt that was so tight around his muscles it looked like the sleeves were about to tear at any second, fitted blue chinos, and white shell toe Adidas with no socks. He walked in and waved at the crowd and went straight to his fiance, lifted her up in his strong arms, and gave her a big tongue kiss. Then he went to give Tiana a hug and sat down next to his fiance. The audience finally settled down and the second part of the interview began.

"*Stan The MAN*! How are you duuude?!"

"I'm doing great, I can't complain. Just living life and loving all on this beautiful young lady right here," Jay said with a smile on his face.

"We can see that. YEEEES! So what is new in your life besides signing that big contract for three hundred million for five years with the Cleveland Back Breakers!"

"Nothing much for real. I'm just getting ready for this upcoming season, so I am training hard."

"I can see that look at the size of those arms," Tiana screamed. "So when is the wedding, you guys?"

"I am leaving it all to my baby to handle. It's her wedding, and she can do whatever she wants."

"See why I love this man? Like I said, he is a dream," exclaimed Iesha. "But the wedding will be after the upcoming season is over. That's what I am projecting. This wedding has to be perfect."

"Okay, Okay. HM. So may I ask, Iesha, what made you decide you wanted to get married? I mean, you two are still like, so young?"

"I love him, he loves me, that is all we need to make it, right babe," said Iesha while looking at Jay with love in her eyes.

"That's right, beautiful."

The engaged couple kissed, and the audience said, "AAAAAWWWW!" Tiana looked at the two and said, "Wow, you two are just adorable! And the way he proposed to you is everything. Can we pull the video up, Robin?" Robin pulled the video up on the screen on stage, displaying the happily engaged couple on a helicopter ride cuddled up. Iesha asked Jay, "Bae? Where are we going?" Jay responded, "Just wait, baby," and kissed her on the forehead. Iesha looked back at the cameraman with a smile and waved. The two finally arrived at a helipad on top of Jay's apartment building, with a staff of chefs and waiters on standby. Once the helicopter landed, the couple hopped off. Once the aircraft flew away, the staff brought out a table, two chairs, a white tablecloth, a vase with a dozen roses for the table, and two plates of surf and turf with vegetables and potatoes. To top it off, the staff brought out a bottle of champagne and two glasses. The couple sat down, ate dinner, and made a toast with their glasses of champagne. After the two finished the meal, a waiter approached the table and presented the beautiful Iesha with her favorite dessert, mint chocolate chip ice cream. When she dug into her dessert, she noticed a gigantic diamond ring peaking out at her. She began to cry, and Jay got down on one knee and said, "Baby will you marry me?" She shook her head, yes, and they shared a kiss.

The video ended and went back to everyone on stage. The audience said, "AAAAAWWWW," and everyone clapped for the couple.

"Wow, that was so sweet of you, Jay. You are an amazing man for doing that for your best friend's ex-girlfriend," said Tiana.

"Tee, I see you're still messy," Jay said, laughing. "But what can I say? She chose me."

"Well, I just hope *she* made a good choice," Tiana said. "Alright, everyone, that concludes the show for the day! Thank you all for joi...."

Chapter 4: Cue Is Here To Help You

Pen turned the TV off and re-lit his cigar. Cupid appeared on the couch beside Pen, wearing cuffed white chino pants, a pink polo shirt, and red sunglasses. Surprising Pen yet again.

"Damn, kid, that was some tough shit to watch," Cupid said as he was sipping on a glass of scotch while watching Pen jump from being startled.

"What the fuck! Dawg, if you're going to be doing all of this, I will need you to at least send me a text or something!"

"Chill, chill, chill, kid. My bad. I didn't mean to startle you. I just couldn't help but watch that painful interview. Phew! I know that hurts."

"It does, but you know what, for the first time in a year, I am not tripping."

"You're not?"

"Why would I Cue? I mean, it all makes sense now. The entire relationship does."

"HM! Is that so?"

"It is. That interview showed me that it was never me that she wanted. She was happy with what I could give. She played the game well, but she probably felt like she got stuck with me. She always loved Jay. It's pathetic and sad because here, my dumb ass was thinking we had something all these years."

"Well, you know, kid, a very fly young lady lives in Las Vegas and has been blowing your phone up since you started watching that interview. So, instead of sitting here rehashing things about your ex, you need to hit her back, big dog."

Pen picked up his phone and realized he had five missed calls from a young lady named Sililoqy, aka Silly. Silly was a very famous model whom Pen had met five years prior. She was five feet eight inches tall, slim but very well proportioned, with thick full lips, long natural hair, smooth brown skin, and pretty dark brown eyes. Pen decided to FaceTime the beautiful model, and when he did, she answered on the first ring.

"Now there's a face that I miss. How are you doing, you handsome man," Silly asked.

"I am doing well, beautiful. How are you?"

"I'm good. I uuuum, I just saw the interview earlier, and I just wanted to call and check on you. You're looking nice over there, short king," said Silly shyly.

"I'm actually fine. I am relieved like a weight has been lifted off of my chest. And thank you," Pen said with a huge smile.

"Wonderful! I'm happy to hear that. I am launching my new business in the next four days and wanted to invite you. I haven't seen or talked to you since I modeled for your last book cover. And... I guess I just wanna see you. It's here in Vegas, so if you're down to come out here..."

"I will be there. Just shoot me the time and location in a text," Pen said.

"Done. Well, I look forward to seeing you, handsome. I have to go and speak with my event planner," she said while winking and blowing a kiss. "Talk to you soon!"

"Talk to you soon, beautiful."

The two ended their FaceTime call, and Pen looked over at Cupid, who was staring back at him with a jaw-dropping smile.

"Look at you youngin! You are a mack! Big Mack DADDY IN THE BUILDING SON," Cupid exclaimed.

"It's not like that. She is just a friend. She has always supported my work, and I have always supported hers."

"Man, she likes you. She probably always has. I'm glad you said yes. "Short King" you deserve to wake up to her in the morning in Vegas!"

"You've got jokes, I see. I will text my one dude tomorrow at the Burke Lakefront Airport and book my private jet, and we are on our way to Vegas."

"*My dude*," Cupid said as he took another sip of his scotch.

That night, Pen slept in his childhood home. When he woke up the next day, the first thing he did was look at his phone. And he had hundreds of notifications. While scrolling through them, he saw that he, his ex-friend, and his ex-girlfriend were all over the news, blogs, social media, etc. The world was going crazy about that interview. But it helped Pen with book sales of his work that had already been published. Because of the publicity from the interview, his books were selling like hotcakes! He hated to get sales that way, but he said, "I'm pretty damn sure my mother is loving this right now." Sitting on the edge of his bed, he texted his contact at Burke Lakefront Airport to charter his private jet. Afterward, he received a phone call from his college friend, Robinette, aka Robin. He let the phone ring for a while, debating whether he would answer or not, but he answered.

"Hey, friend! How are ya!"

With a deep sigh, "Robin, I am doing great."

"Great! So WHATCHA UP TO!"

"Nothing much. I'm just sitting here watching me trend all over social media, news, blogs, etc," Pen said sarcastically.

"OH! That's wonderful! Well, I'm glad I could help with your publicity!"

"Are you serious right now? As soon as I heard about the interview, I knew your name was written all over it. I'm not saying you owed me any explanation for why you did this, but having at least a heads-up as a friend would've been nice."

"Peeeeennnnyyyyy Pen, don't get your boxers in a bunch. It's only business!"

"Unfortunately, with you, it is always business."

"Is it not helping your book sales? Since the interview, you've sold over two million copies of the "*Dark & Dirty Spirits Collectors Edition*." That's a big deal, now thank me!"

"Damn, Ahmad Pen threw a hell of an interception, and Jay caught it and put a ring on it! Pen is cute, but he ain't *"Stan The Man" Jay Stansfield*. That brotha is fine. I can see why she folded. He can fold me any day. Oh, here's another one, Robin. Pen is such a sucka that he needs to go somewhere and kill himself because his writing is trash, and his sex game probably is, too. That's why Iesha went to a real one," Pen said as he recited all of the social media posts about him and his former relationship.

"All publicity is good publicity, Penny Cat."

Pen hung up the phone and went to the bathroom to shower and prepare for the day. After getting dressed in his comfortable joggers and t-shirt, the five-foot-six, bald-headed, light-brown-skinned, stocky/muscular-built author, Pen, walked out of the front door where bloggers and vloggers awaited him with their phones, cameras, and questions. Pen ignored them, pushed through everyone, got in his car, and pulled off. On his way to the airport, he received a phone call from his mother. Pen began to sweat profusely and grabbed his chest due to his heart beating fast. He answered the call, and his mother began to speak.

"Hello, my *sonshine*!"

"What do you want, Mother," Pen asked reluctantly.

"Nothing. I'm just calling to check up on you and see how you're feeling. That's all. You should be feeling great. Look at all the books you've sold since you left the house yesterday. Do you realize that we have made almost one hundred million off of the collector's edition of your series in less than a day? Your girl Robin really did you a favor."

"Mommy, I don't feel good at all. I can deal with people attacking my art, but some of the things that have been said really fucking hurts."

"Stop it. At the end of the day, it is all business. Get with it if you're going to be a businessman and have your *own* company.

You've already walked away from your family's empire. So you should be alright," Lola said.

"Sure, because at the end of the day, it's always *business* with you. Unfortunately."

"You're damn right. If anything, your friend did a great job helping you. And if you're hurt, hey, it's life. Welcome to the real world, son. You treated that bitch of an ex like she was made of some type of fine china. I told you she would break your heart. I told you not to date her. Now, who you should've gotten with was Robin when you two were in college. That girl would have made a fine daughter-in-law. She fits in perfectly with this family."

"Do we have to go there?"

"Yes, we do! Because maybe if you listened to your mother, you wouldn't be in any of this mess. Now your fucking feelings are hurt."

Pen let out a deep sigh as he tried to hold his composure. Then he said, "I'm on my way to Vegas. I need to get away from Ohio for a while." There was a long and awkward silence on the phone between the mother and son. Pen finally said, "Hello, are you there?" His mother responded, "You can run from your problems all you want, but they will always be there until you face them," and hung up the phone. Pen finally arrived at the airport, where he boarded his private jet to go to Vegas. Where only the unknown awaited him.

Chapter 5: A Warm & Wet Welcome To Vegas

Pen finally arrived at Las Vegas McCarran Airport, where a limo was waiting to take him to the Bellagio Hotel. As he rode in the back of the limo, he texted all of his family and friends to let them know he had arrived safely. Then, he received an incoming FaceTime call from Silly. When he answered, Silly was wearing nothing but a sheer robe.

"Hey you," Silly said in a very sultry voice while looking at Pen with nothing but lust in her eyes.

"Uuuuum hey. What are you up to," Pen said nervously.

"Nothing, I'm just thinking about you. Based on your background, I see you've made it to Vegas. I wasn't expecting you this soon."

"I just needed to get away from Cleveland. Better yet, *Ohio,* for that matter."

"I feel it. What are you getting into later?"

"I'm heading to my hotel to get settled in. Then, I will get myself something to eat and relax for the rest of the day."

"Why are you staying at a hotel when you could just stay in my mansion with me," Silly asked while giggling.

"I don't want to intrude," Pen said nervously.

"Are you in a limo?"

"Yes."

"Cancel that hotel reservation. I just texted you my address. Give it to your limo driver and bring your handsome ass over here."

Afterward, Silly ended the FaceTime Call. Cupid appeared right before Pen in the limousine wearing an all-pink suit with a tank top underneath the blazer, two gold rings on each hand in the shape of a heart, and pink sunglasses. This time, he did not frighten the young man Pen because, by now, Pen was used to Cupid popping up on him unexpectedly.

"Daaaaaaaamn son. Shortie is definitely a baddie, son! Fo sho," Cupid exclaimed.

"That she is," Pen said while letting out a deep sigh.

"So what you gonna do, kid? Ditch that reservation and give the limo driver the addy?"

"I don't know Cue. Even though she is madly attractive, I never looked at her like that."

"You sure kid?"

"Yeah, man."

"Maybe in your mind, you haven't looked at her that way, but ya dick say otherwise. Cause you done pinched a whole ass tent in ya pants, kid."

Pen pushed down his erect penis in sheer embarrassment and said, "Not cool, dawg. But forreal forreal. What would you do if you were me?" Cupid laughed at the embarrassed young man and said smoothly, "If I were you, I'd keep my reservation because you've got some writing to do and...." Before Cupid could finish, Pen let down the privacy window and told the limo driver where to take him. The limo driver nodded and took him to Ascaya, a private, luxury community that sat up in the mountains over the city of Las Vegas. When Pen's limo pulled into Silly's driveway, Pen texted her, "I'm here." He exited the limo, told his driver to return in three hours, and walked up to the glass mansion's double doors. Silly answered the door in her sheer robe, completely nude underneath, showing off her beautiful brown skin. She pulled Pen in very close for a hug, leaving no room between them. Once she finally let him go, she kissed him on the lips, grabbed him by his wrist, and guided him to her pool in the back of the house.

"Oh my god, I am so happy to see you handsome," Silly said excitedly.

"Glad to see you too. It has been entirely too long. And damn girl, look at this house. You weren't living like this the last time I saw you," Pen said as he looked around the luxurious mansion while being dragged to Silly's pool.

"Well, after you put me on the cover of your book, my career took off. I was modeling for some of the biggest brands, shooting commercials in the States and overseas. Just living life and making money. Now BOOM! I'm living in a nineteen-million-dollar mansion," Silly said as she pushed Pen down on the lounge chair next to the pool and sat on top of him while wrapping her arms around his neck.

"Well, I am proud of you," Pen said nervously.

"You know... You're cute but even cuter when you're shy and nervous."

"Am I," Pen asked as he looked down to avoid eye contact with Silly.

"Yes.... You.... Are," Silly said softly and seductively while kissing the timid young man on his face and lifting his head up by his chin.

"Silly, what are we doing? What is this? Why is this even hap...."

Silly put her finger on Pen's lips, shushing him before he could finish his sentence. She stood up, put her hand on Pen's muscular chest, and pushed him back in the chair. She kissed him on the lips while shoving her tongue in his mouth, gripping his bald head as tight as she could. Then, the beautiful model unbuttoned Pen's dress shirt while kissing Pen's neck. She made her way down to kiss his chest and his stomach, and then she unbuckled Pen's belt and unbuttoned/ unzipped his dress pants. She proceeded to put her hand inside Pen's boxers and gently stroked his penis before pulling it out. Once she pulled it out, Pen had a full erection. Silly looked up at Pen with a smile on her face and said, "Wow, your ex wasn't lying when she said you had some girth to you baby."

While Silly was stroking Pen's penis and pleasuring him, Pen was breathing heavily. After teasing the erect young man, Silly stuffed her soft and wet mouth with Pen's penis. Pen laid his head back on the chair, rolling his eyes back to the back of his head as he gasped and moaned from the pleasure of the beautiful model bobbing her head up and down on his fully erect penis. As Silly slowly sucked the young man's penis, she ran her hand up his chest, moaning softly. She sucked on Pen for the next ten minutes nonstop. Pen moaned out loud, "Baby, stop, I'm about to cum. I'm about to cum!" Silly's response was, "HHMMM MMMMM," as she continued to suck. Finally, the young man gripped the back of the beautiful young lady's head and ejaculated in her mouth. While doing so, Silly giggled and sucked and swallowed every drop of Pen's sperm. When she stopped sucking, she wiped some of the sperm off of the corners of her mouth with her index finger, licked her lips, and then licked the sperm off of her finger. Pen laid in the chair like a jellyfish with no bones. He was too weak to move.

"Wow, that was a lot to swallow! And you must eat healthy because your cum is so sweet," Silly said as she giggled and licked her index finger.

"Oh my God, Silly, I can't move. I don't think I've ever had head like that before."

"Oh, we're not finished yet," Silly said while looking at Pen seductively.

"Wait, what?!"

"I want to feel you inside of me, Ahmad Pen."

Silly grabbed Pen by his wrist, guiding him through the glass mansion to her upstairs outdoor shower. She took off her bathrobe, exposing her naked body to Pen once they approached the outdoor shower on the balcony. Pen began to undress himself until he was completely nude himself. Silly slowly got down on her knees and put Pen's penis in her mouth again. She sucked him until he was fully erect again, got up from her knees, walked over to her phone, played "*Honey Love by Ye*

Ali ft Kirko Bangz," and used a voice command to turn on the shower. Afterward, Silly grabbed Pen's penis and guided him into the shower.

While in the shower, Pen went into a full squat position, wrapping both of Silly's legs around his neck. He lifted her up from the ground gripping her booty cheeks, and proceeded to suck and lick on her clitoris. Silly gripped the top of Pen's wet, bald head, pushing his face deeper in between her legs. She screamed, "YES! Just like that! Don't stop! Don't stop! DON'T STOOOOOOOOP!"

Pen removed his face from in between Silly's legs and repositioned her in the "*Yourself On A Shelf*" sex position (look it up if you don't know what it is). Silly asked, "Why'd you stop," while breathing heavily and smiling. Pen responded, "Did you not say you wanted me inside of you, baby?" Pen reached for his penis with his right hand and gently slid it inside Silly's tight, wet vagina. The two said in unison, "God, you feel so good!" Pen gently stroked her in the standing sex position as she had her arms wrapped around his neck. Silly screamed, "It's so big. Oh God, it's so big. I love it, I love it, I love IT!" Pen kept his strokes steady until Silly demanded he go faster. Pen picked up the pace, and Silly bit down on Pen's right shoulder and dug her nails into his back until he began to bleed.

Silly began to moan louder, and then she screamed, "I'm almost there daddy! Keep giving me that dick! Keep giving it to me. I'M ALMOST THEEEEERE!" Finally, the beautiful model climaxed. Pen was about to put Silly down, but Silly exclaimed, "WAIT, WAIT, WAIT, WAIT! Boy, how you gone fuck me like that then expect for me to stand?! You better carry me to that bed." Pen carried Silly to the bed and walked away to take a shower. Silly laid in the bed, admiring Pen's wide, muscular body from a distance with a smile on her face.

"You know, I've never had anyone lift me up while eating me out," Silly said as she giggled and smiled.

"I hope you enjoyed yourself," Pen yelled from the shower.

"You have no idea. You were great!"

"So were you. I appreciate the invite to stay over the next few days, but I really need to be in a space to write my next book, so I kept my reservation at the Bellagio," Pen said.

Silly had a look of disappointment on her face. She got out of bed, walked to the shower, and said, "Pen, I know you're working on your new projects. But can you just stay the night? I have plenty of bedrooms for you to work out of." Pen stopped scrubbing his body and let out a deep sigh. He stepped out of the shower and said, "Sililoqy, you know I only came to Vegas to support you and the new boutique you're opening. I didn't come here to rendezvous all five days. What happened today was unexpected." Silly folded her arms and pouted while Pen kissed her cheek and returned to the shower.

Once Pen finished in the shower and walked over to the bathroom mirror, Silly walked up behind Pen and kissed the back of his head while playing with his penis. "Haven't you had enough," asked Pen. Silly smiled and said, "Just stay with me tonight, and I swear the next time you hear from me will be the day of my grand opening. I just don't want to be alone tonight. And you felt so good. I want you one last time." Pen turned around, grabbed Silly by her waist, pulled her close to him, and said, "Baby, I can't. Not tonight." Silly looked at Pen with a look of disappointment.

"I um… I wanted our bodies to do a lot of talking tonight, Pen. All night," Silly said as she ran her fingers across Pen's chest.

"Silly, my limo driver will return to pick me up in less than an hour. But I will see you at your grand opening. If you're free after your event, then maybe we can have some more *us* time."

"I'd like that," Silly said.

Pen finished getting dressed and received a call from his limo driver that he was outside. Pen kissed the model on her cheek, said good night, and left the beautiful mansion to go to his luxury hotel villa at the Belaggio.

Five Chapters of A Preview Later

So, I hope you all enjoyed the first five chapters of "Cupid's Love & Sex Chronicles: Pen's Journey!" The release date is to be determined. The last thing I have to offer you all before ending this book is another story that I began to write, titled "Bloodline Deception." I began writing this story in 2014, maybe 2015? Again, way before I even knew how to format anything. This story is about a young man raised up as an assassin and assigned to work for and protect a family heavily involved in crime. I don't know where I will go with this storyline yet, but it definitely needs some more work before it is complete. So please sit back, relax, and enjoy a preview and draft of the first chapter of this story!

Draft & First Chapter of Bloodline Deception

I can go on for days, months and years talking about all the scandalous things that I've seen. The people I've protected. The people I've lied for. The people I've killed for and the people I've killed. I have a lot of stories. I was a trained killer, and when the time came, I trained others to do the same. For me, it all started from the time I was born in Paris. I came from a family who ran an organization to train soldiers so that they may serve as body guards and assassins to the most powerful and richest families to ever walk the face of the earth. Only the super-rich and super powerful had access to my family's organization because it was a secret society of killing machines. The profession made my family one of the richest families in the country of France, and the most dangerous. All of the assassins in the organization, including myself, were trained at a very young age. The youngest age starting out was seven years old. The oldest might've been seven. For me, it started at the age of four.

I didn't go to school like most kids. I was homeschooled, and my homeschooling wasn't ordinary either. I didn't even have any friends. Even though there were other children in training, we weren't allowed to communicate with one another. Since the organization didn't want us to be friends nor enemies. Granted we'd have to work with one another one day, the heads of the organization didn't want anyone becoming emotionally attached nor build any animosity towards one another out of jealousy. They were children of other assassins in my family's organization and we were a squad, a unit, a team of young murderers. We were taught everything we needed to know, reading, writing, arithmetic, and everything else. But in between, I was taught every fighting style known to man. We learned about every weapon manufactured. We learned about pressure points, bones, everything about the body in order to know how to kill our enemies and how to disarm them.

I was destined for nothing except to be a killing machine. In my culture, when we were born we weren't given names in my family or any other family that was a part of the organization. We were given numbers and with numbers, there was a meaning behind it. For example, I was born with the number zero. The number zero represents the beginning of all numbers. It was the alpha number as far as my culture was concerned. It was a special number. I got that number because of my father being the highest ranked killer in the world and the leader of the organization.

When you became thirteen years of age, you were granted a name because by that age you've earned enough kills under your belt to get a name. You had to earn your name, work for it, kill for it. By the time I was a teenager I'd killed at least 36 men. Probably more. Growing up, when I was in a classroom in my family's mansion with my booooring professors, I'd go on assassination missions with my father and the unit I was in training with. He taught us everything that he knew. He always said when I got to a certain age,he wanted me to go to America and start an empire of my very own and get away from the family business. But I knew regardless of whatever happened, that could never be. My mother knew it too because she always said that my father was "pipe dreaming".

I was my parents only child. My father's name was Jacq Regime Senior. He was the most feared man on the entire planet at one point. He was very tall. He stood about six foot seven, very light skinned fellow with good looks and a charm out of this world. He was smooth, calm, humble, and loving. My mother's name was Helena Regime. She was six feet even, light skinned, with sharp green eyes that made every man crumble. My mother was very nice to everyone, but she was ruthless.

In my opinion, she was worse than my father. I think sometimes he was afraid of her because when she got mad at him, he wouldn't even want to argue or even make eye contact.I loved my father. I never spent much time with my mother because she spent most of her time in the United States under special request from the Ray family, oil and petroleum tycoons, who were worth a couple trillion. She was head of their security. She trained all of their body guards for them and made sure everything was in perspective as far as their combat, weapon mastery, and much more. I loved my mother too, but we never had much of a relationship due to the fact that she was in the United States most of my life. My father on the other hand was always my go to guy. Everyone thought he was the meanest person to ever exist, but to me he was the sweetest guy. It was amazing how calm he was.

I remember when he took me on my first mission, he put me behind a sniper rifle. I was four. He was about to assassinate one of the largest drug dealers in the world. An older distinguished Dominican man who went by the name Estevez Pedro. He flooded every country with coke and heroine. He had a monopoly on drugs and dried up all competition. My first kill was him. I felt awful when I first did it. I pulled the trigger and split his head in front of his whole family at the dinner table. His wife, parents, in laws, his six young children, nieces, nephews, everyone. My father guided me the whole time and he was really gentle with me. He said to me, "if we don't get him tonight son, we'll get him tomorrow." He put no pressure on me at all, and I just pulled the trigger. I had nightmares for about two weeks straight every night after my first kill. My father helped me get through it.

After that killing became easy, it became fun. I absolutely loved it. The older I got, the more missions I'd go on with my father. By the time I was thirteen, my father had given me his name. He said to me it was time for me to carry on his name and carry it with honor. A year later my father was killed. One summer, we were ambushed by a group of assassins. Assassins we'd never seen or heard of. They were unmasked Russian men. There were at least twenty of them. Their fighting skill was a lot different than what I'd ever learned and I knew every single fighting style in the world. At least I thought I did. My father and I tried to fight them off, but they were too strong. We were able to kill the first fifteen, but when we got down to the last five men, my father was stabbed in the shoulder and lost a lot of blood. He grew weak and couldn't perform like himself.

He fell down, gripping his shoulder. I had a hard time fighting these men off by myself. So, they overwhelmed me and three of them held me down. The last two towered over my father and pulled out two pistols. My father looked at me and said, "son, we had a good run. I love you so much." After that, all I heard was gunshots ring out, and my father's blood was splattered all over the place. They emptied their clips on him and walked away like nothing. They spared my life and said nothing. I remember crawling over to my father's lifeless body and holding him in my arms, screaming. I never even thought that my father could be killed by anyone. He was only thirty-two.

After his death, I had no choice but to go off and live with my mother in the United States. In Cleveland, Ohio. When I first touched down in Cleveland and got off the plane, I was expecting to have a driver waiting for me. Instead, it was my mother with open arms. I ran into her arms and we both held each other so tight we could barely breathe. I cried so hard. My tears stained her satin blouse. I blamed myself for my father's death. I felt like I should've protected him. I felt like it should've been me. I'll never forget my mother and I's conversation.

Helena: (Crying) "Son, it isn't your fault. You know that right?"

Me: (Crying) "Yes, it is, I could've protected him, I should've protected him."

Helena: (Sniffle) "Your father knew this day was coming and the last thing he'd want you to do is this. He wouldn't want you to blame yourself. And even though you may not feel this way, but it's better that it was him than you. If it had been you do you think either one of us would've been able to live with ourselves? Live on this earth? We'd both die. You're our baby. Our only child. Now let's go home. Your room is ready, the Ray's are waiting for you. They can't wait to meet you."

When we walked out of the airport, my mother and I got into an armored Cadillac stretch limousine. It was beautiful. I remember on the ride to the Ray mansion was completely silent. We just held each other's hand. When we pulled up to the Ray Mansion, it was like something I'd seen out of a fairytale book. Even though I'd come from big, big, big money it was nothing like the Ray's. They were the richest family in the United States of America, and their mansion showed it. It wasn't even a mansion, it was a damn castle. A humongous castle sitting on 120 acres of land. They had three guest houses, a recreation building, a museum, I don't know how many car garages, and every single acre was covered with body guards. They had everything. The main mansion was amazing. Twenty-five bedrooms, eighteen full bathrooms, fifteen kitchens and dining rooms, sauna, massage room, bowling alley, movie theaters, and everything else you could ever imagine. I know it may sound unbelievable, I couldn't believe my eyes when I saw it, but it was very real. If you didn't want to, you didn't have to leave the estate for anything, whatever was needed, others were sent to pick them up in the city. Food, cleaning products, etc. It was amazing. It was so big, we called it "the palace" or "Ray's Palace."

The Ray family were beautiful people. I remember when I first pulled up to the main mansion, the first person that greeted me was Mrs. Jeanie Ray. She was what you'd call a high yellow woman. She had the sweetest face, high rosy cheekbones, long silky type hair, a beautiful smile like an innocent child. She was beautiful, inside and out. I'd instantly fell in love with her. I loved her like a second mother. When my mother and I got out of the car, Mrs. Ray said to me "Baby, your life changes for the better now and we will carry all of your burdens." She kissed me on the forehead and guided me into the house to the family room where the rest of the family were. That is when I met the love of my life and truly my best and only friend. First, she introduced me to her husband, Co-CEO, Mr. William Ray. He was medium height, dark-skinned slim, cleaned cut, beautiful slicked back hair. All the way around distinguished gentleman. He was a great man, great role model. Then I met the kid that would become my best friend. If anything, he was a brother to me, Andre Ray. He was a couple years older than me, but he took me in like a little brother. Now at just the age of sixteen, he was six foot five, muscle bound, athletic built, brown skinned, hazel eyes, neat afro, very charming with the ladies, but had a goofy upbeat personality. He was loyal and respectful to everyone he met.

Finally, the love of my life, Andrea Ray. Andrea had big pretty hazel eyes, very light skinned, long silky hair just like her mother, a beautiful smile and a body that made man kill for it. On top of that she had a beautiful personality. It was obvious that I had eyes for her when I first got there. While in the family room Mr. Ray looked at me and began to cry.

William Ray: Son, you look exactly like your father. I'm very happy you're here. Welcome to the family.

Me: "Thank you sir, for everything. "

William Ray: "No need to thank me young man. I hope you're hungry."

Me: "I can eat sir."

William Ray: "You heard the young man, let us please go eat. Andre, is the food ready?"

Andre: "Been ready father."

William Ray: "To the main dining room!"

When we got to the dining room, they had a meal fit for a royal family. It was amazing. I remember we prayed before our meal. We always had to prayed before we ate. ALWAYS! If we didn't, as children we were punished in the Ray house. Like I said, they were like another set of parents or grandparents to me, and they treated me as if I were one of their own. After prayer was over, I was about to eat my food, but Mr. Ray slapped my hand and signaled for a taster to come and taste my food before I did. Just to see if there was anything wrong with it.

William Ray: "Never touch your food until you've prayed, and a taster taste it. You understand me son?"

Me: "Yes sir."

William Ray: "Now I will let you know right here, right now, the second you got off that plane, you became one of our children. We will love you, protect you, and treat you as such. You will abide by our rules. You will attend the same schools as my children. You will work for Ray Oil & Petroleum Corporation twice a week. You will be paid for your services. You will also receive stock in the company. You will eat with the family every day for breakfast and dinner, and you will always keep your love, loyalty, honesty and respect with us as we will with you. Do we have an understanding?"

Me: "Yes sir."

William Ray: "My rules are very simple. Follow them and you'll be fine. Now if you ever get lonely or want to be around the other kids, you are more than welcome to spend the night in the main house with us. We already have a room ready for you here. Even though I know that most of your time will be spent with your mother. I am not trying to be mean or cruel. I just want you to feel that you belong, because you do."

Me: "I understand sir."

After dinner, I went to the house that my mother lived in. It was beautiful. Not as big as the main mansion or shall I say castle, but it was huge. I loved it there. I was just so happy to be there with my mother. I'd never seen my mother so happy, yet sad at the same time. Every time looked at me she just hugged me and kissed me. My first night there, we stayed up all night and watched movies and ate junk food. Most of my life I felt an empty void because I never could say that I had my mother in my life. But at that moment, a part of me felt complete. I knew killing was a part of our lifestyle and when we were called, we had to go. So, I never held anything against my mother. Plus, I knew now that my father was dead, someone would have to take over the league of assassins. In a way, I was hoping it wouldn't be my mother, because that would mean we'd have to move back to Paris and I didn't want to do that. Throughout the fun we had my first night, we had a conversation about what the future would bring.

Helena: "You know now that your father is gone, the league of assassins could possibly crumble. We can't afford that. It is your father's legacy. It is your family's legacy. Our family's legacy. We have to keep it going. Not for the money but for the principle. If you were old enough, you could run it but you're not. So, I might have to step up to the plate and run it from here in the U.S. What do you think about that?"

Me: "I wish you'd stay away from it and let Uncle Jason run the organization. He'll be back in France soon to bury dad. Technically he's next in line anyway because he is the oldest brother and he's the most qualified."

Helena: "Your father was in control for a reason. YOUR UNCLE IS NOT FIT TO RUN ANYTHING!!!!! THAT'S THE REASON WHY THAT SON OF A BITCH WAS SENT ALL THE WAY TO RUSSIA BY YOUR GRANDFATHER IN THE FIRST PLACE!!!! HE'S DANGEROUS, EVIL AND CRUEL!!!!"

Me: "But he's the olde....."

Helena: "I DON'T CARE!!!! When we bury your father, I don't want you near that man. You stay away from him. Do not speak, nod, nothing. We will leave for Paris in the next four days. When we get there, you will stay with my sister. I will stay in the family mansion with your uncle.

My mother got up and left the room. She went in the bathroom and she cried. My uncle and mother never had a great relationship. I never knew why in the beginning, but she hated him with a passion. My uncle Jason was identical to my father, except he had longer hair and beard. My mother came back out the bathroom looked at me and apologized.

Helena: (Deep Sigh) "You're almost a man now. You're fourteen and you've killed plenty. You can handle yourself around your uncle. So, you will stay with us in the family mansion. I know how much you admire your uncle, but you can never, ever, ever trust that son of a bitch. He may look like your father, but they're two different people. Never forget it."

Me: "Yes ma'am."

The very next morning at 6:00 am I went to the main mansion to eat breakfast with the Ray's. Every morning at 6:00 am we ate breakfast as a family. But that first morning at the Ray's, I felt like a child for the first time in my life. I didn't have to get up to combat train, target practice, swordsmanship, nothing. For me I was on summer vacation like any other kid. It was weird. I never had a summer vacation a day in my life. It was just homeschool, training, and missions all year round. But I still went to the rec room with Andre to work out and spar. Considering that he had the same exact training as me, because my mother taught him. On the way to the rec room, I'd gotten lost and somehow circled around Mr. Ray's study. Him, my mother and Mrs. Ray were sitting down having a discussion. And I eavesdropped on their conversation.

William Ray: "I'm glad your son is here."

Jeanie Ray: "We both are."

Helena: "I can't thank you both enough for taking him in as you've taken me in. I don't know how to repay you."

Jeanie Ray: "You've already paid us. You've trained our children in combat. You're head of our security staff. You've even brought in some of the best and most loyal soldiers into this thing of ours. You're our enforcer. But.... Enough of that, you said you wanted to talk to us about something. Are there any problems with Jacq Senior's burial."

Helena: "No, no, not at all. As you both know, I will be gone for the next two months and out of those two months, Jacq Junior will be with me only one month. You both know the whole situation, you know the Regime family and how they operate. They're dirty, cruel and power hungry."

Jeanie Ray: "We're speaking of Jason. Never liked that bastard."

William Ray: "His father, my friend, Mr. Hugo Regime. Great man. He tried to teach that boy everything, but he was just too evil. He wanted to become the head of the organization so bad he tried to kill his own father when he was eleven. He tried to kill Jacq when he was a baby. He was an awful child. It hurt Hugo, but he didn't have a choice but to send him to a Russian boarding school. He was too dangerous."

Helena: "He started his own organization in Russia, at least that's what his ex-wife told me. I tried to tell my husband but (sigh) he loved his big brother more than anything in this world. It was almost like he was in denial when it came down to Jason."

Jeanie Ray: "We remember when Jason was born. I saw his future, he would grow to be an evil dictator. No one is stupid. We all know he's secretly running Russia's government."

Helena: "But how? How can he take over a whole country like that by himself? He's just an assassin."

William Ray: (Bangs Desk) He's not just some assassin Helena. He has a gift. The same gift that I have, my wife has, my children have, and your son has."

Jeanie Ray: "I don't think you should handle this situation alone. You need someone who possesses the same powers as he does. You just don't have enough combat skills to take him out. He will kill you and he will try to kill your son."

William Ray: "I think you should just go bury your husband and comeback with your son. Let Jason have the league of assassins. Don't fight him for anything. You've already established yourself here. Besides you have an exclusive contract where you're on payroll as head of our security. You and the soldiers you brought with you are covered. Therefore, you technically have no affiliation with the league of assassins."

Helena: "When were y'all going to tell me this and how did this happen?"

William Ray: "Jacq loved you so much. You were like a delicate flower to him. Perfection. When he married you, he told his father as well as my wife and I that he didn't want his wife to be a full-fledged assassin for the organization, which is why you were never taken to meet the council to be sworn in. Even though you were already an assassin, it was best we kept you out. He never wanted anything to happen to you under the hands of the league of assassins. Hugo was going to do it anyway, but I had Hugo's ear and I influenced him not to do it. (Laughs) You really thought you worked for them? Like, full-fledged? You poor thing (laughs uncontrollably). Why do you think you're here and have been here for all these years?"

Helena: "What about my son? After all these years and he's a full-fledged assassin for the league. Why couldn't he come with me?"

Jeanie Ray: "He didn't want for his son to be a killer. But he was Jacq's only son. He had no choice but to make a killer out of him. He was his bloodline. That doesn't mean he didn't want for his life to be different. He dreamt that he'd be able to come to America and start a new life, but even you knew it wouldn't be possible. You said it yourself."

William Ray: "Listen let's cut this short because now, I grow bored of this conversation. You may be here to protect us, but you're here for us to protect you and your son as well. Russian soldiers came after your family which only means that Jason is responsible. He did this. We must strategize before we make a move on him. So, you will do as we say!!!! Got it?"

Helena: "Yes sir."

To know that my uncle would have something to do with my father's death angered me to a point where I couldn't think straight. I walked away from the door of the study with tears of sadness, but a heart full of hate. I wanted to kill everyone in the world at that moment. I was just confused. Andre saw the look on my face when I arrived to work out and train with him. He said no words. He just held his arms out and I fell into his arms cry. I never felt so at home before. I felt like I'd been with the Ray's my whole life and I'd only been with them for two days. Andre was truly like a big brother to me. At that moment of crying in his arms I knew I truly had a family in the Ray family and they would look out for me.

Andre: "You are family now. You're my little brother now. Always wanted a little brother. Can you imagine growing up with a little sister like Andrea?"

Me: (Crying and Laughing) Thanks man. I appreciate it. But don't you ever tell anyone about what just happened. Got it?

We both shared a laugh. Afterward we trained, and he taught me some of the skills that my mother taught him. Two days later, I was on a private jet back to France with my mother. I remember when I was growing up, every time my uncle came around he taught me something new. He was so fun to be around. Knowing that he had to be killed my father hurt me. I knew I had to kill him, but I couldn't let my mother know that I overheard her conversation with the Ray's. It was hard to do this, but I had to. When we arrived in France, my uncle was waiting for us. He drove himself. No limo driver. No security. I was a bit suspicious of this at first, but I found out he did this just because he didn't feel like riding back seat. He embraced my mother as if he was so happy to see her, but I sensed the phoniness. He kissed me on the forehead and smiled and walked us to the car. On the way back to mansion, everything felt awkward, even our conversation.

Jason: "You've grown so much in a year nephew. I heard how you held your own when your father was attacked. I'm proud of you. There is a place for you in the league after all. I'd love for you to fight side by side with me. It'll be just like you and your father again."

Me: "Yes uncle, I think that'll be a great idea."

Jason: "Good, because there are some things we have to do as soon as your father is buried."

Helena: "Don't you dare start this already."

Jason: "What is that supposed to mean?"

Helena: "He is my son. You don't just pick us up and tell him what he has to do. You have no business talking to him about anything. You talk to me."

Jason: "Sweetie, listen you are not a part of the league, but he is. Which means that now that I'm next in line, I own him."

After that there was dead silence in the car. I was getting madder and madder by the second. Looking at him was almost like looking at the devil. He was the devil. A snake to the core of his soul. When we arrived at the mansion, I was happy, because I didn't have to look at his face. I went up to my bedroom to relax, but I couldn't. the only thing I could remember is laying in the bed with my father when I was five years old while he read me a bed time story. While I was in bed I could hear my mother and uncle arguing.

Helena: "You won't take my son away from me!!!"

Jason: "Oh sweetie come on. Why you must you be so angry. So....... feisty. You know that turns me on."

(Jason steps towards Helena)

(Helena steps back)

Helena: "Get away from me!"

Jason: "What? Are you scared of me? You weren't fourteen years ago."

Helena: "I will never see what your brother saw in you. There was never an ounce of goodness in you. You're pure evil. You tried to kill him before, now you've succeeded!!! Just like you succeeded with killing your own father!!!! But my son?"

Jason: "You mean our son bitch. Our son. And if you think that he's going back to America with you? You're mistaken."

Helena: "You think that you've gotten away with what you did to me. Just because you have a child by me. You're delusional. I loved your brother more than life itself. And there is no way in hell I ever would've cheated on him. (crying) He was my world. He was my first love. My only love"

Jason: "I did nothing to you. I gave you what your husband, my brother couldn't. That was a child with gifts. A child with powers of a God that could take over the world. That kid took a lot of hits and didn't go down. He could've been weak like my brother and died, but he didn't because he is my seed. That kid, (laughs) he admires me. You think for five minutes he's going to believe a word you say about me. Because I already know what you're thinking. And it'll all reverse back on you. You'll drive him right into my arms. He'll rule this world right here with me and you'll be a rotten corpse next to your husband."

Helena: "My son, your son will be the last thing you see when you die. Which is why you're trying to get him on your side now. You're getting older and weaker. And if he ever found out how he was brought into this world, he'd really hate you then."

Jason: "(Laughs) Bitch please. You're delusional."

Helena: "I just wish I had the courage to tell your brother the horrible things you did to me when he wasn't around. HOW MANY TIMES YOU RAPED ME!!!! (Crying) and I couldn't even look at him or touch him. I didn't want the love of my life to touch me because

I felt so disgusting and sick to my stomach after you committed such horrible acts on me."

Jason: (Laughs) I will never forget those nights. Thank you for those nights. I truly appreciated those nights. Especially when my wife wasn't giving it up."

I wanted to kill my uncle. Excuse me, I'm sorry. I wanted to kill my father right then and there. But I knew that with whatever powers he possessed I couldn't fight him. And I had no knowledge of my powers at all. But I had to learn them in order to conquer his strength. The very next day we buried my father. Every single assassin in the world was there. Including Mr. Ray. Which I'd never even heard my family mention him being an assassin. After the services were over, we all met back at the family estate. I remember looking over at Mr. Ray and Jason talking. And it was crazy how Mr. Ray was a man of no expression. He showed no emotions at all. He even hugged Jason and kissed him on the forehead and told him "Everything will be okay." Afterward he walked over to me and pulled me outside on the balcony to talk to me.

William Ray: "You must think I'm stupid."

Me: "What do you mean?"

William Ray: "Boy I will toss you off this balcony if you don't tell me every single word and detail you've heard since your father has passed."

Me: "I'm not my father's son, am I?"

William Ray: "(Deep sigh) You've heard too much. I'm pretty sure you heard what happened back at the Ohio palace too huh?"

Me: "Yes sir."

William Ray: "Then you know what we must do. But you can't go off halfcocked. Your father nor grandfather would like that at all. Follow my lead."

I wanted to go against Mr. Ray so bad, but I thought about something. If my father trusted the Ray's with my mother's life, he had a reason. So, I followed Mr. Ray's lead and didn't act on my anger and hurt. Mr. Ray spent the night in the mansion that night. The next day he woke up and cooked everyone breakfast. And sat down with just the Regime family. He read his newspaper at the dining room table and was in complete silence. He didn't like to talk while reading, and no one could talk to him. Then he sits his newspaper down and begins to speak. But what he said shocked me, my mother and my uncle/father.

William Ray: "(Sucks teeth) The league is dead."

Jason: "What did you just say?"

William Ray: "The league is dead; your Russians are dead. Everyone is dead."

It was just out of the blue what he said. The room was frozen completely. I just remember looking in his face and he was just so cold when he said it. He had ice in his eyes and took so much pride in saying that all the assassins in the league were dead. The man never ceased to amaze me. My uncle was in disbelief.

Jason: "(Laughs) Okay. Let's see about that. Guards!!!!"

William Ray: "They'll be here soon. Just wait."

They came alright. They came dead. Dead bodies of the assassins who guarded the house were brought to us by soldiers who worked for the Ray family. Mr. Ray sat there looked in Jason's face and said, "you must think I'm a new kind of fool don't you bitch?" He was so cool and relaxed, Mr. Ray scared me.

William Ray: "You see my boy...... here's the thing, you had everyone fear you. You thought you had cleared the board by killing your brother. But you forgot about me. Which was the biggest mistake you could've ever made in your entire life. I have access to every single detail about every single assassin in the world. Majority of them work for this organization. I found them, their families and had them all killed. Even the ones on missions, I found them, and killed them. Now you're the only one left."

Helena: "Ho...HOW?! How'd you, do it. Where'd you find the man power?"

William Ray: "That's none of your concern."

Jason sat there with anger boiling inside of him, but I could tell that there was a lot of fear in his heart. I could sense it. He couldn't even make eye contact with Mr. Ray, and Jason feared no man. He was the true definition of a warrior. But Jason did something. Something that woke up an angry, evil, even colder side. He jumped up to attack Mr. Ray. Mr. Ray looked at Jason, pointed his figure at him, and next thing I knew Jason was lifted off the ground choking. I'd never seen anything like it before. He didn't even touch Jason and he had complete control over what happened to his body. It was amazing yet, it scared me. Mr. Ray then stood up out of his chair, he looked at Jason with a smile on his face.

William Ray: "Now my dear boy. Do you have anything you'd like to say now? Because if you do, you better say it now because they'll be your last words."

Jason: "(Choking and gasping for air) Fuck..... you."

William Ray: "Well it was very nice knowing you. See you in hell."

(Jason's neck snaps. Body drops to the floor)

Helena: "Jacq, go pack your things and prepare to burn this place down. This will be our last time ever coming back to France to stay."

And I did just that. I packed what I came with. Picked up a few photos and got out of there as soon as possible so we could place a bomb in the mansion and be rid of it. I felt relieved, scared, and angry. I was angry because I wanted to kill Jason myself. Instead, it was Mr. Ray who had the privilege to do it. We walked out the mansion before it blew up. The three of us were escorted to a limo to go straight to the airport to board the private jet. When we got on the jet, I was too afraid to make eye contact with Mr. Ray. I didn't even want to talk to him. The only thing I could see was him snapping Jason's neck without even touching him. It was entirely too awkward on the plane ride back home, but I knew I'd have to say something to him eventually. This would be the man in my life until the day we both left the face of the earth. Technically speaking, he was my father now. So, I took it upon myself to walk over to him while were still on the plane to say something to him.

Me: "Mr. Ray?"

William Ray: "Well, well, well. Look who decided to come over to talk to me. Sit down here next to me son. I want to talk to you."

Me: "I'm afraid of you."

William Ray: "(Laughs) Afraid? Afraid of what?"

Me: "Of your abilities."

William Ray: "Son listen, I'm truly sorry about the things that you've been through. I'm sorry for the things you had to witness. But listen to me. What I just did, you can do it too. You just haven't unlocked your potential yet. But you've got it. We will teach you everything you need to know. You're family now."

And when he said those words to me again, I felt no fear. I felt comfortable and at ease. I knew yet again that the Ray's would take care of me. When we got back to Ohio, I spent the rest of my summer training with my mother, Andre, Mr. Ray, and the rest of the soldiers. I learned how to use my super natural powers, control them, hide them when needed. I learned it all. I felt stronger and stronger by the day. I made new friends and for once, I could be a kid and have real friends. Hangout, go to the movies, all that stuff. And like I'd said earlier, I was in love with a girl who was my "family". Andrea was just gorgeous. I enjoyed just being around her. Andre knew I was in love with her too. He used to always tease me. It was funny, but she was forbidden fruit. She was something that I never could and never would have.

Time flies by, and next thing I know, summer is over. School is now in session, and this was my first time going to an actual school. I was so excited. I remember putting on my uniform and getting into the limo with Andre and Andrea acting like a jumping bean with a goofy smile on my face. Andrea looked at me like I was so weird. Andre was happy because I was happy. When we arrived at the school, all you saw were other rich kids pulling up in limousines and luxury cars. As soon as we stepped out, it was like we were in Hollywood. It was literally something I'd seen on television, and Andre and Andrea were so damn popular it was crazy. Everyone loved them. Especially Andre. He played every single sport in school and lettered in all of them. He was a legend, and ladies flocked to him like a God. That first day of school was the best day of my life. I had so much fun. Andre introduced me to everybody and everybody seemed to be cool. They all respected me, and I became popular by association. During the second week of school, I tried out for the baseball team and made the team. Girls flocked to me. I made good grades, my teachers liked me. Life was just good.

My first year in school, I'd even become homecoming king. I was the first one to beat Andre for the title in two years. He was so happy for me and proud of me. I remember him saying, "you know your pussy rate is going to go even higher now." He was just a funny guy. And even though what he said was true, I only wanted one girl, and that was Andrea. I tried to get her attention all the time. Even at the palace when we were at home. She was not paying me any attention at all. I was like a ghost to her. I remember Andre saying that I was probably too light for her. I didn't know. I didn't care, it was her I wanted. But that next school year sealed the deal for me as far as my true love. And not in a good way at all. We had new neighbors move in across the street. The Solomon-Ward family. They were the second richest family in the United States and ran the largest pharmaceutical company in the world. Solomon-Ward Pharmaceutical Corporation made the Solomon-Ward family worth eight hundred billion dollars. Not only did they manufacture prescribed medicine, they also manufactured medical devices. Devices such as crash carts, hospital beds, pacemakers, everything. They ruled the world just as much as the Ray's.

The CEO of the company was Cesar Solomon Ward. Cesar was about six foot even, dark skinned, thick long jet-black hair braided in a ponytail, and a beautiful well-kept salt and peppered colored beard. He was a very loud dresser. Flashy, very flashy. His wife on the other hand was a sweet woman. Her name was Rudy-Mae Solomon-Ward. She was a very short woman, no taller than four feet eleven. She was brown skinned, long salt and peppered hair, she looked like a little native woman. Cutest thing you'd ever seen. She wasn't a part of the corporation. She was a college professor. She taught psychology classes at Cleveland State University. They had three sons. Gregory (Greg) Solomon was the oldest, he was the same age as Andre. Greg was about five feet eight, brown skinned, kind of pudgy, but he was handsome, and ladies loved him. The second one, Shon Solomon-Ward. Shon was the heartthrob of the family. People catered to him like a God because he was just that damn good looking. He was the same age as Andrea and me. He was six foot four, dark as night, teeth was pearly white, big, buffed and built like a tank. He had the hearts of many, including the love of my life. The youngest boy was Miguel Solomon-Ward. In all honesty, he was the ugliest brother. He probably wouldn't have been so ugly if he'd just kept himself up. He was brown skinned, completely out of shape, never wanted a haircut, never groomed himself, sloppy dressing, he was just a mess. All he did was layup and eat fast food and read magazines. He barely paid attention in school, and his grades were awful.

We'd all heard of the three brothers, because the oldest two was always in trouble and always made the newspaper. It was almost sad how much trouble they stayed in. Their father acted as if he hated them sometimes. They cost him soooooo much money, and caused their mother a lot of heartache. They weren't classy or sophisticated at all. They were all the way street. They had that bad boy image on top of good looks. Miguel was too lazy to get in trouble. He was too lazy for anything. But that bad boy image stole the show. I remember when Mr. Ray went over to talk to Cesar and introduce himself. They had a great conversation and hit it off well. Mr. Ray even invited the family over to the palace for dinner. When they came over for dinner, all Andrea could do was stare at Shon, and Shon stared right back. They basically eye fucked each other the whole time at the dinner table. It was a fucking disgrace. I was jealous, I'm not going to lie. They were really digging each other. Everyone enjoyed the meal, the family hit it off well, and after dinner was over, it was time for the children to leave the table and let the adults talk.

So, we all went to the game room to shoot pool, and watch tv. Andre and I loved shooting pool. So, it was him and me versus Greg and Shon. Miguel sat down and watched us along with Andrea. During our time together, Andre and I both knew that we didn't like these guys. Not even Miguel because he was sneaky, and not as dumb as we thought.

Shon: "So, some palace y'all got here. I mean I knew y'all was rich but DAMN!!! Our shit isn't this big."

Andre: "Thanks, but I knew the last family that lived in your house. It's a beautiful mansion."

Greg: "It's alright, could be bigger though."

Me: "We've heard a lot about y'all. And I've got to admit, it's crazy what I've heard."

Shon: "Yeah well, that's how we do this shit. We gangsters in our own right (laughs)."

Greg: "What about y'all. I mean, Andre, you the ladies' man. Jacq you the pretty boy with the French accent and shit. You know your popularity is over now right (laughs)."

We all laughed, but Andre and I's laugh was forced. We sensed a lot of arrogance as well as ignorance. As we conversed, Andrea was still staring Shon down as if she wanted to eat him up. I was just sick with it. Then she got up and pretended to drop something and bent over to pick it up. He looked dead at her ass and licked his lips. Andre snatched her up and told her to go in the other room. He was very over protective of her. And he didn't want his sister looking like a hoe. Especially in front of a low life savage like Shon. When she left words were exchanged.

Shon: "Yo man what's up with you, why you got a pool cue up your ass."

Andre: "That is my sister, if she wants your attention there are other ways to get it."

Shon: "Look man she may be your sister, but her pussy gone be mine mane. (Licks lips) I'm just letting you know."

That raised a beast out of Andre. I'd yet to see him angry since I'd been living with the Ray's. He jumped up and was ready to kill Shon. But I caught him in time. It was hard to hold him back, but I did it. But I looked behind me and saw Shon with his fist balled up with blue flames coming from it. At that moment, I knew he was going to be a problem. He had the same powers as us, all three of them did.

Greg: "Now we can all be cool, or we can get into some gangster shit. The choice is yours."

Andre: "You don't know who you're fucking with. I will kill every last one of you."

I diffused the situation and suggested that the three brothers leave. So, the Solomon-Ward brothers left and went home. But their parents stayed and talked to Mr. and Mrs. Ray. While they were still having great conversation. Mr. Ray felt something. You could tell based on how he looked at the brothers while they were leaving. I had a feeling that he knew that those boys would be trouble. But he kept his silence at the time and never revealed to anyone how he truly felt. But it had gotten to a point where me and Mr. Ray was so close, I felt his emotions, and he could feel mine. We had a bond that not even him and his son had. I think it was due to the fact that I was the only one who really had no one except for my mother, so he took up a lot of time with me. But in due time, everything would come out. Everything.

I Lied

ALRIGHT! Y'ALL GOT ME! I LIED! I LIED THROUGH MY TEETH! I DO HAVE MORE, BUT NOT TOO MUCH MORE I PROMISE!!! What you all are about to read is a story that I began writing when I was in grad school at Southern New Hampshire University. For those of you who do not know, I received my Master's Degree in English Literature & Creative Writing in 2021. The title of this story is "A Kingpin's Memoir." This story is about a young man who lost his mother and turned to a life of crime afterward. Little does he know that all of his unanswered questions about himself are answered in ways that he would never imagine. I will give you all a draft of the first chapter. I hope you all enjoy!

Draft of A Kingpin's Memoir First Chapter

As I sit back in my coke white Rolls Royce, while being chauffeured around downtown Cleveland in my Armani suit and my gold Rolex encrusted in diamonds, all I can think about is my mom. Damn, I miss her so much, and I often wonder what life would've been like for us if she was still here. Would I still be the man that I have become? Would we still be in the projects on Woodland? I don't know. One thing I do know is that with all the money, cars, clothes, and even properties I have, she'd probably be highly disappointed in me. Because despite having a BA from Ohio State University and an MBA from Penn State, all of my material possessions came from drug money. Hell, she probably wouldn't accept a dime of my money even if I begged her to take it.

She wasn't the type of woman who was easily impressed by money. She was a hard worker, and she made a lot of sacrifices for me to have whatever I wanted even when I didn't need it. See, when I was a kid, my mom and I didn't have much. She worked at a Mcdonald's right up the street from our project. She didn't make a lot of money, but she always made ends meet. I always had a roof over my head, decent clothes on my back, and food in my belly. Shit, I was one of the only kids in the projects that had a mama that was clean and had a real job. Other kids mama's in the jects was out there sucking dick and hookin in the streets to make ends meet, or for some crack. So to the average kid in the jects I was privileged. I'd get teased and beat up by some of the other kids in my building because I had a good mother, and they didn't. I can't tell you how many times I'd come home with a black eye and bruises because I'd get into so many fights.

I remember some of the other kids would say shit like, "Yo, SAINT!? Mary still sucking dick to get you a happy meal!?" Every time they said that, I'd try to walk away. But they wouldn't stop; they'd just keep going and keep going to try to provoke me. And when I didn't react, they'd put their hands on me and provoke me to fight. Every time I'd swing, I got my ass beat every motherfucking time. And every time I came home with a bruised and bloody face, my mother was always there waiting on me with the peroxide and bandages. I remember on days like that, she'd say to me, "Saint, sticks, stones, fists, and feet will break your bones, but words are just words, honey. Be the bigger man and just walk away. There's no need to fight." But in my head, I was like, "Nah, fuck that shit, don't nobody talk about my mama like that." But I was young, couldn't have been any older than maybe five or six. I didn't realize the struggles of the other kids not having their mother in the ways that I did. But the crazy part about it is that my mother was somewhat a mother to all the kids without one in our project.

I remember she'd bring food home from work and feed as many kids as she could because they were hungry, she'd buy material and sew them clothes in our hot ass apartment while watching Jerry Springer on them old ass tv's with the fat backs on em. She did all kinds of shit. She was a fucking saint, and despite the shit that the other kids would say and do to me, when they were around her, they showed her nothing but respect. And after a while, they begin to show me some respect because my mother demanded it. She was sweet, but she was nothing to fuck with at all. I remember one time I overheard two crackhead women standing outside my building talking about how my mama was about to get robbed by these two low-level gangbangers outside of my building before I was born. She beat the shit out of them and shot one of them in the ass. They talked about how she threw this karate kick up and kicked one of em in the face and how she grabbed the other robber's arm and broke it, took the gun out of his had and shot him. It sounded like an action movie!I couldn't believe it, but then when I asked my mother was it true, she didn't deny it.

"Baby I took up a lot of self-defense classes when I was a kid. My father demanded it. How do you think I fought them dudes off. I had to show em a lil something something. Plus, I was pregnant with you, and they were about to rob me of all the money I had to my name. I needed money for my little Saint, " my mom said while laughing about it. I asked my mom why she named me "Saint" after she told me the story of her robbery attempt. She told me it was because I was born without sin and that everything that was ungodly in her life, I was the best thing to come out of it. When she told me that I wanted to know everything about my mother, I didn't know. So I began to ask as many questions as possible.

"Where did you grow up at, mama?" I asked.

"Bratenahl, Ohio sweetie," she said.

"Isn't that the rich part of Cleveland?"

"Yes, sweetie," she said while laughing.

"How'd we end up in the projects if you're from the rich part?"

"After I got pregnant with you, I had to drop out of college, and my parents cut me off financially baby," she said with tears in her eyes.

The last question was the question that made her break completely down in pain and sorrow. That question was, "Why don't I know my daddy?" My mother got up without speaking a word, and she began to walk to her bedroom, sobbing out loud. She slammed her door to the bedroom so hard that it caused for my baby picture to fall off of the wall and break. I'd never seen my mother like that in my entire life. She was always strong, always laughing, always happy, but that day was the day that she had just completely shut down. When she came out of her bedroom later, she didn't even mention my question. She just cooked dinner like I never even asked her about who my father was, and I never brought it back up. But I felt so incomplete in my early years. Because even though other kids I grew up around didn't have their daddies around, at least they knew who the fuck they were. I didn't know shit about mine.

Another thing that bothered me was that I didn't even know anything about my mother's family. Shit, I didn't know shit about anyone. It was always just my mama and me. And after asking about my father, I was afraid to go any deeper with my questions. After that conversation with my mom, every old black couple that I would see when I wasn't with my mom, I'd wonder if they were my grandma and grandpa. Every black man I saw that looked close to my moms age, I'd wonder if they were my dad. I know that sounds crazy as fuck, but shit, cut a motherfucka some slack. I looked for certain features. Like if the men close to my mother's age looked anything like me. Or if the older people who I thought could be my grandparents looked anything like my mom. I was only five years old. I didn't know. All I knew was that it had to be someone else out there that could help my mom and love her in the way that she loved me, whether it had been my dad or my grandparents. I often questioned why my grandparents would let my mom struggle like they did if they were rich. I mean shit, my mama had to decide sometimes if she was gonna get me clothes for school or pay the electric bill, and every time she chose to get me clothes. It was hard for us a lot of days. And even though she made a way for us to have everything we needed to survive, it began to take a toll on her slowly but surely.

The End

I am so honored to be able to share my works with all of you reading this book. Thank you all so much for the love and support. I hope you enjoyed all of the additional content. The Welcome To 10-5 Series is far from over. The next installment will be titled "***Curse of Cain: Eye of The Gemini!***" The release date will be determined soon. Until then, please make sure you all enjoy the first two installments!

"With Love, Prayer, & Great Vibrations!"
-King Pen Gemini-

Curse of Cain: Eye of The Gemini Preview (Intro)

You know, when I killed my brother, I didn't regret it. Not at all. Instead, I was happy I did it. I fucking hated Abel. He was always a spoiled little bitch. And he wasn't as great as everyone made him out to be. In fact, he was lazy. Entitled. I did the work, and he benefited from the fruits of my labor. And I was punished simply because I was not a part of *God's* plan. I didn't ask to be born, so why should I suffer? And you all want to know something else? I blame my mother and especially my father, Lucifer, for this. Because of their lust for one another, I suffered. I wish that I could die. But unfortunately, I can't. And it is all because God is making me pay for the sins of my father. A father that has brought so much evil into this world.......

This is all you all are getting right now. You'll have to wait until the book comes out.

Curse of Cain: Eye of The Gemini

Ain't No Light In This Bitch.

It's Dark In This Bitch!

www.ingramcontent.com/pod-product-compliance
Lightning Source LLC
Chambersburg PA
CBHW070621310726
48982CB00001B/142
* 9 7 9 8 9 8 5 8 2 2 9 2 2 *